A timely reminder
of your visit.

Best wishes
from the author

Peter Hyson

A Fair Cop

A Fair Cop

the first in

The *Cotswold Capers* series

PETER HYSON

A Fair Cop by Peter Hyson
© Peter Hyson 2023
Published by The Cotswolds Press 2023

Cover design by Emma O'Brien, Illustrator & Maker of Monsters
www.emmajaneobrien.com

This novel is about a typical British English village: I have therefore used typical British spellings.

This is a work of fiction. Any similarity to any events or persons living or dead is unintentional and purely coincidental.

ISBN: 978-1-7393489-1-5 (e-book)

ISBN: 978-1-7393489-2-2 (paperback)

For Sam and Catherine, Tim, Tina, Effie and Iris and for Beckie and Ben who've been such a joy, encouragement and inspiration.

Preface

I'm usually up for a challenge – so when I noticed that a couple of village names nearby where we live in The Cotswolds sounded rather like people's names, I took on not one but two challenges. Firstly, to see how many other place names in the UK could also be names of people and then secondly, to see if I could write a light-hearted series of book s where all the characters are named after and maybe share some similarities with those real places. There were also two outcomes: some wonderfully interesting visits to some very obscure and usually very beautiful villages, hamlets and on one memorable occasion, literally just the name on my sat nav screen; and the birth of *The Cotswold Capers* series of cosy murder mysteries.

The first escapade, *The Taste of Murder*, emerged as a shorter novella. This second book, *A Fair Cop*, picks up a standard length and sees our female amateur sleuth Catherine de Barnes and her cheeky Golden Retriever puppy Dagenham (yes, even the dogs are real places) plunged back into murder and mayhem in the aptly named but totally invented village of Much Slaughter when she discovers the body of their retired village policeman draped in the window of the Police Museum.

Along with previous characters Skye Green and Scott Willoughby, we meet the rather dishy Red Street and the eccentric vet Martin Dales, while entrepreneur Christian Malford steps up with a business offer that could transform Catherine's chocolate-making business and another offer threatens to leave her all at sea.

For more about the characters, their place names and upcoming titles or to sign up for the quarterly newsletters *Continuing Capers* see my website **www.peterhyson.com**.

Chapter 1

Dagenham, my lovely golden retriever, gives me a long pitying stare when I grind to a halt, lungs heaving and face burning. I must have tackled this driveway ten or twenty times and it doesn't get the slightest bit easier, despite my twice daily dog walking. I wipe my forehead on the back of my hand, my blond, curly hair damp with sweat. Sorry, Mum, lady-glow. She regularly recycled that old saying, 'horses sweat, men perspire, ladies merely glow'. Dag, restless to meet his doggy pal Barking, scampers off again, towing me the final twenty metres up to the 1970s vicarage.

My friend Scott Willoughby stands at the open door, and I wonder if he's heard my approaching gasps but as we step into his cool hallway, I realise he can see the driveway from his study, and I laugh.

'Hours of endless entertainment, eh, Vicar?'

He follows my eyeline and smiles.

As we pass from the public arena into his domestic one, I'm greeted by the massive black and grey furball of Old English Sheepdog that is Barking. Or rather Dag is, there's absolutely no interest in me or even Scott, and the two hounds tumble around, through the kitchen and out into the garden.

'Useless guard dog!' Scott gazes after his dog, looking like a proud father watching his child erupt into a playground. 'Good listener, though!'

'Aren't they just!' My six-month-old pup has seen me through many a lonely night since I moved into the village. It was Scott who suggested I needed a pet, though he was at pains to point out I shouldn't see it as filling the hole left in my life by my erstwhile straying husband. He'd even loaned me his own rescue pup Barking for a few days. When my own rescue hound arrived, it seemed only right to name him Dagenham after the London Borough, sure even then that they'd be the best of canine companions. And what a difference Dagenham has made, not only as the ever-willing listener and ever-keen sharer of affection, but also as the most effective finder of friends. Within a week I knew more people than in the previous two months in the village before I got him and there are few in Much Slaughter who don't know him by name. He's been the catalyst to a dozen supper invites. Sadly, no romantic interludes as yet. But hope springs eternal in the Catney breast.

I lower my rucksack carefully onto the floor, which leaves me with an unpleasant damp patch at the bottom of my back, so I'll need to make sure I keep facing Scott. And I'll definitely need to keep my arms plastered to my side. My calves are aching, but all the chairs are plastered with newspapers or worthy-looking books and the coffee table is submerged under the remains of breakfast and a whisky glass I hope was a nightcap, rather than a hair-of-the-dog from this morning.

'No Cherry this morning?' Cherry is Scott's… well, no-one seems quite sure what she is. Partner? Long-term girlfriend? A few other less savoury descriptions have also been suggested but she's actually well liked and arrived here with Scott and has been accepted along with him despite (or perhaps because of) the air of mystery.

'No – she's spending this week working on the renovation of her cottage back in Much Snoring. Unfortunately.' He gazes around the room with a bewildered lost-puppy look. 'Cat, I'm sorry but I can't stop. My clergy colleagues are due any minute and I've got masses to do – sorry, no pun intended.'

I smile. Yes, he does look rather haggard, so I suppose he must be missing Cherry's presence. In more ways than one. He's tall, broad-shouldered and has the classic sharp jawline but his eyes look puffy and dark and there's the start of crow's feet at their edges, even though I reckon he's probably only in his early forties. He's got a couple of days of beard stubble and being black-haired it looks as if it's been drawn with a felt-tip pen.

I take out a box of my favourite chocolate macaroons which I'd baked just a couple of hours earlier and hold them up proudly. 'Fifteen people, I think you said? I've done 25.' And though I say it myself, they're some of my best.

Scott seems pleased. 'Good move, Cat. I have to say that, judging by their waistlines, our local clergy are rather fond of their fodder. They seem to descend on food like locusts – very Biblical but not very edifying! Now, where on earth did I put my clerical collar?' He stands in the middle of the room and spins around, then just stands motionless.

It's disconcerting to see Scott so flustered. I've always thought of him as the archetypal cool, unflappable cleric, hovering saint-like above distractions. 'Look, I've nothing in the diary. Why don't you start in here while I set up the kitchen?' I'm not at all sure what I'll find if I tidy the sitting room, so I reckon I've got the better job.

Moments later, I'm not so sure. Dirty dishes and saucepans are piled in the sink and across the draining board and there are dirty plates, glasses and cutlery on the table, along with a half-empty bowl of shrivelled salad, probably older than last night. It all feels worryingly unlike Scott.

Ten minutes later, with a packed dishwasher churning away, the overflowing items have been washed and sit draining, and the emerging wooden work surfaces have been scrubbed clean. My search of the cupboards has located fifteen matching cups, saucers and side plates, admittedly in the typical shade of church green. Two huge metal kettles rumble away on the gas stove, while my macaroons stand like a valley of pyramids on a large stainless-steel platter.

Just as I drop the final teaspoon onto the final saucer, Scott returns. What a transformation. He already looks so much better. His dog collar has been found and inserted into his shirt, his still-damp black hair is brushed into place, he's clean-shaven, there's more than a hint of Old Spice in the air and he looks – and smells – like the vicar of old. I wonder if he misses Cherry's presence rather more than he'd prepared to let on.

'I hate these meetings, Cat. They can get so, well, argumentative. It's as if they bring all their frustrations from their parishes and vent them here.' He shudders. 'That's why I'm so tense.' The eye contact lasts a moment too long to be convincing and my heart lurches. He leans on the (now pristine) kitchen table. 'It's the only time I ever miss the City.'

'Gosh, yes, I'd forgotten that. Stock market, wasn't it?'

'Investment banking, actually. Twenty years. Sorry – I know, I know!' He holds up his hands in surrender.

'Scott, let's face it. I'm in no place to throw stones. Don't forget, I was ten years managing an advertising agency! Twenty staff and no holidays.'

'Don't you ever miss anything?'

'You mean the ridiculous deadlines, stroppy clients and colleagues and a mound of paperwork? Hardly!'

'Sounds to me like a vicar's job, Cat.' We both laugh, a little falsely.

'And, let's face it,' I turn to face him, 'it was my choice to up sticks and move here, so I can hardly complain, can I?'

He looks so desolate, my heart hurts and I add, quickly, 'I do know your story's very different.'

He stares. 'It felt as if my world was caving in. Getting made redundant and my wife running off. And that ridiculous business in my last parish.'

Now that last bit has intrigued me ever since I first heard there was something. But before I can say anything more, Scott glances at his watch as, bang on cue, the doorbell rings and in his eyes I see the shutters crash down. 'I'll be off and leave you to your vicaring,' I say. His face pales and a vein throbs in his neck, making him look like he's been condemned to a firing squad. 'But, Scott, you know where I am…'

I squeeze his arm and plant a quick kiss on his cheek.

I'm tempted to slip out the back way but even I realise that the sight of someone furtively slinking out by the tradesmen's entrance might not be a good look. Especially a blond babe. *Okay, Cat, in your dreams!*

'Dag – here boy.' Both pups look up and carry on racing around the garden. So much for obedience classes. Although, in fairness, my investigations into the horrible murder at the recent village fête – fair – meant we had missed a few classes. 'Dag – now.' He looks at Barking and I swear he rolls his eyes, before ambling across the lawn, tail drooping, while Barking remains glued to the spot as if he can't quite believe anyone would spoil their fun.

We pass quickly through the house. The open front door reveals three black-coated clergymen whose florid faces and rotund figures suggest they might be better served by a gym session than a meeting. Behind them are three battered old cars. The men push straight past me and don't even greet Scott: they clearly know where they're heading. Even Dag shows little interest in them which must be a first – but maybe he's sulking at being dragged away.

Behind them traipses a woman who seems to have tackled the driveway far more comfortably than her colleagues and looks remarkably cool despite sporting a rather resplendent flowing cardigan that flaps around her calves.

'The Area Dean. A good thing,' Scott whispers in my ear, as if I should know exactly what that means. All I do know is that she's a rather wrinkled woman, probably in her late fifties, with a taste for a long, knitted cardigan. She does at least nod at me as she passes and then greets Scott with a warm hug and, I swear, a flirtatious wink. She pauses and I wonder if she's also noticed something odd about him. But then she rushes inside, followed by Scott. The door closes.

Dag suddenly pulls on his leash, his tail wagging nineteen to the dozen, which is the way he greets long-time friends. All I can see is an elderly man in a purple shirt, his alpine sticks clicking to aid his ascent. His face lights up as he glimpses me, and his smile shows a full set of gleaming white teeth. 'Please tell me you're a lovely addition to our clergy team, my dear. I'm Bishop Norton…'

'Catherine de Barnes, Bishop. Usually known as Catney. And, no, I'm afraid I'm not.'

'Shame – could've done with someone to lighten the proceedings!' He grins, bends down to tickle Dag's ears, thereby wining a friend for life. 'Ah well, I'd better face my penance, I suppose.' He clicks across to the vicarage and disappears.

Good grief, what a motley crew! I'm not surprised Scott… I get no further as a young woman in a bright red MX5 sports car roars up the driveway and screeches to a halt, almost mounting the doorstep in her enthusiasm. She hops out, showing rather more bare thigh than I'd have thought appropriate for a cleric, before following the tribe inside.

This morning's encounter with Scott and the foray back into both our pasts has left me feeling quite disorientated for some inexplicable reason, so I meander across the churchyard and push on the heavy oak door. Inside, it's refreshingly cool and I select a wooden pew about halfway down and sidle in by a pillar. The silence is immediately comforting, and in some weird way there's a sense of being surrounded by hundreds of years of prayers which have soaked into the limestone walls. Everything is plain and simple. Even the altar has only a single wooden cross and a rather battered candlestick on it; these days, the main silverware is securely locked away in a huge vestry safe. That's when I realise my hands are shaking. And it's not the cold.

I stare up ahead at the beautiful stained glass of the East Window and the colourful patterns it throws on the stone floor, my mind a jumble of thoughts and feelings. I have to admit, I wasn't being entirely honest with Scott. Or with myself. I find it quite hard to pretend when I'm in church. I know that might just be me. I'm not religious and I have no idea what I believe. And although I've probably sat in church more times in the ten months I've been in Much Slaughter than in my previous forty-two years, that's simply because it's much more prominent in a village. It's a very good way to meet people.

Anyway, Scott's words have made me realise something's missing. I'm sure it's not the gaudy, buzzy superficiality of the advertising world: that had lost its sheen long before I left. Although maybe I miss the cut-and-thrust of managing a business. I loved my tiny docker's cottage in a trendy part of East London. But the area was also noisy and dirty! So, not that either. And, while I certainly don't miss the philandering lump I called my husband, actually, I do miss male company.

Well, I guess a church is as a good place as any to count your blessings. I have a small cinema half an hour away and several theatres within an hour. And soon after I arrived in Much Slaughter, I realised that I didn't have friends in London, I had acquaintances. Whereas in the country, even if it's taken me a while, I've got my next-door neighbour, Wickham; Scott, of course, and Rose and her niece Skye at the café. Plus at least a dozen dinner guests. Now I've got twice the living space in my house, a huge garden and country walks from my doorstep. And my trusty pup Dagenham and my growing chocolate business. No mortgage and a small financial cushion in the bank. This was the independence I'd been craving. And I love it, I really do. Okay, so a nice hunk of man to cuddle up with would be the icing on the cake, but hey, you can't have it all, can you?

Mind you, a girl could do far worse than that nice Chief Inspector Parva: the man I helped a few months back. Together we solved the murder of a local celebrity chef. Although he did think me an interfering busybody… there have been worse starting points. And recently, one of the village worthies seems to have popped up significantly, more frequently than I'd have reason to expect…

Any further romantic conjectures are shattered as the church door is flung back, the crash echoing around the stones, and Scott's clergy colleagues tumble in. A couple of them seem to be continuing a dispute, something about who wrote some Bible book or other. Another is on the phone muttering about funeral arrangements. The Area Dean emerges from the vestry with all the communion paraphernalia (I never was very good at terminology) and as she arranges them on the altar, she starts a loud conversation with someone else whose church service it appears she's taking on Sunday. Bedlam! I know there's something wrong but all I can do is slip out for a much needed and very strong coffee. Scott has my sympathy…

Chapter 2

'You're kidding me! Men!'

It's a couple of days after my romantic reflections in the ecclesiastical surroundings and if there'd been any divine intervention in the romance stakes as a result, well, it's far from obvious. My internet dating is not going well. And being woken up at 7 a.m. to a highly suggestive and unwelcome text doesn't exactly help. When my friend May had waxed lyrical about this amazing dating website she'd found, I'd been thrilled for her. After all, for a woman in her forties, and rooted in a village of just a few thousand people, her choice of eligible men are, shall we say politely, somewhat limited. And when she'd been our local mayor I can't imagine she had much spare time. But now that her term of office had ended, her personal diary seems to have sprouted like a field of poppies and even I had noticed that she looked blooming. Good for her.

Just not for me. At first, I'd been too raw after my ex had waltzed off with his business partner and set in train a series of events which had catapulted me from a successful career and comfortable if admittedly compact cottage to a new beginning, on my own and jobless, in Much Slaughter. But the divorce settlement had helped, at least financially. And I've never been unhappy in my own company. Now, at last, I'm finally putting down roots, building my chocolate business and cultivating a bunch of amazing new friends.

The unfortunate incident a couple of months back when a celebrity chef had been murdered at our village fair hadn't been quite what I'd envisaged in a quiet Cotswold village. Neither was my role in catching the perpetrator. With hindsight, though, I'd rather enjoyed it, and I realised I missed having something challenging and outside my comfort zone to take part in. Not just because of the dishy chief inspector, of course: I'd been quite happy without romantic complications.

Or so I'd told myself for a while after my husband took off with a girl who hadn't even been born when we'd got married. But the inspector had triggered something, and I'd finally succumbed to May's persistent line of 'what's the harm in something social?' Trouble is, the men on Just Good Friends seemed to assume 'social' meant either a lifelong commitment or a one-night stand.

My latest dating connection, *Chocoholic*, looked as if he might break the mould, until he'd chosen to share in great detail exactly why he was called *Chocoholic* and where exactly he hoped to slather the fondue…

So I wasn't in the best of moods when I grabbed Dag's lead and set out into the autumnal early morning dampness for a long walk followed by a restorative, soothing hot drink at the café. *Maybe Dag's the only*

13

male companion you need, Cat. After all, he's loyal, loving, undemanding and…

'Oh, really?!' A silver Range Rover roars up High Street, its driver oblivious to the tsunami of rainwater that it deluged over me. As if the soggy autumn morning hadn't soaked me enough. Even Dag growls at the receding taillights, then proceeds to shake himself and treat me to a further head to toe soaking before I abandon the walk and stomp into the café. I waddle duck-like to my favourite alcove having ordered 'the biggest, hottest hot chocolate you've got'. God, I hate November. Not only is it cold and wet but it heralds weeks and weeks of the same or worse. Christmas feels remote, although every shop I go into seems determined to convince me that it's just around the corner. And the whole time it's getting darker with shrinking daylight. No, it's fair to say, November is not my favourite month. Nor is it Dagenham's, to judge by the mournful look he keeps giving me from under the table as his fur steams dry.

'Goodness – a soggy Cat and a soggy dog!' Skye laughs as she deposits a huge mug of delicious smelling hot chocolate right under my nose, and slips Dag a doggy treat. 'Sorry, you really don't need me being flippant…'

'Skye, that's exactly what I need, otherwise I'll drown in self-pity! Mind you, I seem to be doing a pretty good job of drowning your floor.' I glance down at my pretty pink wellington boots, now islands in an expanding puddle of muddy water and I begin to prise them off. We both stare at my sodden socks, now starting their own mini-stream. 'So much for new wellies.'

For some inexplicable reason, my perfectly innocent remark reduces Skye to fits of giggles. 'Didn't anyone tell you? Makes you a dead cert DFL.'

'DFL?' I've no idea what she's talking about but it's clearly not a compliment and I feel my face redden.

'"Down From London". City dwellers who think the country is this idyllic sleepy utopia where nothing ever happens. Who kit themselves out with top of the range designer clothes and pretty boots – sorry, Cat – and then complain when they get dirty or leak.'

'Excuse me young lady.' I try hard to look stern. 'Isn't that a case of the kettle calling the pot?'

She tosses a handful of hair over her shoulder and lifts her chin. 'I may have spent all of my 20 years in the metropolis but that doesn't make me metropolitan.' She giggles. 'Especially since Auntie Rose reckons I was living in a commune.'

Running my eye over her, I can see what Rose meant. Her long curly hair could be called unkempt and its colour, bright blue today, seems to change as often as the English weather. She has long, thin hands and a willowy figure and reminds me of a sprite picture.

I sigh. 'These boots cost an absolute fortune.'

'Pop into the hardware shop in Cirencester. They'll sell you a perfectly good pair for twenty quid.' Skye's gaze has wandered to my branded jacket, so I quickly pre-empt further DFL barbs.

'I love what you've done with this place!' Not exactly subtle, but true. When Skye agreed to take over running the shop from her aunt Rose, she'd let us all know there'd be a few little changes. Well, that had proved an understatement. Whereas Ye Olde Tea Shoppe had been everything its name suggested, it's rebirth as the Crimson Courgette Coffee Emporium is best described as quirky: the walls are plastered with vinyl record sleeves, pages torn from 1960s magazines and old bunting flags. The tables are wooden planks in a rainbow of faded paints, fixed onto what look like old sewing machine bases. A dozen small metal watering cans sprout cutlery and are lined up on a shelf above an army of mismatched metal cups of the style I remember none too fondly from childhood camping trips. There are no signs of anything resembling a plate, just a stack of what look like roof tiles. All enhanced, though I say it myself, with a small selection of my best chocolates, supplied by me on a rotating basis, a business arrangement from which we're both already benefitting.

'We've invited people to write messages on the walls.' Skye points to a wall on the far side of the room where a few names and dates have been scrawled across the decoration in bright felt-tip pen. I'm chuffed to see that there's already a reference to 'the amazing home-made cherry bombs,' Skye continues. 'It hasn't caught on yet, so if you felt able to…'

I nod. 'I'll give it some thought, Skye. But if that's the worst problem you've got so far, you've done well.'

'I know. People have been really kind. Some of the older regulars have been rather thrown by it, it's not what they're used to, but I love that they've stayed with us. Even Wickham.'

Wickham Skeith is my next-door neighbour. In his late sixties, with enough whiskers and beard to obliterate most people's entire face, he's still running his bookshop with the energy of someone half his age. He's also about as traditional as they come. And one of the fairest people I know.

Skye is still talking. 'And they reckon that the catering's pretty good as well. They seem surprised. Then I found out that Auntie Rose had told them I used to be the cook in a hippy commune, so I guess they were afraid it would be all lentils and tofu, laced with hash. It was really a dozen friends who clubbed together so we could rent a decent-sized London house but I don't like to disillusion them – and to be honest, Cat, I quite like the reputation.'

I grinned. 'Good for you. Every girl needs a little mystery.'

A group of four German tourists arrive, pointing and photographing every inch of their surroundings.

As Skye sets off to serve them, she calls over her shoulder, 'Before you go, I've got an idea to run past you.'

Intriguing. Although I really hope she's not about to ask for help in running the café. I know I don't have a full-time job and, yes, I do sometimes feel at a loose end. But I prize my new-found and hard-won freedom. Except, I sense Skye is well on the way to becoming a good friend and it's very hard to turn down friends in their hour of need. I lean down to pet Dag, hoping he'll give me some inspiration on how to decline, politely, and run my fingers through his fur. I make a mental note that he needs a good brush now that the dampness has turned him into a tangled mess. Which is another good point: how would I find time for all these wonderful dog walks? And, much as I love what she's done with the décor, this place is still small and cramped and I just know I'd soon find it claustrophobic. Dag seems to sense my dilemma as he lifts his head and licks my hand. Or maybe he's just checking the chance of any titbits because moments later he slumps back down into deep snores.

Skye carries a laden tray to the tourists and after an awful lot of gesturing and giggling manages to re-join me, slipping into a spare chair. It looks as if it's going to be either a long conversation or a tense one if she needs to sit down. I grip my mug more tightly and swallow the last few dregs then, making sure the

German group isn't watching, I run my fingers around the remaining foam, cherishing their final flavours.

When I look up, Skye's grinning at me, which I take to be a good sign. 'Cat, I've been thinking…'

Hmmm, less good.

'You know how much you love chocolate?'

What a slanderous – oh, hang on, no, it's probably true, internet dater Chocoholic apart. I reach across and place my hand on hers, feeling her bony fingers and warm skin. 'Spit it out, kid.' Not sure it's the best phrase for a caterer but she giggles.

'Well, I'm thinking about setting up a takeaway counter…'

Oh no, she's going to ask me to run it, I can feel it coming. How on earth do I…

'And everyone loves your chocolates, don't they?' *They do if they want to be in my good books.* 'So, I wondered if you'd let me expand your chocolates and tarts and things. Quite a lot, actually. I'd increase your commission, of course. And you know how well your small selection is selling.'

Now I hadn't seen that coming. I mean, so far, apart from the half a dozen packets I've supplied for Skye each week, I've just done a few packs for friends and special events. Okay, I've also talked about taking it to another level, maybe even writing a business plan. *Oh, come on, Cat, you know you've always fancied running your own little business.* True, and confectionery does seem to fit perfectly around all the other things I want to do. Although the thought of committing to supply regular items day after day doesn't have quite the same appeal. 'Oh, Skye, I don't know. It would be such a big commitment, I'm not sure…'

Now she puts her own hand over mine and squeezes gently. 'For me too, Cat. So how about we feature them as specials? Then you can do what you want, when you want. And we'll see how they go.'

This girl's good! I give in. 'Okay, I'll give it one month's trial.'

Skye beams and claps her hands. 'I'll get May to do me a Specials sign – she's already carved a wooden sign to go above the shop window. Mind you, she did reckon *The Crimson Courgette Coffee Emporium* would take up more space than the shop front!'

'It's a memorable name, that's for sure! Where on earth…?'

'It just – grew on me, you might say.'

'But, look Skye, I can't start this until after I've finished my preparations for the Harvest Supper. Desserts for 60 people will keep me out of mischief for some time.'

'Oh, yes. Auntie Rose told me all about it. It's quite an event in the annual calendar, here, isn't it?'

'I don't think I'm the one to ask. It's my first one as well.' My stomach's already knotting over what I've stupidly let myself in for. *Just a few petit four chocolates* hadn't seemed much of an issue when Wickham had asked me. But there were a whole lot of other items they'd forgotten to tell me about. Like chocolate cheesecakes and chocolate cherry bombs.

Skye is still talking 'And then there's the famous Harvest Ball – I've got my eye on just the one to take me. He doesn't know, yet, but he will, trust me. What about you, Cat? Who are you going with?'

I sigh. 'I don't know who'd want to take me.'

'I thought you were trying that internet thingy? No dishy dates then?'

How on earth had she heard about that? 'It's a dead loss. I probably won't even go.' I want to play it cool, but I can feel my face burning.

'OMG, you've got your eye on someone, haven't you? An online hunk?' I shake my head. 'Someone local, then? Come on, spill the beans.' She's too smart by half, this one. I'm saved because the door opens for another group of tourists, Americans this time.

As I glance up, wondering what's happened to the old bell that used to jangle with each new entrant, I see the slim, powerful figure of our local GP, Linton Heath, walk past the window, huddled inside a smart, checked, woollen coat, his dark skin glowing. He glances in and smiles the most gorgeous smile in my direction along with a small wave. Sadly, his long powerful legs take him past the window in just a couple of strides, totally oblivious to my now pounding heart and flaming face. At least no-one's noticed. Then I see Skye staring and smirking, she's not missed a thing. Of course she hasn't, she's going to fit perfectly into village life. 'What?' I say.

'Well, he *is* rather dishy, Cat. Perfect for you. If I was forty years older, I might…'

'Whoa, hold on there. Forty years older? Just how old do you think we are?'

She looks confused. 'Erm, mid-, no idea.'

'For your information, young lady, I'm forty-two. And in my prime.'

At which point, I realise the lovely doctor has doubled back and is now dithering in the doorway. 'Ah, um, Catherine…' His deep, gravelly voice sends prickles down my spine. 'I was wondering if… you'd like to go out to dinner with me next week?'

Without waiting for an answer, he bolts like a scalded cat, just as I catch Skye smirking.

'What, young lady?' I say, innocently. 'It's purely social.'

Her giggle echoes across the room and I sigh. She doesn't miss much, that one.

Chapter 3

What do you wear for a first 'encounter'? I refuse to call it a date, because that would jinx even the most promising meet-up. And this one's especially tricky because it's with someone in the village who, let's face it, has generally seen me shrouded in the dubious delights of Barbour jacket and wellies (even though my pink ones have now morphed into traditional green).

If our venue was some distant eating place, it wouldn't matter nearly so much. But it's the local restaurant, which admittedly has a regional reputation, but is also staffed by villagers I pass every day in the street. Which guarantees every inch of what I wear and every morsel I eat will be circulating on the village gossip grapevine long before I've left the table.

Plus, what message do I want to give? After all, I'm a comfortably well-off, comfortably proportioned, mature lady who's (almost) comfortable with life. OMG, that makes me sound so twinset and pearls, which I'm definitely not. On the other hand, nor am I cowgirl boots, tassels and a ten-gallon hat, or the Cotswolds equivalent of this, which doesn't bear thinking about. What clothing says 'sophisticated lady with a zest for life and the hint of a wild streak' who loves her dog and her cottage and chocolate, although not necessarily in that order? And up for a good time – in a respectable way (probably)?

The slinky little black dress is out: it's got too much class *and* cleavage. But my usual evening attire of loose trousers and an even looser old t-shirt won't do justice to the occasion (it doesn't do justice to anything, actually, and should have been ditched years ago, but it *fits* me, if you know what I mean).

Look at it this way, Cat: on a glamour scale of 1-10, where does tonight's supper fall? Good point. Four would be the pub, eight Mortimer Manor, so maybe a six? Seven would be smart black trousers, a cream shirt and my brocade jacket. But six, six is a problem. Hmm – maybe the black trousers, the jacket and no shirt? *Behave, girl.*

After my attempts to choose an outfit reach double figures and my bed is strewn with rejects, I settle for Massimo Dutti tailored blue jeans, a dazzling white cotton vest which hugs my figure in all the right places and a bright red waistcoat, complemented by soft, black ankle boots. A single sweep of my arm moves the pile of discarded items from the bed onto the floor.

Luckily, I'm not one for masses of makeup and I need to be out of the door in precisely thirty-two minutes. Not that I'm counting, you understand. But a girl should be polite – and therefore five minutes late. So, a squirt of discrete perfume, a hint of red lipstick and a dab of foundation leaves just one final dilemma: hair up or down? I love my golden curly hair and during the years in London I must have spent the equivalent of the GDP of a minor country getting it just right. But the Cotswold countryside is a different matter. If I leave it as it is usually, does it look as if I haven't made an effort? But if I hitch it up, it can look like a mop and it's likely to come down anyway. In the end, I settle for as-is. Then I clip a simple gold band around my neck and, with hands only slightly shaking, I'm set.

It's a pleasant autumn evening and the sky is sprinkled with stars, so it's a five minute relaxing amble to the Stroud Road. Sadly, this being village life, the streets are deserted and there's no-one around to appreciate my efforts. But I suppose it does prevent any nosy inquisition.

The King's Bounty has a blazing log fire in full flame and the tables are still only sparsely occupied. A quick glance reassures me there's no-one I recognise, although that won't stop the village gossip flaring into full swing, long before the evening's out. Unfortunately, my own table is also under-populated, there's no sign of our village medic. He, unlike me, certainly won't make it across the threshold without being recognised and acknowledged by all. Linton had warned me that his evening surgery might overrun, so I'm not unduly concerned and settle myself into the upholstered chair, tucking into the jug of water that arrives simultaneously with me.

Halfway through the glass, the wine waiter arrives with a glass of champagne, and I groan. This is never good news: either some bloke fancies his chances and considers a lone female fair game or I'm about to be stood up. Again. It turns out to be the latter because, moments later, my phone buzzes with a text from Dr Heath: *Cat, so sorry, ruptured appendix and ambulance delayed by smash on A419*. There's a string of sad-faced emojis and flowers but it's too late, the evening's ruined and I have to face the walk of shame back through the tables. I know you can't argue with medical emergencies but really, what's a girl to think?

I stomp back home, my mind made up. No more dating a doctor, it'll never work. Maybe internet dating isn't so bad, as some of my friends agree. Time to resurrect *Honeyblond2*. Half an hour later, and still in my glad rags, with my homely supper of soup, bread and cheese, a large glass of wine and two of my largest cherry bombs I pull up my profile to see what's happening. I've notched up eight requests, none of whom look even remotely promising.

*

'I can only apologise for my fellow men!'

The following morning I'm slouching in a comfy armchair at the Vicarage, a weak smile on my face. No wonder Scott Willoughby is such a popular vicar. I'd only stumbled round for a cup of coffee and already I'm sobbing over my dating woes!

He leans back, stretches his legs and waits, his chin resting in one hand.

'And don't get me started on number 3! He described himself on his profile as, "a tall dark and handsome 45-year-old" and turned out to be short, round and, well… And I'm pretty sure he was married: the white circle on the ring finger is a dead giveaway. He spent the whole evening eying up the other women in the pub. I mean, I know I'm no Julia Roberts, but, really! I should have known from his profile: Big Boy Barney!'

Scott's piercing dark eyes lock onto me. 'And Linton?'

'There is no Linton.'

His eyebrows arch and he maintains his gaze. I carry on.

'Okay, it's going nowhere. We've had three attempts and each time "something's come up" at the last moment. He's always really apologetic. But I want to date a man not an empty chair.'

Scott laughs, which seems a tad insensitive given the circumstances. 'Sorry, Cat. But you should talk to Cherry – I reckon doctors and vicars have a lot in common! In our early days it was like my parishioners had a second sense when it came to their emergencies.'

'Really? How did you guys meet?' In all the months I've known him, I realise this is the closest he's come to any really personal sharing. I mean, I know some superficial stuff, obviously, but otherwise, nothing. And I'd never even noticed. He's good at being professional.

'It was in my previous parish. I was new and she was coaching the girls' rugby team when I dropped in to introduce myself, and she offered to help me settle in. It didn't go well.'

He stares out of the window. A clock strikes ten. A washing machine gurgles and churns away. I know there'd been some upset in his previous parish but Scott's never given any sign he wanted to talk about it.

'If you'd like to talk about it…' I rest my hand on his, on the chair arm.

But Scott shakes his head. 'Let's just say, the Bishop got involved. And I didn't handle it very well, either with him or with Cherry.' His body tenses and his eyes glaze over, then he sighs. 'Anyway, Cat, this is about you, not me. What do you plan to do next?

'Join a nunnery!' The words are out before I've even thought them. We both giggle and I'm sure he's thinking it's hard to imagine anyone less like a nun. 'Maybe I'm just not meant to have another man. I hardly made a success with the last one.'

'Cat, he ran off and left you. That wasn't down to you.'

'Maybe if I'd tried harder, listened to what he was telling me. What if he was right all along?'

'Don't *ever* think that.' Scott has gone red and is on the edge of his chair.

'Well, I can't be that attractive. He left for a younger woman. And the men on the dating sites aren't exactly queuing up to romance me. Maybe it's time to

accept it and stick to Dag. At least he never rejects me.'
I was feeling sorry for myself now.

'That's rubbish and you know it!'

'I only wish it was. But what can I do when all the men I meet sound so great and attentive online then when you finally meet up all they ever want to talk about is their ex, their job or their football team?'

When I stop and think about it, it really doesn't seem worth the effort, so by the time I've strolled back to my cosy cottage, I've decided. I just need to log on and delete my profile. And take one last quick look. Ooh, he looks interesting. *Cat, stop*! Delete.

*

The village library is the ideal place to go to wrap yourself up in romantic fiction, in a world of inappropriately dashing heroes and impossible lifestyles, not to mention improbable summers of constant sunshine and picnics, which I float though in fine lace bodices, swirling skirts and black leather boots. Blissfully safe from absent medics and all that real life rubbish.

So, when the tall, slim man in a black rollneck, tightly-tailored light tweed waistcoat, designer jeans and red DMs hovers by my comfy armchair and invites me for a drink, I gawp for several seconds. I'm sure he must be already regretting asking. I glance down at my somewhat muddy trousers.

'I only popped in for a gardening encyclopaedia.' *Great chat-up line, Cat, especially since you're gripping The Secret Loves of Lizzie Law with rather sweaty fingers.* 'That's to say…' I run my hands through my matted curls and a large twig drops out. 'I was, erm, gardening, you see.'

The poor man must be thinking he's just invited a mad woman out for a drink. In fairness to him, his face hasn't shown any panic (so far). 'I thought you might have been.' He nods at my knitted jumper which I now realise contains more leaves than the average hedgerow.

I have a hard and fast rule never to date someone the first time we meet. In fact, currently, no-one, ever, under any circumstances. Except, he does seem ever so slightly familiar, if I could just place him. And attractive…

'Red.' I glance at his boots, wondering why he's stated the blatantly obvious. Then he holds out his hand and I realise he's talking about his name not his footwear.

'Catherine. Catney.' I shake his hand, which feels warm but insubstantial. 'Of course. Sorry, I didn't realise…'

'No reason why you would. Not exactly a common name.' He moves from one leg to the other, tugging the lapel of his waistcoat.

'Well, Red, I haven't seen you in the library before. Do you…'

'…come here often?' He smiles, which softens his face, although his dark eyes still seem a little hesitant. 'I'm doing some research here.'

A tractor trundles past, towing a massive trailer piled high with hay and we both watch it until it's out of sight.

'So, what do you think? About a drink?' His eyebrows lift towards his smooth bald pate.

I glance at my rather grubby hands. 'I'm really not…'

'I'm told they have washbasins in the toilets here.' There's that smile again. It is rather nice. And he seems pleasant enough. *Except, you've given men up, Cat, even pleasant ones.*

True, I think. And I'm only being sociable. If I have a glass of wine, I can down it in five minutes and we're meeting in a very public space, so it's not exactly risky. Or even risqué. *Behave yourself!*

'I tell you what,' he says. 'I'll see you in that trendy place around the corner in ten. Or not. It's up to you.' He marches off.

Oh Cat, what have you done? I'm sure there must be a dating equivalent of buyer's remorse.

Chapter 4

With a suggestive wink, Skye nods her head towards a quiet corner table where Red is already settled in behind a huge mug of hot chocolate topped with a mountain of thick whipped cream and a single roasted marshmallow. *Wow*! I think. *Why haven't I ever been offered anything so gorgeous?*

Skye winks again, giggles, and whispers, 'Tasty!'
Ah, so that's why. Cheeky madam.

My companion rises with a slight smile, and I notice his eyes slowly appraise me from head to toe. I'm proud of the way I've guarded my figure despite my chocoholism and it's always nice to be appreciated. I'd just prefer it to be, well, a little less obvious. *Are you sure this is a good idea?* Probably not, but then, nothing ventured, nothing gained, as my mother used to say. After all, he dresses smartly, seems capable of holding a sensible conversation *and* he has a pleasant face. In the 'potential' stakes, he's above the bar. Which, admittedly, is currently set pretty low.

Skye delivers my own hot chocolate, minus adornments, then apologises as she slops some down the side of the mug. She's too busy making eyes at my companion. *My* companion, Skye!

It seems I've passed Red's scrutiny, as he half-stands and extends his hand across the table. 'Time for a proper introduction: Red Street. Thank you for coming, Catherine. I wasn't sure you would.'

'To be honest, neither was I. But, Mr Street, you had me intrigued.' I raise my eyebrows but my attempt at a Roger Moore James Bond impression falls on deaf ears, so I blush and take a few moments to settle in my seat. I reach for a reassuring fondle of Dagenham's soft ears, but of course, he's not there so I fuss with my handbag instead. It all feels very awkward. But then these first meetings always do, even when there have been several preliminary online chats, which is more than this one's had, so it's hardly surprising there isn't the usual intrigue and anticipation. To be honest, it feels a little foolhardy. Which I realise I rather like.

Red's face is a spider's-web of fine wrinkles, which I reckon must make him a good decade older than me and his eyes, which I'd thought were jet black, are actually light blue but overshadowed by dark rings. He sighs and leans forward, resting his elbows on the table and looks rather intently at me. 'It's good to finally meet you.' Then he leans back, abruptly. 'Sorry, that must sound very freaky. What I mean is, I've noticed you whenever you've passed the library and it's nice to finally have the chance to chat.'

I'm not sure whether to be flattered or spooked. My hand automatically goes to smooth my hair and tuck a strand behind my ear so I suppose I must be flattered. On the other hand, I don't think I like the idea that someone's secretly been observing me. Then again, he's invited me here, so I obviously haven't put him off. I say nothing and Red speaks.

'Sorry, Catherine. I honestly don't make a habit of this.' His gaze scans the room while he talks so perhaps he's as nervous as I am?

'And I don't make a habit of accepting invitations like this one.' I smile at him but there's no immediate response. 'Tell me more about your research. It sounds intriguing.'

He grunts. 'Not really. I've got a passing interest in ceramics, jugs mainly. Nothing pretentious, although I have written a book about them, most of them Wedgewood. There have been some thefts from dealers recently, so I'm doing some research in how long it's been going on. Thought I might even write a novel based on it.'

His last few words fade into silence, so I crane forward to hear. But then I feel uncomfortably close and make a show of getting a tissue from my handbag so I'm at a more suitable distance again.

Meanwhile, Red has resumed staring out of the window. I'm a great believer in closely examining someone when you first meet them, particularly when they think you aren't looking; you can learn so much. It has sometimes got me into trouble for staring but after ten years managing a successful advertising business, I've learnt to do it rather more subtly. And it's served me well. It's amazing how often you can spot a fake, even this early on.

After closer inspection, I don't feel Red's putting on appearances or pretending. And I suppose he does look like a fine arts aficionado. He dresses neatly and there's a certain sense of style and stillness about him. I can imagine him being one of those people who stares at a single piece of art far longer than I spend in the entire gallery. Plus, he has long, slender fingers. *Really, Cat? Long, slender fingers make him genuine? There are no long-fingered murderers?*

I can also conclude confidently that he's not a conversationalist. I've met some men whose sole topic of conversation for an entire evening consists of their pet hobby and need little or no excuse to drone on about it. I remember one dire five course silver service meal in the City where, for the first four courses, I was harangued about racing pigeons, then, for dessert, I'd been treated to in-depth biographies of each of his thirty-four birds. By the end of the evening he hadn't even bothered to ask my name. Wouldn't have happened if I'd been a racing pigeon.

I sit further back in my seat. 'But why the library, Red? Surely their stuff is too out of date to be useful?'

'Oh no. They've got a very comprehensive range of current newspapers and magazines, as well as copies going back twenty, thirty years.' He stares out of the window, still as a statue, but less substantial. More like a painting, perhaps. It's rather disconcerting. In my experience, when you meet someone face-to-face, they come to life, they turn from a one-dimensional screen presence to real life 3D: this man seems just the opposite.

The door rattles as a young mother and her daughter make their way across the café. Red's eyes lock onto the admittedly very attractive dark-haired woman, Spanish I'd guess, and follow her as the two of them settle at an adjoining table. The pair look around at the quirky decorations and giggle, enjoying their time together, catching up on the day, no doubt.

I interrupt his thoughts. 'Sounds interesting. What have you discovered?'

A vein in his neck pulses as he sighs deeply, before dragging his gaze back to me and shaking his head. 'Not much, really.' He shrugs and his mouth forms a smile reaching no further than his lips, while his eyes drift back to the young woman next to us.

'Ouch.' A sharp sting on my wrist reveals the deep imprint of my own fingernails. *Breathe, Cat, deeply and slowly.* At least it drags his attention back. *Don't make a scene.*

'Sorry, Catherine. Where was I?'

'You were telling me…' Already he's back, staring at the pretty neighbour. 'You know what, forget it.' The table lurches as I stand up abruptly, depositing a satisfying dark chocolate stain on the front of his waistcoat.

'But Catherine…' He grabs my arm and I yelp as his fingers dig in and he lets go instantly. Several people glance at us, including Skye, but I shake my head to reassure her. 'Sorry, that was unforgiveable,' he whispers as I sink back in my chair, reluctantly. 'It's the girl, she reminds me of… someone.'

I wait. The seconds tick by. 'Someone special?' I say. Red nods, but instead of explaining he just stares out of the window again. Skye arrives with two more drinks which we haven't ordered and makes a point of catching my attention and raising her very prominent beaded eyebrows. But I can easily deal with this clown.

'No, not really.' Red's voice sounds distant and distracted. 'Well, actually, yes.'

Momentarily, a lump comes to my throat. Then I notice why he sounds distracted. He's staring at Skye's retreating legs. He's still distracted when I slam the coffee shop door behind me, though I suppose he must have noticed my departure.

Wow, Cat, that's a world-first: leaving a hot chocolate untasted. I kick out at a large pile of swept leaves, scattering them across the pavement, then I feel guilty because someone must have swept them up, and I try to scuff them back with my foot. Why are men so absorbed in themselves? Or just sleazebags? Where are nature's gentlemen – the ones like our doctor? *Don't go there, Cat.*

A couple of minutes later, and a few hundred yards further on, my door bangs as I slam it loudly behind me, waking my true beloved, Dagenham. Despite looking startled to be disturbed at this time of the day he instantly scuttles between my legs, forcing me to grab a door post to avoid landing on the stone slabs.

'Okay, my boy, you're the exception to the male rule.' His tail shows his appreciation by lashing my legs and as I bend down to fondle his ears, I end up in a sprawling mess on the floor, where I have to wrestle him off before he can lick my face and clamber all over my chest.

Dagenham is never one to miss an opportunity, so he takes one final tramp over my body and stares at the front door. 'Oh, alright. I guess my baking can wait for another half an hour,' I sigh.

So, less than ten minutes after storming out of the Emporium we're heading off in the opposite direction along the Rodmarton road while I educate my pooch on the evils of men in general and one in particular. His ears flop in sympathy and he adds the occasional supportive woof so by the time we top the hill beyond the village I'm ready to take in and appreciate a perfect autumnal day. All around, the trees glow red, gold, and brown against a cloudless blue October sky and the path in front of me is dappled like a church's stained-glass window. In the valley, the beautiful Cotswolds countryside is picked out in a glorious mix of bright sunlight and deep shadow, and I pause to appreciate so much of my new life here. (Apart from the men, of course.) And I have a large batch of particularly juicy chocolate cherry bombs awaiting my return. 'Woof,' says Dag hopefully.

*

I pop a third bomb into my mouth, run my tongue around the dark chocolate coating and slowly squeeze it between my teeth, luxuriating as the soft ganache and caramel filling oozes around my teeth. Then I sigh. 'It's no good, Dag. The Harvest chocolates won't make themselves. Especially since I've already eaten half the stock.' He licks his lips and stares hopefully at the one remaining chocolate. 'Not good for you, my boy.' Purely in the interests of putting it out of harm's way, I pop it into my mouth. If it's possible for a dog's face to fall, his does. 'But look what I've found...' I flick one of his favourite doggie treats into the air and smile as he springs to catch it mid-flight. Which broadens my smile because in all the months I've had him I don't think a single treat has ever made it back to earth intact. *Clever boy.* Right – chocolate production line, here I come.

I'm barely out of my armchair and heading for the kitchen when my mobile phone springs into life. Saved by the bell! I glance to see whose name has flashed across the screen, panicking for a moment that it might be Red. Forgetting that he doesn't have my number, although it wouldn't be too hard to find. Instead, it's Skye

'Hello, Skye. Is everything alright? I was literally about to start on your order.'

'Are you alright, Cat?' Skye's voice sounds thin and tense. 'You left in rather a hurry. Are you ill?'

'No, nothing like that, Skye.' I take a deep breath. Did I overreact? I know I can be a bit hasty, especially where men are concerned. But then, given my ex, who would blame me? 'It was … just a bad idea. In future I think I'll stick to dogs not dating!'

'Rubbish, Cat. You're quite a babe. For someone your age.'

'Less of the…'

Skye giggles and the phone goes dead. *Hah!* But even so, I feel much lighter as I make my way into the kitchen, and as I line up the ingredients I'm actually humming. 'You know what, Dag? She's right, I am quite a babe,' and I sashay across to the melting pot and flick the switch. 'Alexa, play me some slinky jazz.'

Five minutes later, with hands fully washed and cleansed, sleeves rolled up, and my curls pulled back into a plum headscarf, I'm surrounded by chocolate chunks, a milk ganache, my favourite melted caramel, piping bags, scrapers, gift bags and ribbon ties. Then, I open a drawer and select my favourite plastic mould from the sealed bags: just right for small, perfectly round chocs to pop into your mouth as a little treat, and highly likely to tempt you to eat more. Ideal for the coffee shop and maybe even for Harvest Festival afters. A short while later I perch on a kitchen stool surveying the three dozen little balls of deliciousness separated out in front of me. The question is, what else should I do for Skye's counter? Maybe slices of a chocolate marble cake? What else might Skye be able to sell?

My phone pings with an incoming text. Well, speak of the devil… *You need a NIGHT OUT WITH THE GIRLS. Meet us 7.30 in the Square. Skye*

Excellent. Time to get the glad rags out. And maybe some lippie and heels. Hang on a minute, though. *Girls? Who are the girls?* I like Skye, but I'd hardly class her in my circle of closest friends. My heart drops. I bet she's sent it to me by mistake. After all, I am old enough to be her mother. My fingers shake as I tap out, *Are you sure this is meant for me? CAT,'* hoping the capital letters will alert her to any mistake.

Moments later comes the reply, *You bet, girl!*

Okay, then, I think. *Let's party!*

Chapter 5

Skye was right.

A night out with the girls was exactly what I needed. It just wasn't what I expected. And the girls turned out to be quite the gang: there was Skye, her hair a deep purple and sprinkled with glitter, her aunt – my friend – Rose, dressed to the nines in black velour trousers and a silver top to reflect, she told us, the footloose and free status she intended to 'exploit to the full', Scott's girlfriend Cherry, taking a well-deserved break from renovating her cottage, Rose's friend Mavis Enderby with her cut glass accent and hourglass figure who I've rarely seen in the village but whose hand can be felt almost everywhere, and *her* friend Sandy Lane, who I've spotted around the village looking elegantly fashionable in that effortless way the rich do, a woman I've never spoken to but who turned out to be a disgraceful sixty-two year old whom I loved, instantly.

It turns out a night on the tiles in Gloucester was actually an evening on the roundabouts and swings of Cirencester's Mop Funfair. Which, thankfully for my footwear, isn't held on grass but on the town's pavements. I'd never heard of a mop before so with the six of us crammed into Cherry's car and pootling at a snail's pace more suited to the earlier Roman chariots, Rose took the opportunity, accompanied by surreptitious swigs from a bottle of champagne, to 'explain to the newbies' – Skye and me – that it was where traders would come looking to hire staff. Apparently, the workers would bring something symbolising their trade like a mop or a spade to show they were available and then replace it with a bright ribbon when they were hired. As she talks I giggle as I imagine myself holding a chocolate bomb. Anyway, apparently the mop dates back over 700 years, and the current charter has been in the same family of showmen for over a hundred years. Who knew?

None of which prepared me for the colour and noise of the town's transformation. Market Place and Cricklade Road were jam-packed with huge roundabouts and stalls, all of which seemed so much bigger in the narrow spaces between the shops. And the music was amplified off walls which must have witnessed more than a hundred of these events. As the ever-flowing supply of alcohol began to take hold, I tried to imagine what the walls would have thought about all the changes they'd seen over the years.

Directly in front of St John Baptist church, a traditional roundabout of colourful aeroplanes was filled with screaming, laughing young children, while next to it the ultra-modern Extreme Ride thrust out brightly lit limbs and promised an experience that looked completely baffling, not to say scary. Needless to say, we tried out every last ride, at least where we weren't deemed too old – we did try those as well but were unceremoniously turfed off some, much to the amusement of watching parents. We also made full use of hot dog stands and sampled candyfloss and toffee apples. And possibly one or two of the surrounding hostelries.

My wildly unsuitable short dress and heels did get some admiring glances from a number of rather lovely men, meaning I chalked it all up as an enormous success. Great for the confidence – despite getting a deluge of teasing from Skye, Rose and Cherry who, it transpired, is a dab hand at hoopla so each of us returned with an absolutely huge furry teddy. Dag was not amused, though, and has wasted no opportunity to growl at it.

So, this morning's throbbing head and sawdust mouth as I exercise my pet is a price worth paying. There's nothing like a long, bracing early morning walk to clear the head and I've brought a full water bottle to cleanse the mouth. Plus, I have the luxury of looking forward to a quiet day with some long overdue reading and maybe some even more overdue gardening. Or, maybe not, as any hint of bending currently fills me with dread and a vile taste. Does a full English breakfast really settle the stomach? I'll soon find out.

We trot past the last few cottages in the village and then through the kissing gate into the open fields. Dag catches some scent or other and strains to be let off the lead. 'Sorry, boy, but I'm not risking you getting carried away with all the smells and becoming conveniently deaf.'

His look says only too clearly, 'Who? Me? As if!' But out of respect to farmers and in deference to my own throbbing head, there's nothing doing.

The path is well worn and easy to follow, with the bonus of having walked it most days in the months since Dag arrived, come rain or shine. It's a popular route with a handful of other dog walkers and owners and the pets now have an easy familiarity. Although this morning the only sign of life comes from a startled pheasant who squarks an angry complaint before fluttering back into the bushes, much to Dagenham's frustration.

All of this has become so familiar, it's hard to imagine that this is my first autumn in Much Slaughter. This time a year ago I was still fully established in our London cottage, totally absorbed in frantic office politics and the maelstrom of business, never dreaming I was about to swop the capital for the Cotswolds. And, a year on, I'd never consider going back to that frenetic way of life. Amazing how much can be changed by so little. One text and my boss's summons.

'Morning, Catney!'

I jump like a startled pheasant. 'Oh, morning Skye. Sorry – miles away.'

'You certainly were. I reckon I could have lifted your purse and you'd have had no idea. Something wrong?'

'No, couldn't sleep. Such a great time with you guys - can't believe I've been here for less than a year.'

'Me neither. And I've been here for less time than you. Yet it seems like we've known each other forever. Are you walking my way? I've got at least half an hour before I need to do prep for the café, for the ravenous hordes.'

'I can do. By the way, I'll drop off your chocolate order after lunch. They're just setting in the fridge. I know we talked about after the Harvest Festival, but I thought some preliminary tasters might be good?'

'Thanks, Cat, that's a great idea. They'll sell like hot cakes – if you see what I mean!'

'My pleasure. It'll be good to do something to keep the old creative juices flowing. I mean, don't get me wrong, village life is fantastic. But…'

'It's a far cry from London! I know. It takes a lot of getting used to, the slower pace of life.'

'Tell me about it! I've never lived anywhere where I could see the stars before. Or where everyone seems to be indoors by eight o'clock! And as for all this…' I look around. 'There's so much space. And lovely meadow walks. I even feel safe on my bike without lunatic car drivers trying to force me off the road and then questioning my parentage.'

Skye giggles then winces. 'Quite some night, wasn't it?' It seems I'm not the only one enjoying dubious after-effects from the night before. We walk on in an easy silence, lost in thought and following the path across the field, the ground hard and dry. A cockapoo bounds up to Dagenham then beats a hasty retreat, tail between its legs, as Dag growls his disapproval. Moments later its owner appears, a mobile phone glued to her ear as she ambles through the field some 50 metres away, ignoring the path and the requested leash. We both shake our heads, but she's oblivious. 'DFL,' whispers Skye and we giggle.

At the boundary hedge, Skye pauses. 'This where I branch off.' For a few moments I watch her go, reflecting I'd emerged from my ten years in London with just a handful of acquaintances while in as many months in Much Slaughter I've gained loads of friends. With the added bonus of the smells of harvest rather than diesel and the sounds of bird song rather than sirens. Plus, my wonderful cottage and its oak-beamed history that one day I'll ask Wickham to help me research.

There's a long, slow climb ahead of us towards the Monarch's Way and my calf muscles are starting to protest after being forced to cope with last night's high heels, so I decide that maybe a longer breakfast and a shorter walk is in order. Dagenham looks at me dolefully as we swing back down the hill, then past the Recreation Ground which still reminds me of the unfortunate events from a few months back. Moments later, we're at the top of the main street just as the church clock strikes seven-thirty and I pause to catch my breath.

Ahead of me, High Street is blissfully quiet: the locals seem to have decided it's too early and the tourists are lingering over breakfast. Even the tractors haven't hit the roads yet. A few traders are replenishing shelves behind CLOSED signs but as there's still a good two hours before they open, most shops are as deserted as the streets.

The only movement comes from a handful of cars and vans, funnelling through from the surrounding hamlets and fanning out to workplaces in Cirencester or Bristol, Cheltenham or Swindon.

Over to my left, in our local bookshop, *Bound to Please*, Wickham Skeith is busy changing the window display to showcase works by some famous murder mystery writer whose name I can't remember but who is coming here for a book signing in a couple of days. Wickham grins and makes an exaggerated show of mopping his brow.

'Time for breakfast, Dag.' My pup pricks his ears and picks up the pace, straining on his leash in anticipation of delicious treats.

About halfway down the street, however, just outside the Police Museum, Dagenham stops rigid, growls and refuses to move. 'Come on, boy, we're nearly home and then I can feed... Oh.' I follow his eyeline. Slumped across the Triumph motorbike in the window of the Police Museum is the body of a man. And judging by the bright red stain across his grey roll-neck jumper and the display card below, it doesn't look good. Not again, surely?

*

Almost an hour later – an hour I've spent marching up and down a ten-metre stretch of pavement so many times I ought to have worn a groove in it as I wait to be dismissed by the police – a very portly police sergeant scares the living daylights out of me when he looms over the bike and body, which I resume he must have been inspecting. He stares around for a few moments, spots me and beckons me inside.

He struts into the hallway and stares at me. I stare back with a slight smile because he looks the epitome of the Laughing Policeman I remember from the amusement arcade in my childhood holidays in Skegness. But he isn't laughing. 'I should have known it would be you again, Ms de Barnes. Getting quite the reputation, aren't we?'

'Sergeant?' I nod, rather curtly. After the shock of seeing a dead body on an already queasy stomach from last night, the last thing I need is a sarcastic policeman. 'I can assure you, it's not a reputation I want.'

'Hmm.' His piercing black eyes stare at me for several seconds. 'What can you tell me?'

'I'm sorry, sergeant, have we met before?'

'Indeed we have madam. I was one of the constables who attended your unfortunate encounter with the dead chef. Before I got my stripes.'

'Of course. My apologies. Although as you'll appreciate, it was rather unusual circumstances.'

'But getting to be something of a habit, it would seem, Ms de Barnes.' He stares at me, suspicion written as clearly across his face as if he'd used a felt-tip pen.

'Sergeant, I can assure you I have no involvement, other than as a passer-by. If Dagenham hadn't stopped, I doubt I'd have even…'

'Ah yes, the faithful bloodhound.' He switches his gaze to my pooch, who for some inexplicable reason looks rather proud of the title and licks the odious man's hand. *A bit of loyalty wouldn't go amiss here, Dag.*

'What exactly did you see, Ms de Barnes?' The sergeant then licks his pen like every stereotype of a police officer I've ever seen, and I wonder what he'll do when technology takes over from his little black book. 'Ms de Barnes?'

'Sorry, I'm slightly distracted. It's not been the best of starts. On top of the after-effects of last night.'

The sergeant sighs. 'I'm *so* sorry if this is inconvenient. It's not been exactly convenient for our victim either. So, if we might get on?'

'Of course. Sorry. Do you think I might sit down though? I seem to be shaking.'

A moment of concern flashes across his corpulent face before he quickly masks it and nods to a uniformed constable hovering just inside what looks like an old office. The constable produces a wooden chair which he dumps with a teeth-jarring screech on the marble floor tiles and I perch on the edge, trying to quell my queasiness and gather my thoughts.

'Sergeant, who was it?'

'An ex-colleague, as it happens. Your retired policeman.'

'What, Dean Court? I've heard of him but never met him. And I don't recall anyone say a bad word about him. Do we know what happened?'

'Yes, Ms de Barnes, *we* do. But it's information I'm not at liberty to divulge to the *general public*.' He puts so much weight on the last two words that I'm surprised they can make it out of his mouth. And it seems a little ungracious since, as I recall, my efforts made a material contribution to solving the case of the dead chef.

As if he's read my thoughts, the sergeant shakes his head and announces in his most officious voice, 'Once you tell us how you found the body – if we ever manage to get that far –you'll be on your way and out of our way. Permanently.'

What a cheek. As if I'd asked to be part of this! 'Of course, Sergeant. I'd like *nothing more*.' It's my turn to emphasis the last two words, even though they're accompanied by my sweetest smile. 'I was simply passing, at the end of my customary early morning walk to exercise Dagenham.'

The sergeant looks confused.

'My dog, officer. He stopped outside the window and refused to go any further. And when I looked up, there was the body.' I shudder.

'And you didn't see anything suspicious? Before or after?'

No, Inspector.' I hesitate, recalling what happened. 'As soon as I saw the body over the motorbike, I called you. And then I paced up and down outside the door, which was slightly open by the way, until your constable arrived.'

'And during that time, did you see anyone else?

No, Inspector, it was remarkably quiet, even for Much Slaughter. Which, as you know, is quiet even at the best of times. Except for...'

'Except for a rather high number of murders.' His bushy eyebrows arch.

'Is this is a murder then? I'd assumed it was just some sort of terrible accident.'

'I rather think the knife in his back suggests otherwise. Which is why we leave things to the professionals.' I hastily cover my grin with a hand. He glares at me, realising he's divulged too much in his desire for a hasty put-down.

'Anyway, Sergeant, I was going to say, I saw no-one who looked like a murderer.'

'Which is another good reason why we leave these things to the professionals.'

Goodness, this man is insufferable. It almost makes me want to get involved and prove I'm not the silly amateur he thinks I am. But instead, I concentrate on the very large and very unhealthy breakfast fry-up awaiting me on my return home. I glance at my watch and decide I can now treat myself to one courtesy of the Coffee Emporium.

'Description, please? Of the person you saw who didn't look like a murderer.'

'What? Oh. No, sorry. I didn't mean I didn't see anyone who didn't look like a murderer. I meant, I didn't see anyone who didn't look like a murderer, nor anyone who did – look like a murderer, I mean.'

The officer lets out a sigh so loud and long it could have been a volcano erupting.

'I'm not helping, am I sergeant? What I'm trying to say is, I'm pretty sure I didn't see anyone, whether they looked like…'

I could concentrate much better if I didn't feel under a spotlight. But that's not how it works, it seems. 'If I think of anything else, I'll let you know, Sergeant.'

'Very kind of you, Ms de Barnes, I'm sure.' His lip curls and I wonder whether he sees me as a threat. But then, out of the blue, he smiles, and his fleshy features look so much warmer. 'Sorry, it's a busy time.' His voice takes on a gentle Gloucestershire undertone. 'I know where to find you when we need next you.' *When* not *if?* Interesting. 'And you're quite sure you didn't enter the building?'

'It's not the sort of thing I'd forget, Inspector.'

The sergeant stares down at me for a few moments, then straightens stiffly and resumes the air of a policeman. 'You can go, for now. We'll call you when we need your statement.'

If I hadn't been so hungry, I'd have taken offence at such a dismissal, but the lure of eggs, bacon, toast, mushrooms, baked beans, and coffee overwhelms everything else. Look out, Skye, I'm on my way.

Chapter 6

The summons arrives a couple of days later, just as I'm emerging from a particularly disturbed night's sleep. A ringing phone jolts me out of bed and I race downstairs for my handbag (yes, I am one of those who refuses to have anything digital in my rest space). A female voice informs me, in a lilting Scottish accent, I'm to present myself at the Police Museum at 0900 hours precisely.

On the ninth stroke of the church clock, with Dagenham at my side for moral support, I rattle the wrought iron outer gate of the Museum. Is it deliberately designed to feel like rattling the bars of a cell, I wonder? Moments later, the door opens, and a pale-faced constable who looks about twelve eyes me up and down suspiciously, before unlocking the gate, staring with deep disapproval at Dagenham and finally ushering us both in, no doubt having concluded – correctly – he'd be the one left dog-minding.

I don't know why I'm suddenly feeling so queasy and nervous but, in an attempt to allay my fears, I call out to the receding back, 'Odd place to set up an office, isn't it, constable, in a museum? Or are you hoping to be using the cells again once you've interviewed me? Will two of them be enough, do you think?'

My attempt at levity falls flat as he turns and glares at me. 'Not that it's any of your business, but it saves us an hour's journey back to our headquarters in Gloucester. And it's quite appropriate, given that it used to be a police station. Working up here means we can seal off the museum area from *interfering* members of the public.' He stares at me, pointedly, before swinging on his heels and stomping off down a large hallway laced with old legal textbooks and general artefacts befitting its police and magistrates history in glass-fronted cabinets. while I trot obediently behind him, suitably chastened. On my right, I spot an anteroom crammed with glass display cases of old police uniforms and handcuffs, and beyond this, a tiny office supervised by a uniformed policeman and a black and white toy cat. Dag glares at the cat for a moment before deciding it's not worth a growl. I think it looks rather sweet. Much less sweet is the glimpse into the old police cells with their heavy metal door and bare brick walls.

My guard stops halfway up a flight of stairs and turns to check I'm still there, although quite where he thinks I'd have sloped off to, I can't imagine. But I suppose he's used to dealing with reluctant prisoners rather than willing witnesses; perhaps I should be glad I'm not handcuffed. I grin, causing the youth to scowl and beckon me to hurry.

He leads me into the main upstairs room which, rather appropriately, is still set out as the magistrates' court. I notice I'm not invited to sit in the significantly more comfortable Magistrate's chair but rather to stand in a narrow, raised box which I imagine is where they put the prisoner. Charming. The constable returns to his desk, so as soon as his attention's distracted, I slip round to try the padded chair of power under the stern gaze of another uniformed policeman who stands motionless on the far side of the room. Moments later, another constable arrives, smiles at me and takes her place behind a pile of folders opposite the first officer, who blushes without looking up. Sweet.

It would seem the same demand for punctuality doesn't apply to whoever is due to take my statement, so I'm left to stare from my elevated platform at the wood-panelled surroundings and wonder how many ordinary folk have stood in this very room in the hope of justice. Or, I suppose, lack of it, if you're guilty. And how many have departed for prisons scattered around the Cotswolds, maybe even one I pass on the Fosse Way up to Stratford?

Chief Inspector Glen Parva strides into the room and I frown. The man and I have history. Today, he seems smaller and wearier. The two uniformed constables at their desks sit bolt upright, snap to attention and salute as if their lives depend on it. The atmosphere immediately seems crisper. The chief inspector nods at me and turns away, then swings back abruptly and I swear he almost allows a smile to escape before he barks at the two officers, 'Right, tell me what you've found out.' The young man salutes again. 'Sir, yes sir. We, um, that is, this lady, erm…'

'Oh, for goodness' sake Constable. Pull yourself together.'

'Inspector, maybe I can help?' I step gingerly off the platform. At floor level it feels as if I've shrunk and he's grown, and he towers over me, making an impressive figure. Although he looks singularly unimpressed with me.

'Ah yes, Ms de Barnes. I might have known you'd be involved.' His well-groomed blue jacket sits snugly on his broad shoulders, and I like the fact that he can still button it over his stomach. I'd describe him as well-padded – in a good way. *Come on Cat, you're here for business, not pleasure.*

'Inspector, I'm afraid the death found me, not the other way round. I'm just the one who found the body. At least, from the other side of the window.'

'Quite.' He looks me up and down, his face giving nothing away, certainly no hint that he's pleased to see me. For my part, I smooth my dress and tuck a strand of stray curls behind my ear. One thing you can guarantee about my mop of curls, there'll always be something needing rearrangement. I wish I'd taken rather more care before I'd set off, instead of looking as if I'd just tumbled out from a bad night's sleep. 'Well, actually it was Dagenham.'

'What?' The inspector looks as if he's dealing with a mad woman, then nods at the timid policeman, who takes out his notebook and actually licks his pencil ready for action.

'You remember my wonderful dog, Dagenham.' I wave my hand towards my pooch, who by now has lost

58

all hope of either food or petting and is therefore snoring contentedly beneath the clerk's table. 'He stopped outside the window and refused to budge. Which is when I looked in and saw – the body. Slumped over the motorbike.' I shudder.

He glances at Dag and actually smiles before he realises what he's done and rapidly reinstates his police face. 'The deceased has been identified as Dean Court. A local resident. Ring any bells, Ms de Barnes?'

'Yes, Inspector. I understand he's ex-police and used to be based in the town. But I presume you already knew that.'

The young policeman is scribbling as if his life depended on it.

'I can't say I know much more. You should talk to Wickham in the bookshop, he's been here ages and knows everything about everyone. It's an odd place to kill someone, though, don't you think, Inspector? Mind you, there'll be no shortage of suspects after all those years in the Force…'

The chief inspector winces. 'We don't like to refer to it as the "Force" nowadays. It has unfortunate connotations. We're deemed to be a service.' Behind him, the woman PC rolls her eyes, and I have to stifle a grin. 'And as for suspects, Ms de Barnes, I hardly think petty criminals would have a motive for murder. No, I'm sure our answer lies much closer to home.' He stares at me.

The atmosphere grows tense in the small room. As do I.

'Inspector, you can't be suggesting I'd…'

'I'm not suggesting anything, Ms de Barnes.' As I hop about from foot to foot, under his scrutiny, looking suspicious. The inspector continues.

'What else did you see? Anyone inside, or coming out of the building? Or on the street?'

'No, Inspector, it was dead quiet – sorry, bad choice, it was completely quiet. As I told your sergeant yesterday. Where is the charming soul, by the way?'

I'm sure I see the ghost of a smile on the inspector's face, before he shuts it down. 'Studying police deployment now, are we?' I don't rise to the bait. 'He's out making enquiries. Which, may I remind you, is precisely what you're not to do. You've done your bit.'

'Inspector, I can tell you for certain …'

'No, Ms de Barnes, you can't tell me anything. This is a police matter, and we'll take it from here.'

'All I was going to suggest is…'

'And I suggest you don't. In fact, I suggest you get on with whatever it is you get on with when you're not discovering dead bodies and getting under my feet. We'll be in touch, if we need to. Constable.'

Really? What an arrogant, misogynist man! And to think for a moment I even…

The woman steps forward and as soon as Glen has turned away, she shakes her head and winks at me. 'Don't mind him, Ms de Barnes. His bark's worse than his bite.' She reaches to pat Dag. 'Unlike your lovely dog. He's very good. What's his name?'

'Dagenham.'

She looks puzzled.

'Dagenham – beyond Barking.'

She looks even more puzzled.

'Sorry, I forgot you're not from England.' Oh dear, is that offensive? I have a friend who named his dog Barking – I'm sure you can guess why. They're neighbouring boroughs on the London underground line.'

She just smiles. 'No. I've only been down here about a year.'

'Snap. Except my departure was from London. What made you transfer – if you don't mind me asking?'

'I wish more people would ask. Man trouble. And it seemed like a good opportunity. How wrong I…' She swallows.

'Me too. Mind you, I only left a city and a – not-nice man, not a whole country. And turned my back on a high-powered job that was killing me. Along with the high-powered husband who was killing my self-esteem. Although, strictly speaking, my husband turned his back on me – for a fitter model.'

'Aye, men.' She soaks an impressive amount of feeling into six letters.

'Actually, to be honest, it was all very easy in the end. It all came to a head when I confronted my boss over the way she behaved and threatened to post it on Facebook, except that I used a different piece of anatomy to 'face'!'

The policewoman giggles. 'Why Much Slaughter then?'

'About as different to London as I could find. And I fell in love with my cottage.'

'Aye, it's a bonnie place.' Her accent's getting thicker the more she relaxes. 'But it's nay the Highlands. And truth to tell, I miss me kirk as well.'

'Ah, well on the last one, I might just be able to help. We have a rather dishy vicar here. Though he's spoken for! I'll introduce you.'

'Ah, the best ones always are.' The constable sighs and I see her shoulders sag a little 'I'll give it a bit longer but if it disnae get any better, I'll mebbe move away back tae the heathers.'

She grins as she leads me across the tiled entrance and stares around. 'If you don't mind me asking, why have you got a police museum here?'

We pause in the middle of the hall, the floor of which is now a brightly coloured mosaic of sunbeams filtered through the stained glass door. 'As far as I can work out, both the police station and the courtroom fell foul of financial cutbacks and one of the magistrates wanted to preserve it as part of his heritage. And being a man with influence, well, here we are.'

The policewoman shakes her head. 'Aye, saints preserve us from men with influence.'

And with that enigmatic proclamation, I'm gently ushered off the premises. The policewoman clangs the metal-barred gate shut and peers out. 'Don't give up on him, he really does like you, you know.'

I don't know what to say to that so I bend down to examine the iron framework. Dag takes the opportunity to lick my face with his warm tongue. 'Well, boy, there doesn't seem to be any sign of forced entry, so let's take a look at the lock.'

'Morning, Catherine. How are you doing?' My head jerks up and crashes into the metal door handle and my head threatens to explode. ''My dear girl, I am so sorry.'

'Wickham, it's fine. I'm just a bit jumpy at the moment.' I love my next-door neighbour but years of tiptoeing around his bookshop means he approaches like the silent assassin. *Cat, I'm really not sure that's an appropriate phrase.*

'You poor thing.' He lifts his herringbone tweed cap in greeting, then settles it back onto his thick white curls. 'I hear it was you who found the body.'

'It was.' I lean against the stone slabs of the archway, lowering my voice as a middle-aged couple wander past. 'I've just been interviewed. Unfortunately, it's that dreadful inspector again.'

Wickham's eyebrows arch and a slight smile plays round his lips. I go on.

'Not that I can shed much light, I'm afraid. Apart from discovering the body, of course.'

He leans in closer to me as a tractor rumbles past. 'Maybe you took in rather more than you think, Catherine. Who knows?'

'Oh, I'm not getting involved. Last time was more than enough.'

His eyebrows rise again.

'What?'

'No, nothing, m'girl.'

'Wickham?'

'Well, to be honest, all the time you were being drawn into the events around the chef's murder, you had what I can only describe as a light inside you. Not seen it before. Or after.'

'That was panic, you old rogue. Sheer panic.'

'If you say so.' He taps the side of his nose, then steps back to avoid my friendly swipe. 'I hear the victim was our indomitable Sergeant Dean Court. But since you're not getting involved, you won't want to hear any of my stories about him, will you? Shame. I could have told you tales about him to curl your hair – even more!'

I think fast. What harm can a few tales do? It's not as if I'm actually investigating, is it? It's just a couple of friends, chatting. Even the huffy Chief Inspector Glen Parva couldn't object to a few stories, could he?'

'Mr Skeith, you have my ear.'

He grins knowingly, links his arm through mine and we set off along High Street. My gaze locks longingly onto the Coffee Emporium but he doesn't even pause. 'I have coffee. And a few of those chocolate cookies you insist on quality checking.'

'Mr Skeith, now you have my ear *and* my heart!'

'Cheeky girl. Now, what can I tell you about that rum 'un? I remember, there was one occasion…'

Chapter 7

Within moments the door is unlocked, and I'm treated to a waft of air scented by books and coffee. Wickham has a large professional coffee machine, literally all bells and whistles, and he has it on a timer so that he and any early bird customers get what he calls 'full aroma therapy'. He nods across to the two upholstered wingback armchairs. 'You put a match to the fire while I put cups to the spout.'

Within seconds, I have a bone china cup of freshly ground coffee at my elbow, and at my feet a roaring fire in the grate, with Dagenham lying heavily across my toes and snoring like an express train. It would be the perfect start to the day if it wasn't for the murder...

Wickham boots up his cash register and turns the door sign to OPEN, then drops into the armchair opposite me, stretches out his long legs, adjusts his shirt cuffs and arches his fingers above his waistcoat. The consummate storyteller is building atmosphere. He sips his coffee and regards me over the rim of the cup. 'Now, where to begin?'

We're spared an answer as the shop bell tinkles and I glance up, tight-lipped. 'Hello? Anyone here? Wickham?' Ah, it's the voice of our vicar, my friend Scott Willoughby.

My companion smiles and puts a finger over his mouth. Keep quiet.

I listen to Scott's heavy footsteps as he approaches the counter and imagine him peering over, his 6'1" frame checking for signs of life. Then his voice marks his progress towards the stockroom. 'Wickham, I just wanted to collect that new Bible commentary…'

We're both trying to smother giggles and I'm wondering how on earth he hasn't heard Dagenham's snores when he finally spots us. 'You two! You knew perfectly well…' There's a massive grin on his face as he shakes his head. 'My goodness, that looks cosy. Not interrupting, am I?'

'Not at all. Pull up a chair. I was about to instruct our young lady here in the saga that is our erstwhile bobby.'

'Wickham, for goodness' sake, use plain English.' I punch his arm and turn to Scott. 'He's about to dish the dirt on our murder victim. It was our retired policeman.'

Scott smiles.

'You already knew, didn't you?'

He smiles again, with the merest nod of his head.

'Such a shame you listen to village gossip, vicar!'

'One person's gossip is another's vital information, Ms de Barnes.' He flushes red but nevertheless grabs a wooden spindle chair and settles on it.

Wickham snuggles into the sprung upholstery of his own chair, reaching his hands towards the fire. This lovely man enjoys nothing more than an audience and the opportunity to be a raconteur. He looks at us both and clears his throat.

'Well, where to begin? I know you'll say "at the beginning" – but where is that? I think we'll go back to when our policeman was just...'

We all jump as the shop phone trills. 'Sorry – I should probably get that.' Wickham ambles across to the counter, then disappears with the phone into his tiny office and closes the door.

'Mind you don't fall off that chair, Cat.'

'I don't know what you mean, Vicar. Just stretching.'

'Of course you are. Nothing whatsoever to do with trying to overhear Wickham's conversation.'

'Pure coincidence. Although I think I may know who the caller is.'

Scott's eyebrows rise. 'That's none of our business, young lady.'

'Oh, I think you'll find it might be. But in the meantime, what have you heard about this death?'

'Well, I can tell you, the police can't trace any family so it looks as if I'll be asked to conduct the funeral, eventually, once they've finished. Very sad, really. Seems he kept himself to himself, even though I'm told he's lived here all his life. I was rather hoping Wickham might fill in a few details.'

'Yes, that is sad. I can't imagine how someone could live like that, for that long. Especially in a friendly village like this. Although I suppose, as a police officer, you'd probably want to keep some boundaries.'

We both stare into the fire, mulling this over. There's something mesmerising about real flames in a log fire, the rich red and amber colours, the dancing flames, the…

'…. don't you think, Cat?'

'What? Sorry, miles away.'

'I said I wonder why he was killed in the police museum. Do you think it was simply that the killer found him there? Or…?'

'Yes, I wondered about that.' I reach across and scratch Dag's back, staring into the flames. 'I can't imagine he'd have been killed somewhere else and taken there. That would have needed more than one person and would be far too risky, even if you use the back entrance. But why the museum? What was he doing there?'

'Reliving old memories, perhaps? Maybe he felt comfortable there?'

'An interesting thought. I think I might have spotted him in there a couple of times when I passed. But why would he have been leaning over the bike when he was stabbed? No, I think whoever killed him did the deed somewhere else in the building and then staged it like that. To make a point.'

'What point?'

'No idea, Scott! But I reckon if the police work that out, they'll have…'

'That was your police inspector friend, Cat.' Wickham waves his phone as he slips into a chair.

'Good grief, Wickham. Stop creeping up on me like that, you nearly gave me heart failure!'

Wickham just grins. 'Gone rather red, haven't we, at the mention of a certain officer?'

'Or maybe I'm just rather near a roaring log fire, you old stirrer. Anyway, spill the beans.'

'Not many beans to spill, really. The inspector merely wanted to find out what I knew about Dean but when I said I'd known him since childhood he said all he was interested in was recent times not ancient history. Insisted people who use a knife to kill are acting on recent events, not long-term grudges. I told him, if you want to understand our erstwhile sergeant, you need to go back over all his career here, and maybe further.'

'What did he say to that?' Scott leans forward, mesmerised.

'Let's just say, he wasn't exactly interested.'

Really? I wonder. *Does he know something we don't know?* I look at the others. 'Well, we most certainly are. Though I can't imagine the two of you as babes in arms.' I cradle my arms and mime a rocking motion, offering what I imagine to be a besotted-mummy grin. Not that I'd know.

'Honestly, Catherine!' Wickham grins and carries on. 'No, we don't go back quite that far. More like the early years at secondary school. It didn't take long for him to come to the attention of the headmistress, the redoubtable Betwsy Coed. Nor to maintain it for the rest of his school career. Which wasn't exactly a long one.'

'I can imagine.' Scott distractedly plays with his dog collar. 'I didn't have much to do with him, but he never struck me as the academic type. Nor the police type either, if I'm honest.'

Wickham pats his arm. 'A good insight, Reverend. It took a lot of us by surprise, that did. He'd been quite the young tearaway. Always on his motorbike – dead keen on that, he was. I always reckoned that's why he joined the police, so he could officially race around the countryside like a bat out of hell without getting enough speeding tickets to paper a wall.'

I think about that. 'He must have crossed an awful lot of people during that time, Wickham. Perhaps one of them…'

I watch his moustache twitch as he wrestles with his thoughts wondering if I've sparked a memory. But then his face creases into a huge grin. 'Catherine, this is the Cotswolds, not the Cosa Nostra.'

'Sounds like an uneventful life,' I say, 'to end up being murdered. Surely there must be *something* to know, however insignificant it seems?'

'Not that I'm aware of. Dean kept himself to himself. He never married, although he was a bit of a ladies' man. And there were some rumours, but nothing I ever saw, so that was probably just more village gossip. Mind you, I did see…'

Before we can hear anymore, the shop door crashes open so fast it misses the bell and Glen charges in, like a bull in a china shop. He glances around, spots me and with his face puce and bulging, flings a newspaper onto my lap.' What the hell is this?'

I'm on the verge of replying, 'it's a weekly newspaper' when I catch Scott's warning look – he knows me too well. Then I see the banner headline: LOCAL VILLAGE CONTINUES TO LIVE UP TO ITS NAME. Oh dear, our beloved policeman hates publicity at the best of times. For it to have happened so quickly won't be a good sign.

'Read it,' he snaps. Scott leans forward to look at the article, taking the opportunity to place a gentle hand on my arm. Even so, it's several seconds before I calm down enough for my eyes to focus and my brain to read.

Residents of the tiny Cotswolds village of Much Slaughter were stunned to learn this week of yet another murder in their midst. This time it was popular local bobby, Sergeant Dean Court. Until his retirement ten years ago, he had wielded his truncheon in the cause of justice and peace and haunted the town's police station for more than thirty years. No-one we spoke to had a bad word to say about him, and the town was deeply shocked when Dean's lifeless body was found slumped over a motorbike, in full view, in the window of the local Police Museum, with no less than three daggers in his back. Police say they have no immediate suspects but continue to investigate. Dean Court had been instrumental in setting up the Youth Club in the village. This is the second murder this year, in this unfortunate village, and residents are wondering where on earth the police presence is, these days? Especially since last time, the police only solved the murder with the help of local businesswoman Catherine de Barnes. Our reporter has discovered that it was none other than the said Ms de Barnes (55) who found this, the latest, body. The amateur sleuth had no comment to make about the state of her current investigations. Well, at least our clueless coppers can rejoice that her help is on hand – again.

'Fifty-five! Fifty-five? How dare he? I'm 42...' I toss the newspaper contemptuously onto the floor, causing Dag to look for a moment until he decides it's not worth chasing and lapses back into snores. Both Scott and Wickham are shaking with the effort of controlling their giggles. And then Scott speaks.

'Inspector, were there really three knives?' I look up to see all the colour has drained from his face and he looks horrified. 'I mean, one is bad enough. But three: that's either three people or one very determined killer. Either way, it's serious intent.'

The inspector looks severe. 'Vicar, you know perfectly well I can't confirm how many knives we've sent to Forensics.'

I stare at him, unsure whether his use of the word *knives* was deliberate or not. Judging by the pulsing vein in his neck and the furious look on his face, I'm guessing not. So, there were indeed three knives. Interesting. The inspector is talking.

'I'd like to know how exactly the paper learnt all this so quickly? You've clearly spoken to them. Care to explain yourself, Ms de Barnes?'

Deep breaths, Cat. Count to… 'Allow me to point out, Inspector, that they say I made no comment.' It sounds more like a hiss than my voice and even Dag looks up briefly. 'And the reason I had no comment to make was that they never asked me. So I'm guessing that they heard things on the village grapevine.' I treat him to the fiery look that's withered more than a few advertising execs over my career.

The inspector, however, is made of sterner stuff. 'But you don't deny you're investigating?'

'Of course I'm not investigating. I had more than enough last time. I was merely curious about a couple of things.'

Scott leans over and retrieves the scurrilous publication, pointing to the by-line. 'Inspector, I know this reporter, Stanley Downton. He's from the village of Much Snoring up the Fosse Way, and I had more than a few run-ins with him when I was vicar there. He has a definite axe to grind, if you'll forgive the rather unfortunate metaphor.'

'Well, let this be a warning to you. All of you. Leave this to the professionals.'

'Of course, Inspector.' I treat him to one of my sweetest smiles. He's rather dishy when he's angry and his face muscles tighten. 'Happy to oblige.'

'Humph. Yes, well, see that you do.' Then he's gone as quickly as he arrived. I turn to Wickham.

'Now, Mr Skeith, you were about to dish up some scandal before we were so rudely interrupted.' He stares at me for a moment, and I feel my face flush. But then he relaxes back into his chair.

'Hardly scandal, my dear girl. Although some in this village would have liked to have made it so. Just some gossip that there was finally a love interest in his lonely bachelor life.' He interlaces his fingers across his chest and regards us through half-closed eyes, a slight smile around his mouth.

Scott and I are both on the edge of our seats. Literally. Which of course is exactly what my old storyteller friend wants, so neither of us is willing to give him the satisfaction of asking the obvious question. But life's too short.

'Alright – who was it?'

The old man glances over his shoulder, before leaning forward and lowering his voice. 'That's just it…' He looks around again, then draws even closer so the three of us are virtually nose to nose. 'No-one knows.' He falls back and grins broadly.

'So there's every chance this could be a lover's tiff?' I leap out my chair, causing Dag to leap up as well, anticipating a long-overdue walk. Wickham's face changes.

'The thing is…' Our host lets out a weary sigh and his shoulders droop. 'I think I might know who the person was.'

'Well in that case Wickham, you have to tell the inspector.' I snatch my phone from my bag and start dialling. 'We need to get him back here.'

'I'm not sure anyone will believe me. Even I wouldn't have believed me. Several days ago, I heard them arguing outside my shop. I didn't think anything about it, but then when you mentioned a lover's tiff… Except that this sounded far more than a lover's tiff.'

'Then, for goodness' sake… Wickham, who was it?'

'I'll save that for your inspector, Catherine.'

Chapter 8

The inspector is back, if not exactly friendly. 'Maybe I should just set up a permanent office in this town, it seems to be turning into the murder capital of the Cotswolds.'

'That would be very nice, Inspector,' I smile at him, hoping my ulterior motive isn't too obvious. I swear there's a hint of a smile there, before his police persona snaps back into place.

'So, who is this mystery woman you're so keen for me to talk to, Mr Skeith?'

'She'll be here in just a moment, Inspector. I've asked her to pop in to help you clear up a little matter.'

Scott and I both shake our heads, then Scott slides behind my chair, his elbows resting casually on the upholstery and we both stare at the door. The tension-building of the storyteller has its place but…

The shop bell tinkles, and we all jump in unison like puppets on strings.

Wickham springs to his feet and waves her to his armchair. 'Chief Inspector Parva, this is Mavis Enderby.' He leans on the back of the chair.

Goodness, I hadn't expected to see my new friend drawn in. I smile but she seems too nervous to notice.

'Inspector.' With a slight nod to our host, she settles herself into the armchair, folding her hands in her lap and interlacing her fingers over her tweed skirt. With her hooked nose and small intense eyes flitting constantly between the four of us she has a bird-like appearance, and she has the same wary concentration. 'How may I be of assistance?'

'Mavis, I think you need to explain to the inspector what you and Dean were arguing about in the street a couple of days ago.'

'We weren't. I'm not the sort of person to get involved in public contretemps, I can assure you.'

Wickham holds her stare. It's like watching two birds of prey circling, waiting to see who'll sweep first. Then he crouches to gently touch her arm. 'Mavis, I saw and heard you. You were right outside my door.'

Something flickers across her face, then she lets out a long sigh. 'Ah, yes, of course.' She fixes her dark eyes on Chief Inspector Parva as if he's the chosen dormouse and she's challenging him to break cover. 'But you can take my word for it, it was nothing.'

Anyone less like a dormouse is hard to imagine and the inspector's face tightens. 'Ms Enderby, since the person you were arguing with has now been murdered, I'll be the judge of its importance.'

Wow. The atmosphere between them has enough charge to boil a kettle.

'If you really must know – and I can't for the life of me see why you should – the sergeant had in his possession an item belonging to me and I asked for its return. He refused.'

'That hardly seems grounds for a huge row.' I can't stop myself blurting it out and I'm rewarded by angry looks from both of them.

'As it happens, I agree with Ms de Barnes.' *Now that's a first, Cat.* 'I think you'd better explain.'

'Very well. Perhaps then you'll accept why it has no relevance to your enquiries. Years ago, my house was burgled, and Sergeant Court was the investigating officer. They didn't take much, certainly nothing of any particular value, and there had been a spate of the burglaries. Court reckoned it was probably a gang of local teenagers and he said he'd have a word with a few of them. "Clip a few ears", as he so delightfully put it. Well, the break-ins stopped but Court never recovered any of my stolen goods. The case was closed. At least, that's what I thought. Until that blasted article in *Country Life.*'

Wickham fumbles in the magazine rack by the fireplace and recovers a copy of the glossy magazine. 'I kept this issue because of its local interest for our readers.' He colours and I wonder if there's something of the local gossip about my wonderful neighbour – in a very gentlemanly way, of course.

Mavis shudders. 'What on earth that dreadful man had done to warrant a full interview in such a prestigious publication is beyond me. It was bad enough seeing his name plastered across the page. But when I looked at the photograph, well, there it was, right behind him.'

'What was, Miss Enderby?' Even the inspector is sucked into this mini-drama and he leans forward as Wickham drops the open magazine on the table between us. There in glorious technicolour is Court grinning like the Cheshire Cat while pointing to a display cabinet of clocks, ranging from tiny travel versions through to carriage clocks and a couple of sturdy mantelpiece ones. They're not to my taste, the ticking would drive me mad, and changing each one twice a year would be a nightmare, but they must be collectables and potentially valuable, since on the open door of the cabinet there's a chunky lock and the plates of an electronic alarm. Beside it is another cabinet, equally crammed with ceramic pieces. This is clearly not a man who does anything by halves.

My eyes are drawn to something else. It's a bad habit of mine: when someone wants me to look in one direction, I have to look in the other, to see what I'm not meant to see. This time, it's over Court's other shoulder. At the centre of his mantelpiece there's a large brass clock in pride of place, obviously commemorative and significantly larger than the other four clocks on either side. Maybe a retirement present? There's a small brass inscription plate but it's far too small to read in the photo.

Mavis points at the photo. 'That's my clock.' She stabs it hard with a bony finger. 'One of the items stolen from my house. Bold as brass, on his mantelpiece.'

80

Glen whips out his mobile, takes several photographs, then barks into his phone, 'I'm sending you some photos. Check inside Court's house and report back.' He turns back to stare at Mavis. 'How can you be sure it's yours? There must be hundreds of them?'

'Inspector, that clock was given to me by my dear late husband, you can see the inscription plate. After he died, nearly twenty years ago, it became even more special. So, yes, I think I can say with certainty that it's mine.'

'And that's what the confrontation was about?'

'Precisely.'

Now, of course, I'm not investigating this murder. It's absolutely nothing to do with me. But is some old timepiece, even one with sentimental value, sufficient motive to murder someone? I mean, I could just about understand her slapping him, perhaps, in the heat of the moment. But killing him later, in cold blood? It seems altogether too calculated. There again, what do I know? As the inspector would no doubt take great joy in pointing out.

It seems Glen agrees with me as he sighs. 'Alright, Ms Enderby. We've taken over the office in the police museum – it seems to be the only space to work in this village. Come in tomorrow and one of my officers will take a statement.'

Mavis clamps her hands onto the chair arms, winces and pushes herself rather gingerly to her feet before bestowing a cool smile on us. 'I presume I'm free to go, Inspector?'

She sets off across the shop, rubbing her left shoulder, just as Glen's phone beeps. He glances at it and stiffens. 'One moment, madam.' He beckons her back and shows her his phone screen. She glances at it and all the colour drains from her face.

'Ms Enderby?'

'Oh! Yes. So I'm afraid my earlier account wasn't entirely accurate.'

I'm straining in my seat to see, but Glen's on his feet and just too far away. Scott, however, gently manoeuvres across so he can see the phone and when he sees me looking, raises a single eyebrow, looking shocked.

'Rather more than that, I think. According to the inscription, the gift was *from* you, rather than to you. And to someone who was quite clearly not your husband.'

My mouth gapes. She's so strait-laced and proper. I turn to look at Scott but his eyes are flitting from Mavis to the photo and back. So who did she give it to? And if Court had got his hands on it after the robbery, could he have been blackmailing her? Yet she seems to have made no effort to get into his house and retrieve it.

'Must we rake all of this up? It was a terrible mistake. And so long ago. I can't think what came over me. And with someone like *that*!'

'Mavis, can't you see how bad this looks for you?' I pause and stare at her as a horrible thought dawns on me. What if the clock wasn't the proceeds of crime but instead Mavis gave it to him? What if Court had been her lover?

Inspector Parva's pen is flying over the page as he records every detail.

In a few seconds Mavis has gone from bird of prey to rabbit in the headlights.

I take a deep breath. 'Because if it got out that you and Sergeant Court were, shall we say, pounding the same beat, it would ruin your reputation.'

'Quite.' She shudders, then puts her hand on my arm and produces a sickly smile. 'But, my dear, a besmirched reputation and some old timepiece is hardly a motive for murder, is it? After all, Inspector, my family has faced far worse over the years we've been in these parts. And we're still here.'

Drawing on her generations of aristocratic breeding, Mavis stares hard at Glen as if challenging him to a duel. The inspector slowly and deliberately turns to a fresh page in his notebook, looks her up and down, and refuses to wilt.

Meanwhile, my heart is beating fit to burst and my mind is firing in all directions, trying to make sense of this.

Finally, Mavis sighs. 'Alright, Inspector. You may as well know, my affections fully weren't reciprocated. Oh, he let me think they were, for years. And I wanted to believe him. I so wanted to believe...' She sags and Scott quickly grabs her arm and eases her into the vacant armchair while I nod at Wickham, who bustles off to his office for some tea. I smile as he deliberately leaves the door wide open and his head keeps popping out so he doesn't miss a juicy word.

'But I should have known.' She looks at me and seems to have aged a couple of decades in as many minutes. 'There was a dark side to the sergeant, if you know what I mean.'

I feel myself jolt and notice Scott has paled. Inspector Parva appears unmoved.

'No, our sergeant wasn't the pillar of the police and community he'd have us all believe.' She alternates twisting a hankie between her fingers and dabbing her eyes with it. 'Of course, for years even I'd been fooled. I mean, there'd be the occasional hint, a flash of anger. But I just thought it was him not liking to lose in the pub quiz, especially if he thought someone was cheating. He's an ex-copper so what would you expect?'

Out of the corner of my eye, I see Glen's neck muscles tighten and he's gone slightly red.

'Except that lately, it seemed to get worse. From the moment that *Country Life* journalist suggested he should write a book about his time policing here, and call it Secret Sergeant, he started delving back into his old cases. The slightest thing would set him off. He even got into some kerfuffle or other with Martin

Dales. I thought maybe it was because going back over all those files made him a bit, well, unsettled.'

Dean Court, an author? Who'd've thought it? Maybe the journo was just buttering up an interviewee? *Put those claws away, Cat.*

Scott places a gentle hand on Mavis' arm. She quickly wipes the corner of her eye with her hankie.

'A couple of weeks ago, soon after the article in Country Life, I asked him about the clock. But he just laughed in my face. Told me it was just one of his little trophies. Then stared at me until I apologised. He wasn't someone you wanted to cross, that Dean.'

'That must have made you very angry.' The inspector scribbles frantically.

'Not really. I mean, it was only a trinket when all's said and done.' Glen stares at Mavis for a few seconds, then returns to his scribbling. As the silence lengthens, a thought occurs to me.

'Mavis, do you know how far Dean had got with his book? Did you ever see him writing it?'

'No idea. I know he said he didn't trust computers and wouldn't own one. Although I think he occasionally used the library computer if he needed to research something.'

Goodness! I can't imagine life without a computer. And if that's true, how could he produce his manuscript, assuming he'd even started?

The poor woman stares helplessly at us, as Wickham brings her tea, which, I notice he's managed to put in a bone china cup and saucer. Nice touch. Mavis doesn't notice, and she's now holding her hankie so tightly that it's all crumpled. She sits up taller. 'Inspector, may I remind you, I came here voluntarily, to help you, at Mr Skeith's request. Not to be interrogated like some common criminal.' Glen looks up momentarily, then returns to his notebook.

'I'm amazed no-one spotted you together, you and the sergeant.' Wickham smiles. 'You know this village – even the walls have eyes.' Mavis turns to him, her face blank.

'Dean always insisted we met at the museum. He had his own key. And that we met in one of the cells – he said it prevented anyone else knowing. But now, it seems, well, rather…'

'Sinister?' I blurt out.

She nods, then scrambles through her handbag and extracts a second cotton monogrammed hankie. 'It seems he held most of his meetings in that cell.'

The inspector's phone bleeps with another text message. He stares at it and the redness in his face deepens.

Frustratingly, I still can't see his phone. Anyone would think he's deliberately shielding it. Whatever the message says, it keeps him occupied for some time. Or maybe it's just a police trick to increase the pressure on a suspect. Well, if it is, it doesn't work as Mavis simply continues dabbing her eyes with her hankie and sniffing.

Finally, Glen clears his throat and stares at Mavis. Then he waves his phone at her. 'Hardly an "old timepiece" as you so charmingly dismiss it. According to our expert, it's a couple of hundred years old and worth several thousand pounds. Which definitely *is* a motive. On top of everything else you've told us about unrequited love. Mavis Enderby, I am arresting you on suspicion of the murder…'

My jaw drops. 'Chief Inspector, you can't seriously think that Mavis…'

This is ridiculous. Can't he see how upset the poor women is? I have to speak up. 'In all the time I've been in the village, I haven't heard anyone say a bad word about her. I've never even heard her raise her voice before today.'

'Thank you, Ms de Barnes, for sharing the benefit of your six months' residency. I prefer facts.'

I'm about to protest that it'll soon be a year, but he raises his hand and points to his first finger, as if explaining to a small child. 'Firstly, the clock – worth thousands. No wonder she wanted it back. Especially with her incriminating little plaque on it. Secondly, 'Hell hath no fury…' She finally realised he'd been leading her on all this time, making a fool of her. From that moment, his fate was sealed. Thirdly, she lied to the police, you all heard her.

'But then, if she murdered him in the cell where they used to meet, why would she drag the body halfway across the building, Inspector? Would she even be strong enough? It makes no sense.'

'And why three knives?' Scott shakes his head, sadly. 'Surely one would have been more than adequate for the, um, purpose? So should we assume it's three people? That would be rather crowded, wouldn't it? And far riskier, with more DNA and the chance of more damage – to something other than the body, that is. It makes no sense.' He runs a finger around the inside of his clerical collar.

'Good grief. If it's not bad enough having one busybody poking their nose in, now I've got the local vicar as well. Listen, Reverend, when you've been at this as long as I have, you learn murder doesn't make sense. What I will tell you is that we don't believe there're three killers. There were only very partial fingerprints on any of the knives, but Forensics are sure they're from the same person.'

We stare at the inspector. Scott's right, this really doesn't make sense. It's not that I can't accept knowing a murderer. After all, it wouldn't be the first time. And I've watched enough cop shows on TV to know that it's often the least obvious person. But Mavis, and over a clock? And a love affair that by all accounts hardly got off the ground? And, more importantly, it doesn't *feel* right. 'Inspector, I beg you...'

Glen snorts like an angry bull, along with the flaring nostrils. 'Ms de Barnes, I really do suggest you button your tongue before it gets you into serious trouble.

He links his arm through Mavis's, causing her to wince, and leads her outside to a waiting police car. Within seconds they've sped away, watched by several open-mouthed villagers.

I turn to the others. 'Guys, we can't possibly let this drop.'

Wickham puts a hand on my shoulder and squeezes tightly. 'Cat, you heard the inspector. Let him do his job.'

'If only he would! He's made up his mind and now he's ignoring anything that doesn't fit. If the clock is so important, why didn't she try to get it back the minute Dean was dead? We can't possibly let an innocent women go to gaol because the pig-headed inspector won't look beyond the end of his nose. Snout. Whatever.'

Scott's voice is barely more than a whisper. 'Cat, this isn't your battle.'

He's right, of course. It's what my colleagues in London used to say. 'Cat never knows when to give up', like it was the epitaph on my tomb. Which come to think of it, it was, workwise, after I marched into my boss's office and told her she was bullying one of my staff. *And you promised yourself no more hasty decisions.*

I glance around. 'Guys, I need a few minutes?' They nod and Wickham goes off to potter with a coffee machine I know needs absolutely no attention since it cost him a small fortune to ensure it was self-sufficient. Scott moves to the other side of the bookshop to stare intently at a shelf of books, then stiffens and I giggle because he's wandered into the Erotic Fiction section. *Move on quickly, Cat.*

Settled in the comfy armchair in front of a warm blazing log fire, it all seems simple and straightforward. If I'm to have any chance at all with the dashing inspector, I can't keep poking my nose in where it isn't wanted. Or needed. After all, the inspector is a perfectly competent officer. And look what happened last time. I was exhausted. Which I can't afford this time, not with all the chocolates I need to get ready for the Harvest celebrations. And for Skye in the Coffee Emporium. And if I don't make a go of it, well, then I've wasted my time and money on the chocolate course and all that equipment. To say nothing of my reputation.

With a deep sigh, I scramble to my feet. 'Guys, you're right. I can't get involved.' My heart sinks, but my head announces very firmly it's the right decision.

Scott reappears fast from his accidental foray into Erotic Literature, grateful for anything that covers his blushes. He drapes his arm over my shoulder. 'It's okay, Cat, we get it.'

Wickham comes to my other side and places a proprietorial hand on my arm. 'We just needed to make sure you do what's best for you. After all, hell hath no fury like an *inspector* spurned!'

'Thanks, guys. I need to get on. I have a dog who won't walk himself and chocolates that won't make themselves.'

Then I spot Mavis's soggy white hankie, discarded by her chair and my throat seizes up. 'Although, I have got an idea…'

Chapter 9

The following morning the sun is just above the horizon as Dag and I splash through the overnight puddles. At least, I assume it is, heavy grey clouds and an autumn mist blanket it well. The mist is doing a pretty god job of blanketing my eyebrows as well; I feel as if I'm walking through a dense Amazonian jungle. Minus the heat. Even my darling pooch had to be dragged out of the door and he's still throwing me the occasional disgusted look. Several times he's made a point of standing still and showering me as he shakes his fur, then looking at me as if to say, 'Well, you dragged me out in all this.'

But these are valuable thinking times. Only the most dedicated owners venture out, so in an hour I'll encounter perhaps three people, and they'll be as keen as their pets not to dawdle chatting. Over the last few months, I've learnt to set my brain a puzzle as we walk through the garden gate and then let it get on with it. And at some point, an idea will pop up. Usually.

Today's brain teaser is how to explain to people, including close friends, that my U-turn was triggered by a discarded hankie, because it looked so forlorn, so forgotten? The answer arrives as we trundle past the Police Museum. *Don't explain, ignore it and carry on as if it wasn't the biggest volte-face since Mr Darcy's courtship of Elizabeth in Pride and Prejudice.*

*

'Maybe if we do find something, we can drop the inspector a hint? Perhaps anonymously?'

The three of us are snuggled in the warm, dry Coffee Emporium, the sole customers. I love what Skye has done with the place, but I have to admit, I miss Rose's presence – her new-found freedom has seen her flitting all over. She's away for a few days, visiting friends.

Scott and Wickham grin at each other and simultaneously shake their heads. 'I knew she wouldn't be able to resist, Vicar.'

'Like dangling a toy rabbit in front of a cat, Wickham.'

'Er, excuse me. I am here, you know.' I try to look stern but fail miserably. 'And for your information, all I'm proposing is a brief check-in, and if we can't find anything, well then I'll be forced to accept the inspector might be right.' I shudder, mainly because I don't want to think of Mavis being guilty, but also because I can just see the smug grin he'd wear every time we met from then on. *But Cat, how are you going to see him again? Surely you're not proposing more murders?*

Wickham raises a bushy eyebrow but wisely keeps quiet.

'There must be something we're all missing. Where's the article?'

I scan the page, then stab it with my finger and swing round to my two companions, trying to keep the excitement out of my voice. 'Of course! That's exactly where we need to start…' My phone suddenly bleeps loudly, almost causing a heart attack. 'Sorry – got to go and get ready. I've got a lunch date in Cirencester.' I wiggle my eyebrows. Scott shakes his head and Wickham merely tuts at my rapidly receding back. *Maybe this'll be the one…*

*

Or not! A few hours later and with my spirits significantly lower than the pavement under my feet, I march through the drizzle towards the sanctuary of Wickham's bookshop. Dag seems intent on wrapping his lead around my legs and depositing me in puddle after puddle, probably as revenge for deserting him for lunch. 'You'd have been far better company, Daggers, my boy. If I ever hear one more word about Gloucestershire Old Spot pigs, I'll…'

Luckily, I'm distracted as the door of the doctor's surgery is flung open and the delightful doctor emerges to brighten my day. *I thought you didn't want anything more to do with him, Cat?* True. But in the dating stakes he's also the best of a bad bunch. And today he does look particularly handsome in a long, sandy gabardine raincoat and a colourful peaked check cap. The doctor smiles and beckons me across. *Faint heart ne'er won… Cat.* And I could do with a fresh pair of eyes if I'm to help Mavis…

'Cat, again, I'm so sorry about…'

'Linton, I'm sorry as well. I do know you can't ignore your patients.'

His smile warms me like a summer day. *Ugh, you have got it bad, girl.* However, much as I'd like to turn this into a romantic interlude, especially after my dreadful lunch, there are more urgent matters.

'Have you heard? Our former police sergeant has been stabbed to death and Chief Inspector Parva has charged Mavis Enderby with his murder. But I know she didn't do it. She'd never stab anyone. Is there anything you know that might help? Anything medical, perhaps?'

He looks straight at me for several seconds while his specs fleck with raindrops, before he shakes his head. 'You're right. She couldn't. But patient confidentiality…'

Ah, so she was his patient. And that's an interesting choice of words, *couldn't.*

'Given that she's under arrest, I hardly think her patient confidentiality is likely to be high on her list of priorities, doctor.'

'Possibly not, Cat. But it's still not my decision to make.' In fairness, he does look mortified. Then he brightens, whips off his glasses and tucks them into his coat pocket. 'Come on, we need to find the inspector.'

Linton splashes across High Street to peer in the bookshop window. 'Nope.'

'What about the Coffee Emporium? Otherwise, if he's still in the village, he'll be in the Police Museum.'

We track him down just a few yards away surrounded by coffee, scones and a mountain of files. He doesn't look pleased to see us. 'Just my luck. Another five minutes and I'd have gone.'

'Then it's your good luck, Inspector. We're just in time to stop you – that is, Dr Heath is just in time to… At least, I think he's…' I suddenly realise I have no idea why Linton wanted to catch the man.

The inspector raises a weary hand. 'Ms de Barnes, I've already warned you.'

Linton raises his own hand. 'Inspector, in fairness, I do think you need to hear this.'

The inspector shakes his head and sighs, but he does at least wave us to a couple of chairs. 'Make it quick then. I'm needed back at headquarters.'

Linton nods, but he still takes a moment to shake some of the water from his coat. 'Inspector, you understand I'm bound by patient confidentiality. And Mavis Enderby is one of my patients. However, you might want to get her to demonstrate how she'd stab someone. It will be… very illuminating. Especially if Sergeant Court was killed by the knife?'

The inspector looks up, warily. 'He was.' He sighs, dials, then mutters into his phone, taking very obvious care to avoid us hearing, then returns to his files, ignoring our presence.

Linton and I move to one of the few free tables in the mid-afternoon rush. 'What was all that about?'

He smiles, his face softening and a large raindrop settling cutely on the tip of his nose. 'Patience, dear Catney, it's the heart of all good medicine.'

Maybe, but I'm no medic. He smiles and it's abundantly clear the doctor's not for turning. Thankfully I'm distracted as the ever-attentive Skye delivers a plate of shortbread and two steaming drinks. Yes, I know, I've just come from lunch. But the unfortunate encounter coupled with Linton's intrigue seems to have left me feeling peckish.

Linton sighs contentedly. 'Well, isn't this nice, Cat? An unexpected bonus in my day.'

'Until your phone rings.' The words are out before I can block them and he looks crestfallen. 'Sorry, Linton. I am trying not to go on about it. It's just this wretched murder business.'

He rests his hand gently on my arm, causing a very pleasant jolt. 'How about we play it a bit more informally, more last minute? I'd hate to miss out on seeing you.'

The inspector's phone rings, causing the three of us to jump, so I just smile and nod at Linton. It seems that nothing about this relationship will ever be straightforward. *So maybe just accept it as the way things are.*

The inspector listens for a few seconds, then slams his phone down on the table and calls across to us, 'Turns out, you were right.' My heart leaps as he waves us across to join him. 'Seems Ms Enderby has a frozen right shoulder and couldn't possibly raise her arm high enough to stab him. Nor could she have moved the body. Or cleared up the mess.'

I beam at him. 'That's wonderful news, Inspector. Now we can get on with finding the actual murderer.' The inspector scowls.

'Don't push your luck. Who's to say she didn't hire someone? She's not out of the frame yet.' He pauses to push his ever-present sunglasses higher up on his nose. 'What I will say is that the coroner confirmed that Court did indeed die from the daggers in his back. But he also had significant bruising to the back of his head consistent with a single blow, administered before death. Which means he could have been knocked unconscious first, somewhere else in the building, then dragged and placed on the motorbike.'

'And three knives. It seems like... someone was determined to make sure he was dead!' *Well done, Cat. At least I avoided calling it overkill!*

'Which will provide one of the planks in our investigation. You, however, Ms de Barnes will not be investigating. We've managed perfectly well without you so far.'

'But why three knives, Inspector? Stabbing someone three times, that could be understandable in a fit of anger. But going to the trouble of three knives?'

But Glen Parva remains tight-lipped, scoops up the files and with a final, 'I hope you realise just how much more paperwork you've caused,' is gone.

Linton glances at his watch and I sigh. 'I know, you've got patients to see, forms to fill out.'

'Actually, no. As it happens, I'm free for the next hour or so.'

'Unless the butcher slices his arm off or there's a motorway pile-up…'

He grins. 'Or someone goes into premature labour. Quite.'

He really does have the nicest smile. I feel myself weaken. The doctor continues.

'Now, tell me how your chocolate habit's going.' He leans in and I'm treated to a heady whiff of cologne.

'Eating or making?'

'Oh, I thought we might share a few by a warm fireside?' He wrinkles his nose, causing his glasses to bounce. And those amazing blue eyes, so deep. He could be a seriously good alternative to chocolate… Or combined with it… *Stop, Cat, you're in public.* I've gone as hot and as red as a bunch of cherries. *Whoa, stop that image right there…* I cough, loudly.

'Well, I've been trying a few new recipes. Some for when I start my display here, some for the Harvest

Supper. Maybe you could pop home with me to sample my bonbons at Bedside Manor. Oh, that is, I mean, …'

Linton's mouth trembles and his eyes water but he simply announces, 'I'll look forward to that.'

Deep breath, Cat. 'The idea is, I try a few lines out in here, see which ones are popular and start to build some trade. Or not, as the case may be.'

'Oh, I'm sure you'll do really well, Cat. After all, who could resist your bonbons?' His cheek is rewarded with a spluttered mouthful of my hot chocolate. Goodness, I like such a dirty sense of humour. It bodes well.

'Look, doctor,' I giggle, 'I need to exercise my pup. How about you join us and then I can offer you a bite…' I wait for his eyebrows to rise then add, 'of afternoon tea. Scones, jam and cream on the menu today, chez de Barnes.'

Linton tips his cap, inclines his head and takes my elbow to help me stand. Which is useful because, for some inexplicable reason, my legs turn to jelly the moment he touches me.

Dagenham opens his eyes, looks out of the window then gives me a look of complete disbelief. As we promenade out, Skye treats me to a kissy-kissy grin and several other customers regard us with open curiosity.

The cold damp hits me like a rushing train and we shiver more tightly into our coats. 'Are you sure about this, Catherine?' The dashing doc looks truly concerned. And it's a long while since a man has shown me concern.

'Have dog, will exercise.' I'm not about to admit it, but not even a full-blown tornado would make me miss this opportunity. He links his arm through mine and my legs threaten to go on strike again, but I manage to shift them into gear as I thrust my shoulders back and lift my chin. Yes, Much Slaughter, I am indeed walking out with your very eligible medic. Unfortunately, driving rain soon forces my chin back down and the narrowness of the path as we leave the village and head towards Monarch's Way makes us walk in single file. Plus, the awful weather means there's no-one to see us. I don't think there'll be a protest from any of us if I make this just a pee-and-run exercise.

As if he's read my thoughts, Dag trots across to the nearest tree and duly obliges, then fixes me with such a baleful look I have to laugh. 'It's okay, Daggers, we'll head back.' He wags his tail in approval and trots off the way we've just come. Linton, however, looks quite disappointed. 'All the more time for tea and scones, doctor.'

My phone pings and we both exchange glances. Thankfully it turns out to be just a text message. I scan it and turn to my companion. 'Mavis sends her grateful thanks and undying love.'

A concerned look flits across his face. 'Do you think she'll be alright? It's quite some ordeal your friend's been through.'

'She'll be fine. And I'll fix a catch-up in a few days. But she's built of stern stuff, that one.'

Just a few minutes later, we cross the threshold, all of us shaking out the dampness onto my tiled floor. 'I'll just pop the heating on. The kettle's in the kitchen, as you'd expect.' Actually, it's more of an excuse to peel off soggy wet trousers and slip into something… dry. *What did you think I was going to say? I'm a nice girl. Well, at this stage.*

Back in the kitchen, the lovely Linton has not only put the kettle on, he's also found a couple of mugs, my best teapot and a loaf of bread. 'Sorry, Cat. I've no idea where you keep your PG Tips.'

'I keep my PG Tips to myself, my good man. But you'll find some Earl Grey in the caddy over there and the Darjeeling and Assam in that cupboard. If you prefer builders', it's in the cupboard over there. We're not a tea bag establishment.' I grab a plastic tub from the freezer and toss it into the microwave, crossing my fingers it'll be scones and not dumplings. My culinary labelling is not as robust as it could be.

At which point, the atmosphere is ruined as the theme from *Scrubs* blares out and Linton scrambles for his phone. I'm tempted to grab the damn thing and toss it into the microwave but beneath the thwarted romance a little voice reminds me there could be someone in need. *Apart from me, you mean?* A shrill female voice seems to be explaining something at great length as Linton mouths 'sorry'. Then the microwave pings and he mutters to his mystery caller, 'I'll be back in the surgery shortly.'

He lifts his mug in a toast. 'Carpe diem.'

Resisting the strong urge to seize more than the day, I settle down to the most pleasant afternoon tea I've had in ages, before the marvellous medic pats his lips with a linen napkin (I'm not completely uncouth, you know) and wends his way back to his surgery with, I like to think, a parting look of enjoyment. Leaving me thinking that maybe this isn't quite so impossible.

Chapter 10

Within less than an hour the doubts set in. After all, what's changed? He's still a doctor, at the beck and call of any ingrowing toenail or wheezy cough within a ten-mile radius. Yet we managed a whole teatime together. Well, okay, there was that one phone call. But he did put her off, to spend time with me. And he seemed to be enjoying himself. At least, I think so. *And* without me being glammed up. Surely you don't laugh like that with someone if there's no spark? Although, he spends his life around people, he will have learnt a few social skills. *No,* I decide. *Admiring my bonbons is definitely more than being polite.*

Desperate for distraction, I open both *Country Life* and Dean's newspaper coverage and spread them over my dining table. Most of the material is barely relevant, it's all about his work with the youth club, how much he loves living in the village and his passion for collecting clocks: 'hardly what you'd expect from a humble village copper,' he notes. *You can say that again.* Then a phrase leaps out: *thirty-two years of summary justice.* What does that mean and why has it caught my attention? Not so much the thirty-two years, I'd already known that, although it is an impressive employment record. No, the use of summary justice. A two-minute laptop search tells me that although the phrase properly means speeding up the legal process by omitting certain formalities the phrase can also refer to taking the law into your own hands. But he was the law. So, why does it seem to have a rather sinister ring to it?

Scott's answerphone clicks in on the third ring. Wickham, I know, will be tied up with stocktaking, and for just a split second I'm tempted to ring Inspector Parva. But it is just a split second, like when you're tempted to toss a £20 note onto a bonfire, just to see if you can, or blow your whole month's allowance on one amazing dress. You're not really going to do any of these things but just for that moment…

My phone buzzes. 'Hi, Cat. I'm sorry I missed your call. I was on the phone.'

'Excellent timing, Mr Vicar! I wanted to sound you out on something, if that's okay?'

'You want to throw everything up and become a nun?'

'What? No! Of course not.'

'A priest?'

'Scott, be serious. I wanted to ask you what comes to mind when I say, summary justice.'

'Wyatt Earp? Al Capone? Oh, wait a minute, does this have something to do with… Of course it does. Well, I've just been talking to the funeral director. I needed some background for Dean's funeral next week. I tell you, that woman could find gold in a lead mine. I need to take a Home Communion in twenty minutes, so I'll pop in on my way past.'

'I'll put the kettle on.'

'Argh, no, please don't. I must've had at least ten cups on my rounds already. People are far more keen to offer their tea than their – facilities.'

He's hammering on my door well before I've had time to brew my own tea, his broad grin rather incongruous against his black clerical shirt and official dark suit. He pointedly checks the time as I escort him into my sitting room, and we settle either side of a roaring fire. 'Spill the beans, Cat. Why this sudden interest in summary justice?'

'It's a phrase from the magazine article about Dean Court. The writer said he'd spent three decades doling out summary justice. Now to me, that has sinister overtones and almost suggests he's a vigilante. What do you think?'

The vicar stares into the fire and drums his fingertips on the chair arm. 'I wouldn't necessarily disagree. And, as I said, I've been doing a little background. Seems our sergeant did have something of a reputation, but mainly just for clips around the ear for naughty youngsters when they strayed into minor stuff, graffiti, shoplifting, noisy drinking, that sort of thing. With kids who were likely to get exactly the same from their parents, if they found out. There was the odd hint about some speeding motorists getting 'lucky' and the suggestion that his paperwork wasn't the most meticulous. But nothing serious.'

'Hardly seems to warrant his murder. Especially years later. If anything, you'd think the parents would thank him. No, Scott, there has to be something else. Or else we're barking up the wrong tree.'

'The thing is, Cat, this is hardly a crime capital, even for the Cotswolds. According to a friend of Court's who I spoke to, he joked that in thirty years, the biggest case Court had been involved in was when whisky was sent in a coffin to Dr Beeching when he closed the local train station at Trouble House, which was also a pub. And back then, *Court was only a babe-in-arms*. As far as I can work out, he never had a major crime to investigate. No drugs gangs. No art heists. Nothing.'

'Tell me about this friend of Dean's you mentioned. Who's he?'

'Red Street. Lives in the village. Sad story, lost a daughter, Evie I think her name was. Road accident.'

My stomach knots and my mouth goes as dry as a camel's armpit. The odious 'ceramics' man who, throughout lunch, was all too interested in the wrong sort of jugs.

'You okay, Cat? You've gone very pale.'

'Fine. Just realised I've met him, that's all.' No way am I going to share such embarrassing detail with him. Or anyone else, for that matter. It's safely confined to the deepest vaults and labelled radioactive.

Scott nods. 'Well, they'd been friends since childhood, apparently. Street lives on the Green, in that big gabled house opposite the pub. Nice guy.' I splutter and a mouthful of tea goes back in my cup but I turn it into a cough. 'Now – I must fly.' He springs up, pausing in the doorway to look back at me. 'Remember, Cat, you're not getting involved.'

'Of course not, Reverend.'

He runs his hand through his dark hair and rolls his eyes. 'Whenever you call me Reverend, I know you've not listened to a word I've said. I'll let myself out.'

Once he's gone I take stock. Of course I've listened but there's still a murderer on the loose. If I'm going to solve this case, I need an excuse to run into that horrible man, Red Street. But what? There's no way I'm going to offer a hint of another date. And I can hardly rush up to him and demand he tells me all he knows about his recently departed best mate.

After ten pointless minutes staring into the flames, I'm no nearer inspiration. There's only one thing for it: to put myself under pressure and trust it will forge an idea. It usually works. And let's face it, what's the worst that could happen? That I look an idiot in front of him? In that case, he can join the ever-expanding group.

Ten metres from Street's front door as Dag and I tramp through a forest of autumn twigs covering his path, I'm no nearer inspiration. Even bending to tickle my hound's ears and pretending to extricate a rogue twig from his fur brings nothing to mind.

But inspiration finally strikes. In the centre of Red's front lawn is the most magnificent Acer, still clinging onto its golden leaves, even in October.

Whereas mine barely made it into July. What could be more innocent than gardening advice, even if it means I'll have to endure goodness knows how much mansplaining?

The cast iron door knocker produces a window-frame rattle but there's no sound from within. Naturally, I have to peep through the window in case he hasn't heard my knock, even though it threatened to raise the dead across several counties. Through the small window panes the sitting room looks tastefully expensive, although chintz upholstery isn't to my taste. The chairs and sofa look cosy, there's a real log fire set ready for lighting in what I'm sure is a genuine inglenook fireplace, and a welsh dresser with willow pattern china that I recognise from my grandmother's house. But of Red Street, not a sign, so I tramp across the grass and peer through a smaller window. This proves to be the kitchen, although the word hardly does justice to it: the room looks larger than my whole house and is equipped with enough stainless steel to glint like an operating theatre – and with enough knives to equip one. Everything looks pristine and he's either one of the tidiest people in the world or the house is hardly ever used. Either way, there's no sign of its owner.

'Ah well, Dag, can't win 'em all.' Dag wags his tail against my legs and carries on sniffing his way down the path. A street light flutters on and our breath steams as the day cools – a fact that hadn't entered my planning when I slipped out of my toasty cottage. Both of us pick up an eager pace back to my log fire.

At the bottom of the Green, Skye has just locked the coffee shop and waves me across. 'Glad I caught you, Cat, I was about to hammer on your door.' She hands me a glossy A5 leaflet about some business do or other. 'Someone came in this afternoon and left a wadge.'

'Ah, so I'm your conscience recycling, am I?'

She looks hurt. 'No, Cat, I genuinely thought you might be interested.'

'Sorry, sorry. Bad day. I'll check my diary.'

'Read it, you chump. I thought it might be good for your chocolate business.'

I glance at it and see it's from the West of England Business Awards. 'I don't think I'm ready to sponsor anything yet, Skye.'

'Not sponsor, you numpty, enter. It's a competition, for new businesses. Even if you don't win, it would be great publicity and we both get to go to a posh lunch and hobnob with the great and the good, so get the date in your diary. I'm entering in the under-thirties category – so, don't worry, I won't be overshadowing you!'

'Frightened of the competition, are we?' I grin.

'Actually, I think it would be fun to do the application together. It only needs a few details. Oh, and a business plan. But I'm sure you've got any number of those up your sleeve, haven't you?

I can't quite tell if she's being serious or not. So, given discretion is the better form of valour, I choose not to answer. I have got a business plan, of course I have. Even if it was literally jotted on the back of a bar menu a few months back, in a moment of drunken enthusiasm.

Skye slips her arm through mine and before I can argue, she's leading me across The Green to her new flat above the village store.

'Not seen inside yet, have you, Cat? It's my first real place of my own. The start of putting down roots. Only rented, of course. But one day…'

Dag looks at me with imploring brown eyes as we're trotting in the opposite direction to my warm fire. 'Don't worry, boy, we'll only be a few minutes.'

'Of course we will, Dagenham.' She pats his head briefly and gives me a rather strange look. Dag looks decidedly unconvinced.

I'm not sure what I expected Skye's flat to be like – but it isn't anything like it! The walls are a very restful shade of red, her huge, padded sofa is a lovely cream colour that's picked up buy a deep pile carpet and we both pause at her front door to take off our shoes and leave them on the mat outside the door.

Dag sits politely while Skye bustles into the kitchen and returns with a large cloth. With his feet dried, we all tramp across the carpet and settle down. Skye disappears into what I assume must be her bedroom and reappears moments later with a laptop. She hands me a large pad of paper, along with a pencil. 'I thought if we filled out my application online, you could make some notes and then we'll pop back to your place so you can fill yours out.'

She's now settled cross-legged on the floor and is almost bouncing up and down in excitement. With dread, it dawns on me that there'll be no backing out.

'Here it is! Now, let's see what they need. Name of business. Address. Nature of business. All very straightforward, Cat. Now, let me just have a look at my latest business plan, before I attach it. This will be a doddle for a professional like you.'

I wish I shared her confidence. How do I explain to a bright-eyed Gen Z that, in the past, people were paid to produce business plans and cashflow forecasts? When I was managing the Agency, I could read them, even pick up the flaws and potential problems, but writing one is a very different kettle of fish.

Skye taps away merrily for several minutes as I watch in awe. Then she stops. 'Oh, for goodness' sake. Time for a very large glass of wine.'

'Problem?'

Climbing to her feet, she sighs. 'Not really. It's just they want the business plan in their own template. Which means I've got to transfer everything across rather than just attach a file.'

As she trots over to an elegant G-plan sideboard, I breathe a sigh of relief. After all, if they give you a template, how hard can it be to make up a few words and figures? Especially after some wine…

An hour and three glasses of wine later, we get to our feet, Skye carefully holding a data stick. 'It'll be so exciting, Cat. When we get shortlisted, there's a formal lunch. They have the press there and a whole load of local dignitaries. I'm going to suggest they find a local social media influencer to attend. We could even put a small box of your chocolates on every table.'

'Don't you think that might look like I'm trying to influence them?'

'So? All's fair in love, war and business.' She giggles and so do I. It's possible we're just a little tipsy. Which might explain why, two hours later and against my better judgement, I press SEND and my own application is submitted.

As I finally get ready for bed, I'm thankful that we saved the applications on my hard drive because I realise I have absolutely no idea what's in that business plan. But it's been a useful exercise and I'm getting quite excited. Plus, we had a fun evening and as I drift off to sleep I imagine walking past candlelit tables filled with the cream of the business community, all of whom are watching admiringly as, wearing a fabulous long black dress and pearls, I process towards Richard Branson to receive a glittering trophy from him. Meanwhile's stuffing boxes of my chocolates into his jacket pocket, and paparazzi cameras flash madly, like it's the Oscars.

Chapter 11

Just as I'm nearing the stage and eying the glitzy trophy in my dream, an odd whining sound starts up. I glare at the sound engineer who just smiles and waves. The sound gets louder and more persistent and I glance at the nearest table to see if it's some sort of weird business cheer. But they're deep in conversation and ignoring me. The noise gets even louder, followed by a scratching sound, rather like a giant electronic mouse might make. A mouse that barks, just like...

Dragging my now throbbing head from the pillow it finally dawns on me that it's Dag. I stumble through the semi-darkness to open my bedroom door. My heart breaks and I sink to my knees to smoother my pup's head in kisses. I've never seen him look so sorry for himself. Mind you, a glance at my clock shows it's 4 am so I've probably never felt so sorry for myself either.

As I cuddle him, Dag lets out a yelp, followed by a long plaintive whine, which is when I see he's holding his left paw off the ground. It's not a good sign and there's worse to follow when I reach down to feel it and he places his teeth gently but firmly around my arm, then sinks onto his tummy.

'Stay there, boy. Let's see what I've got.' My stomach lurches as I hurry to the bathroom cabinet and return with a huge roll of bandage. Dagenham can't know what they are, but it doesn't stop him growling at me as I approach his paw, something he's never done before. My hands are shaking as I stroke his head and try to reach his leg before he notices. But he's much too smart and all I get is another deep growl. No way is he going to let me touch it, so I lie down and cuddle him, twisting my body round to see as much of his pad as I can. There's no obvious injury and I can't see how it could be broken but he's still not happy so I nip across to the airing cupboard and get my best woollen throw, drape it around the two of us and lie there stroking him, whispering in his ear until we can reasonably call the vet.

Around eight in the morning I figure it's not too early to ring. Dag seems to be asleep but as soon as I stir he yelps so I carefully lay his head down, tuck the blanket in around him and retrieve my phone from the sitting room. A few seconds later, our wonderful village vet is advising me to take Dag round. 'You can't be too careful with that sort of thing, Ms de Barnes.'

That, however, presents a problem. Dag is more than a little reluctant to put paw to ground and it takes what seems like a lifetime for me to half-carry and half-drag him downstairs. Then I have an idea. 'You're not going to like this, my boy. But you'll like limping round to the vet's even less.'

Which is why, a few minutes later and with the village still in darkness, I cross the Green with my pup folded into my large metal wheelbarrow, his front paws draped forlornly over the edge and a look on his face saying *I can't believe you're doing this to me.*

Martin Dales' surgery is an extension on the back of his small, red brick bungalow. The first time I had an appointment there I completely missed it. Not only was there no sign but my attention was riveted by the fact that he had a very realistic tunnel painted on his garage door, so realistic I half expected a train to come tearing out of it at any minute. As it transpires, there's a gate on the opposite side of the bungalow and you follow the path to a small brick-built extension. There's still no sign, though, just an open door leading to a wooden reception desk.

Inside, there's the unmistakable sanitised smell of anywhere vaguely medical and the room is painted a bright clinical white. Most of the walls are covered in posters for pet insurance plans and proprietary medicines but one wall is given over to photos and posters from various animal welfare groups, including a rather pointed one proclaiming, '*animals have feelings, too*'. Given how significant farming is locally, I'm surprised he can get away with it, but I guess if you feel strongly enough to take a stand, it doesn't matter if you risk a client or two.

On my previous visit to register, Martin had been on sabbatical and a locum had taken our details and given Dagenham his required injection, much to my pup's disgust. Today, the vet is already behind the wooden counter, his bald head gleaming in the light from an overhead fluorescent tube. He is busily buttoning a white coat.

Martin has a warm smile and while he leads us into the main room and prepares the long table – which Dag eyes with deep distrust – I take the opportunity to study him in detail. He must be in his early fifties, and while bald, has spikes of hair that suggest it's shorn rather than natural. He's clean shaven. He has an unusually small mouth and eyes. He also seems to be a man of few words, although he does hum while he prepares.

Preparations complete, he tickles Dag behind his ears and looks into the dog's eyes. 'Well now, young Dagenham, what seems to be the trouble?' My pup gives his hand a desultory lick but he's clearly still wary. Even more so when the vet carefully lifts the injured leg and stares at the damaged area.

Martin nods to me and we hoist Dag from barrow to table, accompanied by several yelps and a forlorn howl before Martin crosses to unlock the drugs cabinet and returns with a vial of clear liquid and a scarily large syringe. He glances at my face, which even a hangover and sleep deprivation can't mask, then smiles and pats my arm. 'Don't worry, not only am I fully qualified, I even know what I'm doing.' He nods at the wall behind me, where a black photo frame displays his (numerous) professional qualifications. 'It's just a mild anaesthetic, to numb the area first. Safest for all of us.'

While we wait for the anaesthetic to take effect, I glance around the room. As well as the wall directly in front of me dedicated to showcasing his professional prowess, the wall directly facing him has several posters by the RSPCA (the Royal Society for the Protection of Animals), and the Animal Welfare Foundation. Less prominent but oddly more attention-grabbing because of it, is a poster for the League Against Cruel Sports. Even more startling is it that hangs next to a small photo showing Martin in his white coat amongst a gathering Hunt. I frown, trying to make sense of it.

He follows my gaze and smiles. 'It surprises you, seeing me at a Hunt?'

This is an opportunity too good to miss. 'I suppose so. I mean, it's not really any of my business but I wouldn't necessarily have seen the two as compatible. Although I suppose, now it's not live animals being hunted…'

He plonks down on a high stool, being careful to hold Dag's paw, his gaze switching from Dag to me and back. 'I have a professional interest in looking after all animals – after all, they don't get to choose how they're used. That doesn't mean I support hunting, I don't. And, to be honest, I wanted to keep an eye on Sergeant Court, who always seemed to be there whenever they met. I don't think I was the only one who thought he might be a little too keen to get in with the Hunt people and even more keen to deal with any protestors. Not exactly good with animals, that one.'

He glances back at Dag, then reaches for some surgical pincers, and I look away and stare at the RSPCA poster as if it was the most interesting thing in the world.

After what feels like a lifetime, he snorts, 'Got the blighter' and waves a disgustingly large thorn triumphantly in the air. 'I'll just dab a drop of antiseptic on, then we'll try a bandage to keep it clean. But if it causes him too much annoyance, pop back. Otherwise, he should be fine in a couple of hours.'

'But it's huge, Martin. Where on earth could he have got that from?'

'There really is no way of knowing with dogs. Sometimes it can get trapped in their fur or between their claws, then it gets dislodged, they step on it, and, well, you've seen what happens next.'

Dag stares at the bandage and I fear he's about to yank it straight off, but then he looks at the wheelbarrow and seems to decide anything's better than *that* indignity. He tries a few tentative steps and then paws at the door to be allowed to escape.

Outside, it's fully light now and the sounds and smells of the village coming to life filter across the garden. Dag declines to get back into the wheelbarrow and limps along the pavement slowly, looking sorry for himself, and no doubt seeking sympathy and hence treats. I'm perfectly happy with the slow pace as it gives me time to think about Martin, the Hunt and Sergeant Court, although how my latest information helps the investigation I really can't fathom. But something about the vet leaves me vaguely uneasy. Is he perhaps a little too smooth? Is there more to this Hunt thing than meets the eye? My gut rumbles, so I know something will eventually make sense. Meanwhile, I'm more than occupied trying to manage Dag's lead and an empty wheelbarrow, which, as you might imagine, gets quite a few puzzled looks and some decidedly unhelpful and universally implausible suggestions. The sooner I drop the thing back home, the better.

Thankfully, the lights are already on in the Crimson Courgette and I can see Skye getting ready for the day's business, which reminds me I've promised her another batch of chocolates today so, with a brief apology to the hapless Dag, I settle him in his basket in the hall of my cottage and set to work.

A couple of hours later, a dozen bags of mixed chocolates are ready to expand my new career, or alternatively, to help it sink into oblivion. We poddle down to join Skye in her café. She takes one look at Dag's impressively bandaged paw and ushers us towards a roaring log fire. Dag is rewarded with not one but two treats and a whole lot of sympathy before he settles down in front of the now-blazing fire and snores his way into making up for lost sleep, occasionally sniffing his bandaged front paw with a look of absolute disgust. I, meanwhile, ignore the mid-morning hubbub of customers and stare across at

Bedside Manor, dreaming of the lovely Linton in full sexy scrubs, surrounded by a bevy of admiring nurses (not too admiring, though, thank you) and saving life after life with his long, delicate hands…

A loud snore from under the table jolts me back to reality just as a hefty blast of cold air announces the arrival of a group of tourists, who settle in the far corner while casting envious glances at my place in front of the fire.

Skye greets them and then waves her arm across at the counter where she's invested in a large brass carousel so she can display my chocolate goodies in pride of place. It strikes me that this is an excellent excuse to monitor sales, because apparently, according to Skye, my business plan says I'm currently undertaking a period of intense market research. Who knew? And it's also proving a useful way of disposing of my trial runs for the Harvest Supper next week. I'm eying one of the ruffled packs when the policewoman from Scotland comes in. My goodness, she looks as if she's carrying the world on her shoulders. I nod a greeting which gets a wan smile but then she turns on her heels, blows her nose and hurries out without ordering anything. Very odd.

At precisely 11 o'clock, my phone pings with a distracting text from Linton that sets my pulse racing. Apparently it's an admin morning and he's on his way across to join me. I have a dreamy couple of minutes imagining those skilled fingers busy on the keyboard and files rather than on scalpel and suture before Linton emerges from his surgery. In place of full scrubs he's wearing slinky slim-cut chinos and a yellow cashmere jumper over a crisp white shirt.

Maybe this is the way to take it with the medic, literally as the moment seizes us. He bustles in, kisses me briefly on the cheek, which produces enough sizzle to charge a medium car, then hurries over to the counter and returns with a steaming black coffee and one of my sample macaroons, which he tucks into with the enthusiasm of a true lover – of chocolate, that is. Please, what kind of a girl do you think I am?

All too soon, he's finished his drink and treat. He smiles at me with enough warmth to melt all of my chocolates. 'Cat, that was lovely. And I don't just mean your macaroon.' He wiggles his eyebrows and grins. 'We really must do this again soon.'

'How about tomorrow?' *Goodness, where did that come from, Cat?*

'Right answer!'

We stare at each other for a moment and I notice a thin line of chocolate staining the side of his mouth. *Dare I? Have we reached... Yes, we have.* In one smooth motion I snatch a napkin and dab his soft skin. For a moment he looks startled, with a rabbit-in-the-headlights look, then he grabs my fingers, gives them the lightest of kisses and is gone. As am I, lost in my cheeky audacity, and the pleasure of it.

Which is short-lived, as Rose slides into the chair recently vacated by the lovely doctor.

'Morning, Cat. Going well, I see?'

'Morning, Rose. One of your rare visits, is it?'

Rose grins. 'Well, no point being freed from running the café if all I ever do is mope around the place.'

'I'd say your days are anything but crappy, Rose. Where was it this time?'

'A long weekend in the Peak District. Very – restorative.'

She looks around to check no-one is sitting nearby, then leans in across the table and lowers her voice. 'I've just run into Wickham and he tells me you were asking about Sergeant Court. Is this part of your investigation?'

'Rose, I'm not investigating.'

'Of course you're not, my dear. Anyway, Wickham thought I should tell you Court told me some time back – and with some relish – that his memoirs were causing no end of consternation. He said it made all the research into his old cases positively worthwhile. He reckoned Sandy Lane, for one, was positively quaking in her boots and it takes a lot to shake her, I can tell you. He also said it served her right. And a few more like her. I must say, I saw another side of him. And not a pleasant one.' She sighs and stares into the flames while I'm trying to make sense of what she's just said. I know I've only really talked to Sandy on the

123

Cirencester night out but I liked her and she'd been great fun. It was hard to imagine her quaking in her boots. But I suppose you shouldn't judge a book by its cover, however glamorous. I'm intrigued. Does Rose know more about her than she's letting on? Either way, my gut tells me I'll probably get more out of her if I let her take her time. And it's not as if I've got anything else on; I can do my customer research perfectly comfortably from here.

'You know he never owned a computer? I mean, these days, who doesn't have at least a laptop or a tablet?' I meant it as a throw away remark, more to keep the conversation going.

But it jolts Rose back and she looks around, thoughtfully. 'I always thought there was something not quite right with that policeman. He was just a bit too full of himself.' She stared into the fire, nodding to herself. 'Everything was always about him. Talk about secretive: if you asked him to give you the time, he'd look at his watch and then keep it to himself. And he always had to be right. They do say – and I'm not one to gossip – that when he was on duty, he was always on the scrounge for some free food and drink. And who knows what else? The shopkeepers used to dread him appearing, like Houdini, in the doorway.'

Clearly another book not to be judged by its cover. The whole Sergeant Court thing needs some serious rethinking and Rose's comments have opened up a range of new suspects the man might have upset over the years. Although, even if he'd been pushing his luck over freebies, surely none of that would be enough to get him killed?

I glance at her. 'Does the inspector know about this?'

Rose snorts, causing Dag to look up and several customers to turn around. 'To be honest, I don't think that policeman is pushing too hard. In my opinion, he's never quite got over suspecting Mavis to really consider anyone else.'

I pause. Maybe there were more grudges than I imagined against our rather unsaintly Officer Court? Especially if there was someone who didn't want an old case being brought into the light of day? Or maybe Court uncovered something he'd forgotten and decided he could use it to his own advantage? After all, if he wasn't averse to a few food freebies, who knows what else he might think he was entitled to? If only I could find out which cases he'd been reinvestigating. Or whether he'd kept a copy of his manuscript. Somewhere, in the back of my mind, there's a voice whispering an answer. If I could just... No, it's gone.

Chapter 12

I need a bigger kitchen!

A few days later and with the Harvest Supper only days away (how did it come round so quickly?) every work surface is covered with catering boxes of coconut and tins of condensed milk, the egg output of a minor chicken farm and enough slabs of plain chocolate to build a decent sized house. To say nothing of three whisks, an industrial mixer blender, all three of my melting pots and my entire collection of spatulas and catering spoons. Plus a couple of huge brown ceramic mixing bowls. Also laid out on the counter is butter, three types of sugar and enough flour to liberally coat me, every work surface and the floor, as well as go in the recipes.

Some time later, and drying my hands on my third soggy tea towel, I survey the debris. My dishwasher trundles away on its fifth load and the timer on my cooker reminds me I have 8 minutes and 45 seconds before the next batch come out. Just enough for some clearing away or for a coffee. Coffee it is, then.

It's also the perfect opportunity to sample my wares. I don't understand chocolatiers who are put off the goods by their work. For me, it's one of the main benefits. Which is why my coffee is enhanced by a mini-mountain of crumbs and cream from a chocolate coffee cake and two chocolate macaroons, whose peers are on perched on cooling racks covering every spare space. The first macaroon tastes wonderful, soft and moist, the soft coconut top being just right to balance with the hard chocolate base. But of course, that may be the exception, so I need to try a second one...

As I add my plate and mug to the mountain of other dirty pots, the buzzer reminds me to check on the remaining goodies. Through the glass door, they look perfect. But I'm all too aware that opening the door too soon can lead to the collapse of even the best-looking cake, so I give it another 30 seconds, then open the door very slowly and ease the contents onto my final cooling tray with a sigh of relief.

Tucking an escaping curl of hair back into my unflattering blue hairnet, I set about making the cream filling, spooning some instant coffee granules (the only time you'll ever see such a travesty anywhere on my property) into a large brown ceramic bowl, followed by several tablespoons of caster sugar and some boiling water, which I then whisk until the mixture is gorgeously light and fluffy. The inevitable finger dipping/licking test satisfies me it's the right taste and consistency for topping the first sponge. Once cooled and iced, it can join the others ready for boxing.

In the distance, the church clock strikes one. Lunch time. But even I can't nibble chocolate all morning and still face food. Dagenham would have no such qualms about eating too much – although I shudder at the impact it would have since it's a complete canine no-

no – and right on cue, he scratches at the kitchen door. 'Okay, boy, I'm on my way.'

I grab a handful of his biscuits and toss them to him in the hall while I peel off my flour-and chocolate-stained cooking gear in exchange for wellingtons and waxed jacket. Time, tide and walkies wait for no man (or woman). And I have a job to do in the library on our way back.

The early mist and dampness have given way to one of those nondescript autumnal English days: neither warm nor cold, nor dry nor wet, the sky a light grey with broken cloud that might easily move into blue sky or black rain clouds. Not that Daggers is in the least bit interested in such niceties. If it isn't torrential rain, he couldn't care less. And as far as I'm concerned, today my need is for fresh air and a flour free environment, so we both spend a wonderful 45 minutes tramping out of the village and following a footpath through the muddy, barren fields behind the church before we complete the circle, re-enter the village and do a loop around the recreation ground.

With perfect timing, the clock chimes two just as we reach the top of the Green. A quick glance at Red's house suggests it's still empty.

But across the Green, our enthusiastic new librarian has made a point of opening the doors at least five minutes before the advertised time, so I make my way inside and fire up the lone public computer. With a quick glance to check no-one's watching and a quick prayer that the new librarian is more of a stickler for prompt opening than for prompt clearing of browser history, I watch it trundle into life. Yes. Excellent. Nothing's been cleared for weeks and for the next couple of hours I scroll down, making the occasional note on my phone of any URLs and websites that might conceivably have been part of the sergeant's research. There are a few newspaper reports, and when I click through they're about crimes where he's mentioned as the investigating officer, but as I've already learnt, they're really only minor infringements. Nothing murder-worthy. And, of course, there's nothing to show who did the searching.

The history also shows how amazingly diverse our village inhabitants are in their browsing, from the predictable exotic holiday locations to the bizarre: face masks of Papua New Guinea and the GDP of St Vincent and the Grenadines. Presumably some slightly odd school project?

An hour later, with Dag nudging my leg with increasing urgency, I've had enough. My back aches, my shoulders are stiff and my eyes are itchy from glaring at the small screen. This has been such a waste of time and effort! I start to close the pages down when something Rose said floats into my brain.

Moments later, I'm staring at the Facebook page for Sandy Lane. It turns out to be disappointingly spartan unless you really want to know that she's an old girl of St John's School in Marlborough and read

Sociology at Nottingham University. Although there are a few photos showing her muscular body in various yoga poses and taking part in what looks like wild swimming. According to the web, she has a large house on the outskirts of the village, but appears to have joined no interest groups and has a sum total of four Facebook friends, including Mavis. A little odd for someone who'd seemed so carefree and vivacious, but maybe she just prefers to live life in the flesh rather than through the ether. Another dead end.

'You know she used to be a magistrate, don't you?' I look up with a start, to find Scott squinting over my shoulder. 'Apparently, she was there one day, gone the next. Resigned. No-one seems to know why. Lots of rumours, though. Some sort of impropriety.'

'You little gossip! How on earth do you know that?'

He taps the side of his nose. 'Actually, I can't remember. Probably someone told me at some party or other. Certainly wouldn't have been Sandy, I've hardly spoken to her.'

'Not one of the flock, then?'

'Sadly not. Doesn't make her a murderer, though. Why are you so interested?'

'According to Rose, Court said he had Sandy, and I quote, "quaking in her boots". Do you think it could be anything to do with her being a magistrate and him being a policeman? Perhaps a case they clashed on, here in the village?'

'I'd be surprised. From what I can remember, the Magistrates' bit was closed long ago. Hang on.' He leans over my shoulder to tap a few keys, staring at the screen. 'Yes, closed in 1969, so that idea's out.'

My shoulders slump and I bang my fist on the table, before remembering I'm in a library.

Scott clamps a firm hand on my shoulder, causing me to wince. 'Catney, you are *not* investigating. That's what I came in here – to remind you.'

'I'm not. I'm just – intrigued. Anyway, how did you know I was here? Were you spying on me?' The trouble with living in a village is, everyone knows your business.

'Saw you through the window and hoped you were researching chocolate recipes, not recipes for murder. Come on, they'll be closing in a few minutes, and I need a mug of tea.'

He links his arm through mine and pretty well drags me outside while Dag, my trusty protector, simply wags his tail and trots beside us. I need to have serious words with that dog if he's to remain in my diplomatic protection squad… *Hold on. Is that who I think it is?* Across the Green, a security light has flicked on outside one of the cottages, illuminating a slim well-dressed man who's about to put a key into the door.

'Scott, can we just divert for a moment? I need to speak to Red. At least, I need you to start a conversation with him, so I've got an excuse to talk to him.'

One of the many things I like about Scott is his instinct to know when to shut up and act.

'Red,' he bellows, 'got a moment?' He bustles across the grass with me trotting a few paces behind. 'Just wanted to ask whether you'd like to do a reading at Dean's funeral? You having known him so long.'

Red looks from Scott to me and back. 'Oh, I'm not sure, Vicar. I'm not really a speaker, you know. I'd just offered to help him publicise his book idea. And a little bit of research.'

It would take a better excuse than that to thwart my favourite vicar. 'You must have seen quite a lot of him then. That would be really interesting to hear – for the eulogy, you know.'

For a split second, the man looks positively furious, before he smiles and nods towards his door. 'I suppose so. Why don't you come in for a minute?' He virtually pushes Scott towards the house, then throws me a look of anger I'm sure is designed to stop me in my tracks, so he can shut the door in my face. But I'm not easily deterred, especially with Scott there to watch my back. Dag gives a sharp woof to remind me I have him as well and I just hope he'll be more protective than he was when the vicar kidnapped me from the library.

The lounge furniture proves every bit as comfortable as it looked through the window. The china proves to be mostly Wedgewood, its signature blue and white displayed on a significant number of plates and dishes of all shapes and sizes. Scott and I perch on edge of a cream and green sofa while Red serves a large plate of shortbread biscuits. I hadn't realised how hungry I was until the plate appeared, and within moments I'm doing full justice to them while Scott looks on in amusement and Red in amazement. Well, I did skip lunch.

'Nice place,' Scott nods, looking around as Red beetles back into the kitchen, soon reappearing with a tea pot and three mugs commemorating the centenary of the Dragon School in Oxford.

'Milk? Sugar?' Red spots the rapidly depleted plate and raises an eyebrow. 'And I do have more biscuits…'

Scott takes a sip of tea and puts his mug back on the table. There's a motto printed on the inside rim: *arduus ad solem* – which means 'reach for the sun', if my school day Latin serves me well.

'Must have been an interesting project, Mr Street, helping Dean with his book.'

'Yes, it is. Was. Would have been. Sorry – this is all quite a shock.' In fairness, he does look quite upset.

Scott nods his understanding. 'I suppose it all comes to a halt now?'

'Yes, I suppose so. We were only at the drafting stage really, listing old cases, that sort of thing. We were due to meet in the museum the night he died., to take some photos. I'd told him they would ensure his eternal fame. How ironic.'

I quickly return my mug to the table before I slop it everywhere. 'You were with him the night he died?'

'Yes.' He glares at me. 'Well, no, actually. If you must know, he didn't turn up. I just waited around in the hall for, I don't know, maybe fifteen, twenty minutes.'

'So, if he didn't turn up, how did you manage to wait in the hall?' This is starting to get interesting.

A look of pure delight passes over his face. 'Simple. It was unlocked. In fact, it was slightly ajar when I arrived.' He delivers the statement as if it's the punchline in some epic court case.

I groan inwardly as I realise an unlocked door means pretty much anyone could have got in at any time and the whole list of suspects is blown wide open.

Time to take back some of the initiative. 'What time did you get back here?'

'I suppose I got back about ten, just in time for the news. Look, how's this going to help the eulogy, Vicar? It's rapidly turning into more of a police interrogation.'

'Sorry, Red. You're quite right. Just curious, that's all.'

'Actually, Red,' I smile at him in a way I hope is warm but reserved, 'it's possible you might be able to help. You know the police arrested Mavis Enderby?' He nods. 'But there's no way it could have been her.' Another nod. 'So, from your little bit of research, was

134

there anything else you thought was, shall we say, unusual?'

'Nothing that would lead to murder, no. I did discover one interesting thing though: he was the reason Sandy Lane quit the Bench. But as soon as I mentioned it to him, he snapped my head off and told me in no uncertain terms to drop it. I thought it would make an interesting subplot if I do decide to write that novel.'

Scott and I lean forward in unison. I'm still digesting that titbit when Scott asks, 'And did you drop it?'

'Of course I did.' Then, glancing at Scott he blushes. Yes, actually blushes, bless him. 'Well, to tell you the truth, Vicar, not exactly. You see, I was curious about why he was so angry, so, yes, I did do a little more digging.'

Scott stares for a moment. 'But presumably you didn't find anything – or you'd have told the police?'

'Well, that's just it. I did – and I did. But that inspector seemed so sure he'd already got the murderer, I don't think he was really listening. And before you ask…' he swings his gaze back to me, 'he's not been back in touch.'

I stare at the entwined dragon on my mug, the three of us lost in our respective thoughts.

Hang on a minute. What if…? 'Red, what exactly did you discover about Sandy and Dean?'

'Well – I suppose it's a matter of public record. Providing you look in the right records, if you get my drift.' I don't but it doesn't seem the moment to ask. 'She got a caution from Sergeant Court. For assault. Couldn't find out any more details though.'

Now that is interesting. It gives me another line of enquiry. Which I'm not doing, of course. Enquiring.

Chapter 13

Early the following morning, the day of Dean's funeral, Dagenham's frantic barking drags me downstairs. He's pawing at the front door. I have to take a firm grip of his collar and forcibly drag him back before I can open it. He's never behaved like this before which makes me more nervous than wondering what might await me on the other side.

As it happens, there's no-one there. Just an enormous bouquet of flowers: red and pink dahlias, their almost perfectly symmetrical petals glowing in the early morning sunshine. There are also several Chinese lanterns, a half a dozen rich burgundy chrysanthemums and four white ornamental cabbage flowers, their green stems and leaves adding depth and pulling the whole display together. Very impressive.

Odd, though, there's no card, no clue about who to thank for this unexpected pleasure. I remember, back in the summer, complimenting Linton on the display in his front garden and saying how much I enjoyed flowers, but to be honest, he didn't really seem to be taking it in, and moments later his phone rang, and he was off on some urgent house call. And that had been ages ago. *Bless him, he must have finally remembered.* With a grin as big as a child on Christmas morning I'd picked up the bunch and searched for a note, my heart thudding with the anticipation of what he might write. Except there wasn't one. I even searched around in case it had dropped off, blown down the path or whatever. Nothing. How like Linton to add a little mystery to the romance. *Really? Can you hear yourself, Cat?*

After my shortest shower on record and high-speed makeup application, I lock my front door to the accompaniment of the church clock striking eight. Hopefully, there's just enough time to show my appreciation before morning surgery. Unfortunately, though, while my v-neck jumper dress shows my figure to its best advantage, it also exposes too much skin in the chilly morning air, so I duck back and grab a woollen knitted poncho. Decorum rather than décolletage, I think, on this occasion. My dress hemline leaves a minor gale blowing round my nether regions, but I'm determined not to sacrifice my showpiece legs. Not if I'm going to stick with these crippling shoes. *Let's face it, Cat, it's only a five-minute stroll.*

I nod good morning to Wickham, my next-door neighbour, on his way to his bookshop and smile, as out of the corner of my eye, I see him staring after me. Otherwise, the village is still and silent. Until a battered old Rover rumbles past and stops in front of the Museum with a crunch of gravel and a puff of exhaust smoke and out climbs Inspector Parva. He's directly in front of me so avoidance is out of the question. Mind you, it's worth it as I watch him cast an approving eye over me, then blush and bolt inside. This

138

is as good a moment as I'm likely to get to update him on what I've discovered and maybe, if he's still feeling wrong-footed, I might even wheedle something useful out of him. 'Inspector…'

He stands in the middle of the tiled hallway, looking as guilty as if he'd been caught with his fingers in the cookie jar. 'Inspector, if you have a few moments, I wanted to update you with what I've learnt from talking to several people in the village. Seems to me both Sandy Lane and Red Street had an axe to grind against Dean. Sorry, poor choice of metaphor.'

He stands still, not indicating that he wants to take notes, and to all intents and purposes more interested in my poncho than my ponderings. My voice trails off.

'Thank you for your interesting observations, Ms de Barnes, but I can assure you that we're pursuing our own lines of enquiry which I'm certain are about to bear fruit.' He raises a hand. 'And before you ask, no, I'm not going to share them with you. Now, perhaps you'd like to go on whatever date you're dressed up to the nines for, and leave me to get on with my date with my paperwork.' *Goodness, Cat, is that jealousy? Amazing.* He marches away and moments later a door slams. His voice echoes off the tiles: '*Constable…*'

'Has he gone?' A deep baritone voice scares the living daylights out of me. I spin round to come face-to-face with what looks like a grizzly bear and I jump back with a squeal.

'Gracious, dear lady, I do apologise.' The man stretches out a large, well-groomed hand from a cufflinked sleeve, gently lifts *my* hand to his lips and plants a soft kiss. 'Boothby Graffoe. Wing Commander. Pleased to meet you.'

His sudden appearance renders me speechless so I can only stare. He's dressed in a beautiful dark suit, obviously tailor-made, with a crisp white shirt and a tie sporting two shades of blue on a deep red background. But his most striking feature is the extraordinary white, bristling moustache jutting out from his cheeks at forty-five degrees and seemingly as wide as a Spitfire's wings.

'Has he gone?' the man says again and he glances around the hall. 'He would've made a splendid sergeant-major, that one. Definitely an army type. Not RAF, that's for sure.' Graffoe shakes his head. 'I heard him giving you a dressing-down and thought it better to stay hidden, what?' He nods across to one of the cells. 'That's the only time I've felt safer in there than out here, don't y'know?' Then without warning, his face creases into the biggest smile I've ever seen. 'Just made a brew. You look as if you need one.'

He leads the way through a door to my left into a modern office and goes to pour tea from a brown teapot. 'Perks of being the duty volunteer,' he grins. 'I don't often get the treat of an elegant young lady like you coming in, though. If I'm allowed to say it, these days.'

After his initial shock appearance, I must admit I'm warming to the man. 'Of course you may, Wing Commander.'

'Oh, Boothby, please. Retired now, what.'

'Catherine de Barnes. Catney or Cat to my friends.'

He hands me a very welcome mug of steaming tea, just the right shade of brown, and indicates a wooden chair opposite the desk. 'Rum do, this murder business. And in here, of all places.' He plonks himself down behind the desk, then ducks to open a drawer and from the muffled sounds it's not hard to imagine something bracing being added to his brew.

'Did you know the sergeant, then, Wing – Boothby? I gather he came in here quite often for his research?'

'A lot more in the past couple of weeks. I wondered if he was angling to get a model made of himself, eh?' He chuckles, his blue eyes warm and sparkling.

'How did he seem? Had he changed in any way recently?' I've no idea why I'm asking this, but all the TV detectives ask, so it must be important.

'Funny you should ask that. He had, actually. Just in the last couple of weeks. Got quite excited, although come to think of it, not in a good way. More, a rather unpleasant gloating. Not sure he did much research, mind you. More writing and holding court.'

'I don't suppose he left any notes or anything here, did he?' Although if he had, the police would have taken them by now. Whatever else you might say about Inspector Parva, he was efficient.

'No, he was always very careful to take everything away with him. He even used to check under the table and rifle through the wastepaper basket. Seemed a bit over the top to me, to be honest. But then, you know these police types. They like to pretend they're being methodical, but most of the time it's just mindless over-caution. Wouldn't last five minutes in the services, not even the army.' He raises a pair of huge bushy eyebrows. *Ah well, another dead end.*

'Well, thanks, Boothby, it's been an unexpected pleasure. And thank you for the tea.' If I don't get a move on, I'll be too late for my unofficial appointment with the lovely medic. I stop. 'Oh, by the way. Did you say he was holding court?'

'Oh yes, I'm surprised he didn't set himself up on the JP's bench. And one of them was the woman you were telling the policeman about. The one who sounds like a road.'

'Sandy Lane?'

He grins, his face beaming again. 'Aye, that's the one. And whatever they were talking about it wasn't something pleasant, from what I could hear. Not that I was listening, mind. But let's just say, a lot of his meetings were held at such volume it was hard not to.'

'So, you know what they were discussing?'

'Well, that would imply I was listening. Which I wasn't.'

I smile at him and gently rest my hand on his arm. 'I know. But it could be useful.'

'From the snatches I did hear, without trying to of course, she was begging him not to put something about her in his book. Something about a police caution, I think. She said it would ruin her reputation and wouldn't do anyone any good.'

'Yes, I'd heard that. I don't suppose she mentioned any details?'

He shakes his head, making his bristly beard shake quite alarmingly. 'Sorry, you'd have to ask her. I don't think it went very well though. I heard him mutter something then she shouted, "You're disgusting," and flew out of the building like a bat out of hell. I never saw here again. But I'm not here each time we're open. And Court did have his own key.'

Oh dear, two steps forwards, one step back. I smile. 'Thanks anyway, Boothby.' With a bit of luck, I might still get to the surgery in time. How bad would it be to feign illness and get a last-minute appointment?

'Catherine?' I glance back to see the lovely Wing Commander has got up from behind the desk, a look of concern on his wrinkled brown face. 'None of my business, of course, and it's a good thing you're doing, but just – be careful. We still have a killer on the loose. And maybe more than a few foxes flushed from their lairs. Which could be dangerous...'

What a treasure! He's only known me five minutes and I just know he's got my back. Much Slaughter is full of such lovely people. *And a killer, Cat.* Speaking of lovely people…

My heart sinks as I hurry past the coffee shop: there are already five people queuing by the surgery door, which opens for business just as I reach it. But one thing you never ever do in a village is jump a queue: they'll be talking about the offence thirty years later. I'm just wondering whether to ask the fire-breathing receptionist if she can tell me what Linton's doing over lunch when the inner door swings open and the good doctor emerges. He scans the room apprehensively, no doubt assessing what medical matters he'll be served today. When his eyes catch mine his face lights up. 'Catherine, I didn't…'

'I haven't.' Oh, the language of romance: our conversation's already reached the banality of a long-married couple.

He glances at his watch, then at his receptionist. 'Five minutes?' Her glare is as fierce as the others in the queue, although I know they're already considering whether to be offended by the delay or intrigued with the prospect of some ripe village gossip. Personally, I couldn't care less as I bound into the consulting room, admiring Linton with more relish than is decent in public.

He gestures to the patient chair and flops down on the doctor side of the table. Personally, I'd have preferred the consultation to take place on that very enticing leather couch…

'What can I do for you, Ms de Barnes?' I'm not sure whether his stiff professionalism is because he's in doctor mode or because he thinks ears might be firmly planted against the door. As it turns out, it's neither: his face cracks into a huge grin as he seizes my hand and places my fingers to his lips sending shock waves sizzling down my spine. I guess if I'm going to swoon, this is just the right place.

'No, seriously, what can I do for you?'

Ah, so he's going to play this with a straight bat, is he? Well, two can play that game. 'Oh, I think you already know, doctor.' I wiggle my eyebrows and adjust my poncho to better effect.

He continues to look blank. I'm so glad I'm sitting because only two moments into the conversation my legs are already like jelly, he looks *so* sexy in his tight-fitting open-necked blue shirt.

'I wanted to thank you.'

'Riiight.'

God, he's good at this. 'For my little – gift.' I cross one long leg over the other, secretly enjoying the fact that he stares for a moment, blushes and suddenly has to study a huge medical textbook on the other side of the room. I can't help it, I twist my bottom slightly on the chair so my hemline rises a few centimetres, as seemingly, does the doctor's temperature. Well, the gorgeous creature deserves a nice thank you.

'Cat, I have patients waiting outside. And lovely as it is to see you, I have no idea what you're talking about.'

'My bouquet, of course. The ones you left on my … My heart stops. You didn't, did you?'

He shakes his head and my blood runs cold. My face goes so hot it's about to spontaneously combust and I'm certain I'm going to die of embarrassment on the spot.

'I certainly wish I had, though, if this is the thanks…'

But by then, I'm halfway out of the room and charging from the surgery at breakneck speed, leaving five twittering gossip-riven villagers staring open-mouthed at the fleeing madwoman. How will I ever show my face in here again? I'll be a laughing stock. I'll have to sell up, leave the village and become a nun.

All of this I tell Dagenham with my face buried in his fur, quite certain I'll die of embarrassment or disappointment. Or both. Dag rests his head on my lap, while his tail thumps the floor rhythmically, in sympathy.

My phone rings and stays unanswered. After three attempts, whoever it is takes the hint and the house returns to quiet, until a bleep alters me to the arrival of a text. I ignore it. I'm never going to answer my phone again, nor will I ever leave my cottage, so it really doesn't matter.

The screen displays WE NEED TO MEET and fades.

Chapter 14

One thing you can guarantee about a village funeral is that the church will be packed. At least three hundred and fifty people are jammed into the bone-numbing pews, with another fifty or so, mainly men, shuffling around at the back. Although from what I've learnt about Dean over the past few days, I have a sneaking suspicion they're here to make sure he really has departed. *Cat – behave*. Even Inspector Parva has deigned to put in an appearance, which I find oddly warming, although other police are conspicuously absent, even the Scottish lass.

Considering how little he had to go on, Scott has done an amazing job. The front of the service sheet has a photo of Dean in uniform, leaning on a police motorcycle outside the museum when it was still a police station. Scott has managed to weave a few pieces of information into the service, including a rather tongue-in-cheek reference to the *Secret Sergeant* memoir truly living up to its title as no-one seems to be able to find out anything about it. Which is an interesting thought: what if it was simply a ploy by Court to, what? Get him some attention? Settle a few scores? Even blackmail a few guilty consciences? After all, there was Sandy's sudden resignation from the role of magistrate – that would be something she wouldn't want people to learn about. And as for Red, who was probably the last person to see him alive, did

Dean have something on him? Is that why he wanted to keep him close by? You know, keep your friends close, keep your enemies closer? But what? As far as I can see, Red's main flaw was an eye for the ladies.

As we near the end of the service, Scott invites Wickham to 'share some stories from the time they were both youngsters in Much Slaughter'. The poor cleric looks relieved to have someone else take responsibility and I'm fascinated to learn how my neighbour will deal with the murky past of the enigmatic policeman.

Wickham mounts the pulpit steps and gazes around at the congregation. He polishes his glasses, shuffles his notes, clears his throat and bends to gulp from a glass of water. Finally, he lifts his eyes above and beyond the people in the church. 'It hardly seems possible, but I have known Dean Court for over 50 years, ever since we were both teenage tearaways here in the village!'

A few titters rumble around the space while I'm trying to imagine my neighbour and the prim and proper bookshop owner as a delinquent.

'In those days, Dean seemed almost surgically attached to a stream of motorcycles, going back to a battered Honda 50, nearly as old as him and getting progressively larger and faster. It came as a great surprise to many of us when he applied to join the police, and even more so when he was accepted. All became clear though when Dean the policeman became Dean the motorcycle officer. And some years later, it was even more of a surprise when, almost overnight, he stopped riding and became our local beat bobby. Looking back, I suppose we shouldn't have been surprised. He would often drop something as if it was hot coals, even though two minutes earlier it had meant the world to him. Because Dean was a man of sudden impulse, something which continued throughout his life, whether it was motorbikes, his football allegiance, his passion for collecting clocks then ceramics and even his latest favourite – beer. Dean Court was nothing if not unpredictable.'

As usual with anything that lasts more than a couple of minutes, my mind starts to wander and I'm reminded of that photo of Dean's front room, crammed with clocks and ceramic pieces, not what I'd have expected of the man. Not that I'd known him.

Wickham clears his throat. 'As final proof, none of us would ever imagine he'd feature in *Country Life* as an expert horologist – a collector of clocks. And still less that he'd write a book. All I can say in conclusion is there was much more to Dean then met the eye and I'm glad to have known him.'

Wickham returns to his seat, giving his glasses a defiant polish, as several people shake their heads and a few tut. But I think he did a pretty good job talking about a man who had, shall we say, a rather chequered past? There don't seem to be many in the congregation genuinely mourning his death. I sigh. Try as I might, my surreptitious glances don't detect anyone looking especially pleased or suspicious. A spot of divine intervention and a flag of guilt would be most welcome at this point.

Inspector Parva seems convinced that the use of three knives shows premeditation rather than it being a crime committed in the heat of the moment and I suppose that makes sense. I can't imagine many people wander around Much Slaughter with one, never mind three, knives stashed away on their person. *As far as you know, Cat. After all, they'd hardly flash them around as if they were one of the Three Musketeers, would they*? An interesting thought though: what if there were three people, each with a knife? That would also explain how the body was moved … But then, why only one set of prints?

The people around me shuffle to their feet as the final hymn puts a stop to any further thought and a few minutes later we file out of the draughty church into the even more draughty churchyard. There's a light drizzle, the sort you don't necessarily notice until you suddenly realise you're soaked through. Scott however is wrapped in a huge black clerical cloak and has the final part of the service, the committal, printed on a laminated sheet. He's clearly done this before.

No-one has been able to trace any family, so half a dozen of us trudge from the church to the open grave watching the undertakers slowly lower the coffin. I spot Inspector Parva hovering midway between the church and our little gathering, still carefully scanning people as if he suspects one of our group is the perpetrator. Given that it consists of Wickham, Mavis, Rose, Boothby, Scott's girlfriend Cherry and Martin the vet and, as far as I can tell, was a spontaneous decision made just moments ago, it seems unlikely.

A strong gust whistles across the surrounding barren fields and makes us all shiver and I'm personally very glad when Scott concludes the few prayers and the blessing. We continue to hover, looking at each other, uncertain as to how long to linger in order to be respectful before giving in to the worsening rain and cold wind. My ears tingle and my nose is dripping and must be as red as Rudolph's. The smell of damp grass is overwhelming.

Eventually, Scott makes the sign of the cross, and trundles toward the church hall and the wake, giving the rest of us an excuse to leave. I'm about to head for warmth and shelter when my arm is grabbed, and I'm very firmly guided in the opposite direction. 'We need to talk,' a woman's voice hisses in my ear. There, at my shoulder, is Sandy Lane. 'Didn't you get my text?'

'Oh, that was you? I had no idea.' How had she got hold of my number? I feel slightly uncomfortable. Sandy's face is taut, her lips drawn into a grim line.

'Of course it was me. I hear you're saying I killed Court.' This unexpected accusation unnerves me and I swing round to face her, digging my heels into the sodden grass, which stops our progress.

'Sandy, you said you wanted to talk. So let's do it here. And, for the record, I certainly haven't accused you of anything. I was simply interested in your history with the sergeant.'

'Fine,' says Sandy, sounding anything but. She looks around the empty churchyard. 'But first of all, you must understand that you can't go round accusing people. Especially when you don't know the facts. There are consequences. As I well know.'

My heart thuds: she does look angry and I take a step backwards, trying to assess my route to safety. Isn't this exactly what a murderer would say? I hesitate and go on. 'Sandy, all I wanted to do was to understand. And, let's face it, isn't it better that's it me rather than the police?'

Sandy grunts. 'I suppose you'll find out anyway, like you did with that chef murder. If you must know, I committed a minor offence over in Dorset, nothing very serious. But enough for Sergeant Court to hear of it and give me a right royal ticking off. And for me, being a JP, as I was then, if it had got out, it could compromise any future cases I sat on. So I resigned.'

'But you said it was a minor offence: that would hardly be a resigning matter. What exactly did you do?'

Sandy turns to gaze over the misty countryside, her back to me. I'm starting to think that's all I'll get when she lets out a huge sigh, shrugs her shoulders and announces over the gravestones, 'I hit someone. In a

153

pub. He tried it on – which no-one saw – so I slapped him, which lots of people did see. He refused to press charges, but it was enough. Which is why I haven't touched alcohol ever since.'

I touch her lightly on the shoulder, causing her to jump. 'Sandy, what on earth makes you think anyone would care?'

She nods. 'No, you're right. He lost that hold over me years ago. But I care.' She pulls a tissue from her sleeve and carefully dabs the corners of her eyes. 'These days, I'd probably be applauded for giving the groper exactly what he deserved.'

Which is probably just what the murderer would say. Although she does seem quite convincing.

As if she's read my mind, she turns to look me firmly in the eye and adds, slowly and deliberately, 'It was certainly not a motive for me to murder him. Life's too short. But there are more than a few local publicans' wives and daughters you might want to ask about Dean: if the rumours were anything to go by, the sergeant's personal life was nowhere near as shiny as his uniform buttons. Especially when it came to bars and women.'

'What are you accusing him of, exactly?'

'Accusing? Nothing. It's none of my business, just rumours really. But worth a look, I'd say. You never know what you might dig up. I've always been sure there was something, but I couldn't find it.' She shrugs, her head held proud and marches away, the image only slightly spoilt when she skids on the wet grass and grabs for a handy headstone.

I, however, have a last minute lunch appointment with my dishy doc. Unfortunately, however, with that thought I've tempted fate because when I check my phone there's a text full of sad-face emojis: I'm being stood up in favour of a pile of sick notes, lab reports and poo sticks. Good to know where you stand in the relative order of priorities. *Come on, Cat, you know that's unfair. He'd warned you in his text that this might happen and that lunch was a long shot.*

It's my turn to slither and slide through the churchyard, past the now-raucous wake in the church hall, and moments later into the safety of my cottage, my favourite armchair and a consoling supply of anything chocolate.

*

By late afternoon, however, Dag is threatening to leave me if I don't take him for a walk. More importantly, I'm out of chocolate and the shop's about to close. I know the commercial stuff isn't a patch on my own creations, but it's a choice between an hour up to my elbows in my kitchen or a ten-minute round trip. Today, there's no contest.

Pausing only for Dag to relieve his bladder on the verge by my gate, we set off in pursuit of figure-threatening pleasures. But I'm brought to an abrupt halt barely halfway to the shop when the door to Bedside Manor opens and Linton ushers out an attractive raven-haired beauty who I don't recognise. I drag Dag into the Museum doorway and watch in horror as he puts his arm round her, kisses her and then waves her goodbye, before glancing up and down the Square and ducking back inside. *So much for admin, the swine!* I don't want to imagine what he's been administering with that one. It makes me so angry, he's obviously just like my so-called husband. Men – they're all the same! I'm much better off on my own.

Just then, Wickham appears in the bookshop doorway and beckons me over. If he notices my distress, he's far too gentlemanly to remark on it and simply shuffles me to the fireside while he rustles up some tea. He also roots around under the counter and finally emerges, waving a magazine.

'I think we need to take another look at that article about Dean. Maybe we missed something. Have a read while you drink your tea.' He wanders away to serve a customer who's planted a huge pile of hardback books by the till.

Glad of the distraction, I skim the glossy pages, resisting the lure of the latest trends in country house decoration or top ten places to meet the rich and famous this ski season. And there it is.

'During my thirty years in the Force, I was proud to mete out summary justice to my fair share of shoplifters, graffiti artists, speeding motorists or noisy

drunks,' said popular retired police sergeant Dean Court. 'And in those days, that meant a few clips round the ear, I can tell you. Not that you'd get away with that now. But it worked. Plus the fact that I knew all their parents and brothers and – more importantly – they knew me! Good old-fashioned coppering it was back then. Most of the time, all it needed was for them to hear the roar of my motorbike and they'd scarper quicker than rats down a sewer.'

When our reporter asked him to identify his biggest case, the intrepid lawman modestly responded: 'My only claim to being in on a big case was when empty whisky bottles were despatched in a coffin from the Trouble House pub, when that hatchet man Dr Beeching axed the local train line. Although, in fairness, I was only a babe-in-arms at the time! No – much more interesting is the research I've done after my retirement. That's starting to uncover all sorts of worms from my old casebook... Oh, yes, my little memoir will ruffle a few feathers, I can tell you – you'll definitely be after another interview then. The Secret Sergeant will blow open a whole lot of secrets people would rather were kept quiet'.

That's interesting. Is our killer now in possession of those secrets? I wonder. I glance up. 'Wickham, did you ever discover what happened to that little notebook Court mentions in the article?'

'No. At first, I assumed it must refer to his police notebooks. But when I re-read the article a few days ago I wondered if he meant the research for his book, bringing his cases up to date. After all, the book was going to be some kind of sensationalist name-and-shame from what I could work out. It obviously got him really excited. And also probably looking over his shoulder, he once said something about an old case he'd been re-examining that he reckoned was going to catapult his sales. And, before you ask, he wouldn't tell me anything about it, other than smirking over his title, Secret Sergeant.'

'Didn't he give you any clues at all?'

'Well, he did tell me about one rather unpleasant incident.'

Annoyingly, a tiny carriage clock on the mantelpiece tinkles 5.30 pm and Wickham stops in his tracks. 'I've got to close up now. I'm out tonight.' He winks at me and bustles over to the till, ready to cash up. 'You'll be at the Harvest Supper tomorrow, won't you? I'll tell you more then.'

Chapter 15

The next evening, I hurtle into the Crimson Courgette, my arms loaded with six heavy cake tins, my curly hair flapping, my nose dripping. Wickham grins and recites in an annoyingly smug voice, *'"It ain't what you don't know that gets you into trouble,"* Mark Twain is reputed to have said, *"It's what you know for sure that just ain't so."'*

'Where else would the Harvest Supper be held but in the church hall?' I snap, nerves frayed. 'How was I to know?'

His eyes twinkle, he can be really maddening at times. 'Well, most people read the ticket.'

'And clearly I'm not…' The poor man is spared further vitriol as a dog-collared Scott swoops over.

'Cherry thought you might like to join us this evening.'

'Love to. Cherry's always great fun.'

I glance around to see if the handsome doctor, the philanderer, has the brass nerve to turn up. I'm pretty sure it's his rear view I see, over in one of the alcoves. Part of me is relieved he can't see me, the other part would like the chance to obviously ignore him.

Scott startles me as he puts an arm around my shoulder and leads me to the far side of the coffee shop where Cherry is hedged into a corner by our local solicitor, Carlton Curlieu,. He rises and kisses me on the cheek, although the only previous time I've met him was at some dinner or other. One of the many things I love about village life is that once you've met someone, you're automatically considered a friend, there's no need to have met someone at least five times before making any conversation deeper than about the weather.

Cherry folds me into a deep hug as if we're bosom pals. Speaking of which, she's wearing the most gorgeous, skimpy green satin dress that hugs her figure to perfection, not at all what I'd expect from a Mrs Vicar.

I dump my bags on the table, feeling decidedly dowdy, and peel off my waxed coat to reveal black velvet slacks, a white lace blouse and a long, knitted jacket. Although I do think my soft black leather knee boots make a statement, especially as there's rumoured to be dancing later. 'Just need to drop these off.'

With my precious tins of chocolate coffee cakes and chocolate bombs safely deposited in the kitchen, I can now settle down to survey the room. Several days ago, Skye had celebrated the start of autumn by decorating her coffee shop with bunches of dried wheat and autumn berries plus strings of tiny digital fairy lights and now she's added a large wheatsheaf, beautifully decorated with birds and tiny animals. There are also several freshly baked loaves, plus a huge display of vegetables. The whole place smells of a gorgeous mix of bread, earth and hay bales, which have replaced the chairs this evening. It literally takes my breath away. The occasional Harvest Festival I'd been to in London had consisted of tinned goods, pictures of fresh produce and lots of cheques, and I feel myself proud to be part of a proper country one.

Scott told me they'd sold over fifty tickets and seeing how people are jammed in around the tables, I can well believe it. What pleases me most is that I can name or recognise most of them and nearly all nod warmly in my direction, even if a few then nudge their neighbour and whisper.

Scott leaps up and bangs his fork on the table so every eye swivels to him, just as I wipe my damp forehead. Isn't that just the best timing? He looks around the room until even the children have quietened down, then announces in his best vicar voice – which I've never heard him use before except once when he was rather tipsy – 'Let us pray.' He can't keep it going, just grins and then announces in his everyday voice, 'Gracious God – for all your gifts and especially the gift of harvest, we give you thanks. And for those less fortunate than ourselves… prod our consciences and unpick our wallets. Amen.'

There's a deafening cacophony of cheers and banging of cutlery as the kitchen doors swing open, revealing Skye and her Auntie Rose dressed as Harvest Mice and clutching trays of steaming soup.

'Homemade, I presume?'

Scott blushes. 'In the vicarage kitchen, actually. Not by me, I hasten to add. A bevy of villagers have been brewing the cauldron all day. I was barred.'

Wickham ladles a generous spoonful, licks his lips in appreciation and turns to me. 'You do realise, don't you, that every ingredient is locally grown?' The others nod with pride.

I, however, feel decidedly ill. 'Not all. I'm afraid my desserts have let the side down. I'm so sorry – I didn't know.' Why doesn't anyone ever tell you about these village traditions?

Cherry giggles. 'Relax, Cat. I think they realised when they asked you, that your chocolate couldn't exactly be grown locally. And as for those poor saps where tradition is more important than taste, well, they'll have to make do with the locally-grown fruit salad. Personally, I know which way *my* cookie crumbles.'

A fair point, I suppose. Although somehow, I still feel I've failed. Or maybe I'm upset at not knowing about the tradition. Would it have stopped me baking? Probably not. So perhaps I'm just worried about upsetting the fruit salad traditionalists.

I'm enjoying my first taste of the hot soup when Skye sidles up and whispers, 'Did you like the flowers, Cat?' causing me to splutter and narrowly avoid spraying the table with hot liquid. 'Just a little thank you for the first three months of our chocolate partnership.'

Cherry and Wickham look at me in some concern.

'Just went down the wrong way,' I wheeze, apologetically. Well, I'm glad that little mystery is solved, but I also notice that I feel disappointed, a reminder of just how much I'd wanted them to be from Linton.

After a large sip of water, the thick, creamy parsnip soup does make me feel slightly better, especially after a second generous helping. It seems to have had a similar effect on my table companions as it's consumed in virtual silence. Apart from Carlton's rather noisy slurps, that is, and Wickham's very uncharacteristic appreciative burp as he carefully mops up the last drop with a chunk of fresh bread. Then he leans towards me. 'Now, about what I mentioned last night.'

He's chosen a good moment because as everyone finishes the first course the chatter rises to a deafening level. 'A couple of weeks before Dean was killed, Martin Dales came into my bookshop absolutely spitting feathers. He threw himself into one of my armchairs so hard I thought he'd break at the least the springs if not the legs. Anyway, after he'd downed three cups of coffee, he beckoned me over and announced that he'd just been accused of being a closet hunt supporter.'

'You don't think it could be true then?'

'About the vet? I've no idea. Although, from what Martin said, it was quite a forceful encounter.'

'It certainly was. I heard it myself,' a voice announces in my ear. I swing round as Sandy continues in a highly conspiratorial whisper from the next table. 'The argument was quite heated. It lasted several minutes.'

'But who was accusing him?' I said, though I'd already guessed.

'None other than our murder victim, Sergeant Dean Court.' Sandy nods several times as if to underline the importance of her testimony, even though it's the Harvest Supper not the Old Bailey.

At which point, Scott bangs his fork on the table again, preventing any further cross-examination – sorry, conversation. 'Ladies and gentlemen, as is customary at this point…' I wince and tense, 'the gentlemen on each table will now swop places so you get the chance to annoy some different people!' Much hilarity ensues as the attempts to move around result in the men getting totally confused, with several back exactly where they'd started.

I mouth at to Cherry, 'They should have left it to the women,' and she agrees with a very giggly thumbs up. Our table, surprisingly, given the calibre of men present, succeeds quickly and smoothly and I find myself with Cherry on my right and Carlton on my left. On the table behind, Sandy is now diagonally opposite me, well out of range and she shrugs. I turn to my neighbour.

'Love your dress, Cherry.'

'Really?' She touches my arm and giggles again. 'I wasn't sure it was suitable, which is why I decided to wear it.'

My kind of girl. She grabs a handful of her frizzy chestnut hair and tosses it back, revealing a rugby player's strong, muscular neck and shoulders.

'Haven't seen you around much since we hit the Mop Fair, Cherry?'

'I'm keeping a bit of a low profile. And I've, erm, kept my cottage over in Much Snoring... mainly because I'm still renovating it.' She glances around the room, and I raise an enquiring eyebrow. 'Well, to be honest, our departure from Much Snoring wasn't exactly in a blaze of glory.' She leans back as a group of local teenagers, looking absolutely amazing in white tops and black trousers, swoop in to remove our soup bowls just as the two Harvest Mice deposit a dish of steaming Shepherd's Pie and a tureen of mixed vegetables centre table. Carlton then proceeds to divide the mashed potato pie into six precise segments and serves them onto white plates, which we dutifully circulate round the table, followed by the tureen, so it's several minutes before I can turn back to Scott's partner.

'It's hard to imagine either of you doing anything to warrant leaving under a cloud. You're both so lovely.'

Cherry smiles. 'I didn't say we did anything to deserve it. But you know what villages are like. Scott upset one of the village prima donnas and we had to stop seeing each other for a while. I guess I saw a different side of Scott and it left me feeling a bit insecure. This is a new start for both of us.'

'You seem so good together.'

'Yes, maybe now. I think we're over it. Which might be because I still have the bolthole. And I do love it here. Everyone's so welcoming and I don't think we could ever have had an evening like this in Snoring.'

'Well, I for one am very glad that you both ended up here. Scott's made settling in very straightforward, he's so easy to talk to. And such a wise head on his shoulders.'

'He's learnt a lot over the past couple of years. Now, how about some seconds? It's a shame to let the men have all the goodies! Including the wine – pass the bottle, Wickham. And before you ask, Cat, yes, it is a Cotswolds vineyard so it would be rude not to enjoy it, fully!'

I'm just helping myself to wine when a crash like the Bells of Hades echoes across the room, producing instant silence. Scott makes great play of returning the saucepan lid and wooden spoon to Skye. 'Dearly beloved brethren… we come to the final part of our meal, with one last change of tables. And this time, it's a free for all. To your places!' In the ensuing scramble, I realise that Scott hasn't moved and just sits there, smiling benignly, at the chaos around him. Crafty so-and-so.

Time for me to have a complete change of scenery, so I head for the far side of the room. I'm on the point of settling at a table when I see Linton sitting there, so at the last moment, as he's getting to his feet, I swerve away and drop myself down at a table of four, scrunched into an alcove. Red Street and Sandy Lane look startled at my hasty arrival, just as the bulky figure of Wing Commander Boothby Graffoe throws himself on the remaining hay bale and promptly sinks from view into the straw. He reappears moments later and beams at the three of us. 'Well, well, well, the perfect final formation,' he purrs, twiddling his giant moustache. 'Couldn't be better company, what?'

I'm inclined to agree, although probably not for the same reason. It occurs to me that I've seen Sandy around much more since our graveyard encounter yesterday, as if she's keeping tabs on me, and I wonder if I should start taking a few precautions, such as making sure Dag is often with me. Anyway, for the moment Boothby has engaged her in some complicated business to do with a planning committee or some such thing they're both involved in, so I can concentrate on Red, sitting to my right.

'Did you recall else about your research since we last spoke, Mr Street?' I've had enough beating around the bush with him, especially as he's so elusive. If

Sandy is trying her best to bump into me, Red seems to be doing his best to avoid me.

He baulks slightly, reaches for his wine and when he realises I'm not going to be distracted, lets out a large sigh. 'I thought you'd stopped all that nonsense. No. Absolutely nothing else. And…' he glares at me, '… even if I had, I'd tell the chief inspector rather than you.'

Hmmm, I think. Quite a change from the charming man who'd invited me for lunch. This was getting me nowhere, it was time to do something creative. 'Red, you and Dean were seen going into the Police Museum together on the day he was killed. *Furtively*, I think was the description.'

For a split second, the man looks stunned and for a moment, I think my guess might have worked. But he quickly recovers, his voice now cold and harsh. 'For your information, Ms de Barnes, he wanted a photo for his memoirs – one of him inside the cell waving one of the museum's truncheons. He thought it would be ironic, and I wanted a photo for the publicity.'

'And you didn't think to share that little gem with the police?'

A sickly smile spreads across his face. 'I might have done, except for one little detail – as I told you before, Dean didn't turn up. So either your witness is making things up, or you are. Trying to catch me out, Ms de Barnes?'

'Who's making things up?' The Wing Commander swings round, his whiskers quivering and eyes sparkling. 'I love a bit of intrigue.'

Red, naturally, has spotted the perfect get out. 'Oh, just some Amazon delivery person. But I'm glad I've got your attention, Boothby, I wanted to talk to you about next year's air show over at Fairford. I gather you're after a lift?'

From his look of pure delight, Wing Commander Boothby Graffoe, RAF, retired, is settling down for a long conversation – or monologue – so I can safely turn back to Sandy on my left.

She pours herself a generous portion of wine, takes a sip, wipes her lips on a paper napkin and leans in to breathe copious wine fumes over me. 'It was quite some set-to, I can tell you. I overheard them.'

It takes me a moment to realise she's shunted back to Dean and Martin.

'They almost came to blows. So maybe this whole sordid affair is about settling an argument?'

'I'm not so sure, Sandy. It's an interesting idea, but I don't think it had anything to do with an argument. Even Inspector Parva thinks it had to be cold and calculated.' *Okay, maybe he didn't say that, exactly, but I'm sure that's what he must be thinking. I am.* 'And according to Wickham, although he was angry when he came in, by the time he left Martin was more amused. He could have been putting on an act, of course, but to be blunt, he doesn't strike me as the actor type. No, I think this has much more to do with an old grudge, something from his police casebook.'

The colour suddenly drains from her face, and she staggers to her feet. 'Excuse me, Cat. I think I'm going to be…. I need some fresh air.'

Before I can follow her, Linton slides into her vacant place. 'Catherine, can we talk?' He looks particularly handsome this evening, his crisp white shirt and black sleeveless waistcoat a perfect complement to his deep colouring and dark eyes, those deep, dark eyes a girl could... I pause for a moment, fully expecting his phone to ring. But it seems I'm not going to be spared a difficult conversation, so I stand. 'Linton, I'm sorry. I'm very tired and this really isn't the time or the place.'

Moments later, I burst outside, but Sandy, sadly, is long gone.

Chapter 16

The next morning, bleary-eyed and anything but bushy tailed, I arrive at the door of Skye's coffee shop at half past eight, as requested, clutching another ten bags of chocolate cherry bombs. Apparently, they're 'flying off the shelves', which had necessitated me prising myself out of bed before six. No-one should ever be up before six am, especially on a Saturday. It's not right. Dag is in full agreement as it meant his customary walk had been shortened into a brief stroll round my garden, and he's now beside me but still not amused. On the other hand, the early start has given me a couple of hours to review last night's supper conversations, which have certainly raised more questions than provided answers for my investigation. Non-investigation.

My mind works best when left to its own devices, often the middle of the night when it's free from clatter and chatter. But sometimes it also needs other views, fresh insights and a jolly good shake-up. Which after a flurry of early texts it's about to get.

Skye's shoulders are sagging and she rubs her bloodshot eyes several times as she unlocks the door. Her café smells rather odd, a mixture of stale cooking and sweat. 'Don't worry, Cat, it'll soon go.' She throws the door open and rams a chair in the doorway to stop anyone coming in early. The draught whips small pieces of leftover straw into eddies, although the customary chairs have now replaced last night's bales. I wasn't the only one up early.

'You did a good job last night, Skye. Lovely food.'

She smiles, tossing her long hair over her shoulders. 'I think the costumes helped. The first time is always tricky. Glad to see you've been busy. Coffee?' She starts unpacking the presentation packs. 'Keep this up and I'll definitely be expanding the range. I'm really pleased.'

'So am I, Skye. I really had no idea how they'd go.'

'Speaking of which, how are things going with the dishy doctor?' She wiggles her eyebrows.

'They aren't. Honestly, Skye, there's just no way it'll work. It's bad enough when he keeps getting called away but then I saw him hugging some raven-haired beauty. I had that with my ex.' I turn to the side and dab my eyes as I'm reminded of the cheating lump.

Skye pauses. 'That doesn't sound like Linton. Are you sure?'

'Saw it with my own eyes, in broad daylight. Coming out of Bedside Manor. And anyway, how would you know what he's like, you've hardly been here five minutes?'

That sounds sharper than I'd intended. Skye stares for a moment, then shrugs. 'Don't forget, there were all those summers years ago I spent helping Auntie Rose in the tea shop. I may be a newcomer – but I'm not a stranger, you know.'

She shakes her head and returns to stacking my chocolates.

I sigh heavily. 'I'm so off men. By the way, there were more interesting conversations last night, especially with Sandy and Red.'

'Not that you were fishing of course. It's not as if you're investigating, is it?'

'No, I'm not. But can I help it if people keep talking to me? I can hardly tell them to shut up, can I?' Skye raises an eyebrow. 'What? I can't.'

At which point, Scott arrives, and to my relief he hooks his arm through mine and leads me away to the quietest alcove.

Scott sits down and stretches out his long legs, the bottom of his jeans revealing a pair of thick walking socks and heavy leather walking boots. He's dressed in the chunky red roll neck jumper, and gilet of his off duty uniform. 'Haven't got long, Cat. Cherry and I are off to the Water Park later. I need some fresh air and Barking needs some serious exercise, he's getting far too pudgy.'

'I had a really nice chat with Cherry last night, Scott. She's lovely'.

'I know. Now, your text said it was urgent?'

'I really need to talk through what I've discovered in the last couple of days.'

'That would be about the case you're absolutely not investigating?'

173

Oh, for goodness' sake, why does everyone assume, as soon as I ask a question, that I must be meddling and investigating? *Possibly because you are, Cat?* I pause and go on. 'Can we take a few moments to run through the possible suspects?' Scott stares at me for a moment, then shrugs. 'Who do you have in mind?'

I take a deep breath and then count out on my fingers, 'Sandy Lane, Martin Dales, Red Street – and I suppose we must include Mavis, although I'm quite sure she had nothing to do with Court's death.'

Scott stares over my shoulder. 'Do you think there might've been more to Sandy's magistrate's work than meets the eye? I mean, we know why she resigned, but it was so unexpected, and she was so respected, so involved in it all. I just wonder if the resentment lodged far deeper than she'd have let anyone know?'

It's a good point. I think back to her sudden departure at the Harvest Supper. 'Maybe the prospect of Dean's memoir brought it all back to the surface? She certainly seemed very upset last night when we talked. Perhaps after all these years, she couldn't stand the possibility of the incident being dredged up again.'

'Agreed. But, Cat, is that really enough motive to kill someone? And with a knife? In fact, three knives.'

'Yes, why three? It could be three people. But I suppose one person could have done the job perfectly adequately. Is it just meant to confuse us? If so, it's certainly working'.

'Who's next? Your ex-boyfriend, Red?'

I shudder. 'Below the belt, Scott.' He raises an eyebrow and I giggle. 'Behave yourself, you're a vicar. Look, he was helping Dean with his book, maybe he found something there. But, if so, I don't know what. As far as I know, they had nothing to do with each other until the book. Though, let's not forget, he might well have been the last person to see Dean alive.'

This doesn't seem to be getting us anywhere and my brain feels as foggy as a winter's day on the hills. We sit staring into the fire, lost in our own thoughts. Then an idea strikes me. 'Scott, they both collected ceramics, didn't they, so maybe it was something to do with that? What if Red found out something about Dean's collection? I mean, there were certainly parts of Dean's past that were decidedly shady. Or, perhaps it was the other way round. Did Dean discover something shady about Red's collection and threaten to expose him?'

'Yes, I can't imagine Red Street would take very kindly to being threatened. There's no doubt it would give him a motive. And he certainly had the opportunity. Let's keep him on the list. Next?'

'Our vet! We know he and Dean argued, we have a witness. And the more I think about it, the more I wonder if the way he was with Wickham was a front. If what Dean said was true, perhaps it gives Martin a motive. I mean, demos at hunts often seem to get decidedly ugly. If it got out that Martin was involved in those, it might stop the hunt supporters using him as their vet, it might even finish his business.

'When I was researching my sermon for Dean's funeral, I learnt that Dean volunteered to police the Hunts. I know it was years ago, but what if he was planning to make a big deal of it for his book, maybe even naming Martin as involved in some way? Maybe he found out something even more sinister?'

Skye arrives with two mugs of steaming hot chocolate, deposits them on the table between us, and hovers at my shoulder before whispering, 'Don't forget you've got the Business Awards later.'

What, no, it can't be that already. 'Anyway, I thought we were *both*…'

'To be honest, I only went through the motions, to persuade you to enter. It's far too early for me. Maybe next year.' She grins. 'In the meantime, it's free food, free booze and a change of scenery. And, no doubt, some very eligible men. What's not to like? I've already booked you a taxi. Go and get your glad rags out.'

I know when I'm beaten and in the ensuing silence I make the most of the opportunity to lick the thick cream and chocolate topping, forcing my mind to move back from what I'm going to wear to how to make sense of murder and motives. Objectively, can I really imagine the kindly vet Martin, who took such trouble to remove the splinter from Dag's paw as a cold-blooded killer? Even if Dean was posing a risk to his business? Then again, if your livelihood's under threat, who's to say what you would do? When you're faced with life and death on a daily basis, do you see things differently? Oh dear, this isn't getting me very far. And I can see Scott's beginning to fidget.

'Yes, I know you need to go soon, Vicar!'

He grins. 'Sorry, but days off are very precious. And a day off when Cherry's free as well, that's doubly so.'

'Point taken. There's only Mavis left, and we've already dismissed her. Are we missing someone, or something so obvious, we can't see the wood for the trees? Is there some other reason we haven't yet discovered for Dean to be killed?'

'Well, it certainly wouldn't be for his money,' Scott grins. 'You'd never describe that cottage of his as the height of luxury. And you don't get to stash a fortune away on a police sergeant's salary.'

'Hang on, Scott, that's not such a bad idea. What if there was more to his clocks than meets the eye? After all, it would only need one rare piece and he could have been sitting on a fortune. What if he recognised something in the evidence room? Much Slaughter's a small place, I imagine he was often the only police presence in the village, I'm sure it would have been simple for something to, let's say, get lost.'

Scott looks thoughtful. 'How would we know if anything had been taken? An inventory? And would

177

anyone still have those records? Maybe you should have a chat with Inspector Parva?

I wince. I'm really not sure I can face another dismissal at the moment. 'Perhaps. Now, go – and make the most of your day off, before it rains. I've got a day to get on with.' He looks at me as if I'm crazy which, to be fair, is probably not too wide of the mark.

'Thanks. If you're sure?' I nod and he leaves. I glance at Dag.

'Come on, boy. Time to go home.' He fixes me with such a doleful look I almost relent and order another drink. But I've got an awards do to get ready for, glad rags to iron and makeup to apply if I'm to be ready for lunchtime.

*

It's the first time I've been in Cirencester's King's Head. And very swish it is, too. Thankfully, after Skye dropped her bombshell reminder in the coffee shop, I'd dug out the application pack and noticed that the ceremony was billed as 'formal dress', which seemed rather pretentious for midday in the Cotswolds, where it would generally be either barbours or brogues. Now I'm inside, though, I can see why. A large electronic board flashes the WEST OF ENGLAND BUSINESS AWARDS logo and indicates where the Business Awards Ceremony will be held. In my calf-length black velvet dress, my curly hair brushed but barely tamed and a single tiny diamond shimmering in the choker at my neck, I dawdle a little to bask in some very admiring glances from the women and a few open-mouthed stares from the men.

When I open the function room door, I gasp. Around fifty people are inside, all in smart suits or gowns, with champagne flutes in their hands. The conversation is buzzing. But it's the room itself that hits me. It's only about twelve feet high, tunnel-shaped and made of the most exquisite stonework. It's lit by a combination of half-concealed lights in the ceiling and downlights that twinkle on an incredible polished wooden floor.

A tuxedoed waiter swishes by, a tray of drinks balanced on his upturned hand, followed by a similarly clad waitress sporting a tray of fruit juice. A split-second decision has me opting for fruit juice so I can truly take everything in and as I lift the beautiful cut-glass goblet, the girl flashes a perfect white smile. 'Good afternoon, madam. And welcome to the Awards Ceremony.'

Moments later, I feel a hand on my arm and another receive another shock as Linton smiles and guides me to a table with a spotless and creaseless white linen tablecloth and silver service cutlery.

'Catherine, I wanted to catch you before the ceremony starts. Firstly, of course, to say well done, you've done brilliantly with your business and whether you win or not, I'm so proud.' I stare at him, open-mouthed. For one thing, I've never seen him look so handsome: he's wearing a black dinner jacket with black velvet lapel, a dazzling white wing collar shirt and a perfectly tied red velvet bow tie – the ideal garb to show off his handsome features. *And that smile!* It's a good job I'm sitting down. *Cat, remember he's a thing of the past.* 'Well, Dr Heath, how on earth…?'

'Easy, Ms de Barnes.' His grin is infuriating and intoxicating. 'Skye told me you'd entered the competition and, since I'm also a member– don't look so surprised, we have to run as a business as well, you know – I decided to get a ticket. When you refused to talk to me at the Harvest Supper, I thought, well, at the Awards lunch, she can hardly make a scene. So, here I am.'

I don't know whether to be angry with him for forcing me into a conversation I don't want to have or excited that a man would care enough to do all this. Before I can decide, he locks eyes with me. 'I know you've been avoiding me, Cat. And I do understand, I really do.'

'You do?'

He takes my hand, and a jolt of electricity sizzles up my arm and through my body. Every cell in my body urges me to keep quiet. But I just can't. 'Who is she?' I say.

'What? Who do you mean?'

'The woman I saw you with two days ago. Coming out of your house. The one you hugged like there's no tomorrow. It's bad enough when you drop me for a patient. But when it's for someone like her... raven-haired and with an hour-glass figure. I had too much of that with my ex.'

Linton looks blank, then slowly he starts to smile. *The swine.* 'Two days ago? Cat, that was one of our drugs reps. I've known her for years. She's happily married with a small baby. I'm his godfather.'

Suddenly, I'm desperate for the ground to open and swallow me up. Fortunately, I'm saved by the Master of Ceremonies calling everyone to their seats. Linton is still holding my hand and his eyes are still locked onto mine. 'Cat, will you do me the honour of attending the Harvest Ball next week as my guest?' That's not what I'd been expecting him to say and, as relief floods through me, I realise I've already nodded my agreement.

I'm only dimly aware of other guests filing into seats around the table and my conversation goes into polite automatic mode. I'm not even aware of various announcements, all sounds being pretty much drowned out by the roaring confusion in my brain. Only when Linton nudges me and nods toward the master of ceremonies do I realise my name's been called, and like a zombie I march to the front, shake hands and accept the proffered certificate and a small plaque. The press photographer's flash startles me and as I weave my way back through the congratulations to my table,

I glance at the card in my hand and realise I've been *commended*.

Linton looks like the cat who's got the cream but the rest of the event and most of the drive back passes in a whirl. Only as I open my front door to the sound of my telephone ringing and Dag barking his annoyance at being deserted does reality kick in.

A few minutes later as I replace the telephone handset, I sink to the floor. I thought the day couldn't get any more surreal. How wrong I was.

Chapter 17

'Good grief, Cat, you look awful.'

'Thank you, Vicar, lovely to see you too.' It's a couple of days after the Awards lunch and we're filing out of church in an orderly queue to be greeted by Scott, still in Sunday's full Holy Communion garb. It's a cold, dull morning where our breath hangs in small clouds, at least as far as I can tell through my sunglasses and half-closed eyes.

'Are you okay?' He turns away from the line of parishioners, glances over my shoulder and nods to Cherry. 'What on earth has happened?'

'Scott, can I talk to you both?'

Cherry slips in beside me and gives me a huge hug, before gently manoeuvring me out of the procession and into a quiet corner. 'Come over to the vicarage and stay for lunch, Cat. We don't eat until mid-afternoon, so there'll be plenty of time to talk.'

Her kindness and concern make my eyes water and after the unexpected phone call and a sleepless night, I'd like nothing better than to curl up in a corner and howl. Except the church isn't the best place. 'I couldn't impose. Just a few minutes to chat would be…'

She swings me round to face her and stares into my sunglasses. 'Catherine de Barnes, we learnt a long time ago to always have some extra food for Sunday lunch. When you're with a vicar, well, you just never know who'll turn up!' She grins. 'Besides, you'll be doing me a favour, saving me from a rehash of Scott's sermon. Please.'

'I'll need to see to Dag.'

'We can all go for a walk. Barking will be only too pleased to see his best doggie mate.'

She who hesitates is – committed to Sunday lunch, and Cherry propels me firmly through the tower door and towards the vicarage. Turns out it's quite hard to resist a determined rugby coach so moments later I'm snuggling into a comfy armchair beside a roaring log fire, with a glass of sherry in my hand, one that glows beautifully in the light from the flames. Cherry has gone to potter in the kitchen, I suspect deliberately, giving me space to collect my thoughts and Scott time to disperse the rest of the queue.

Just as I finish the sherry, the front door bangs and moments later, Scott pokes his head round the door looking concerned. 'Two minutes.'

Moments later, Cherry scuttles in with the sherry bottle on a tray and two more glasses, and by the time she's filled theirs and replenished mine, Scott is back, restored to clerical shirt and black jumper.

Scott and Cherry take a couple of sips, each holding their glass up to the light and inspecting it, as if it's a thing of great beauty. I'm grateful for their sensitivity. But, where to start?

'Something's happened, right?' Scott still seems to be addressing his sherry. Just as well, since I can't look him in the eye. I nod. 'Something that's obviously really thrown you?' I nod again.

'An email?' I shake my head, no. 'A phone call?' A nod. 'Who from?'

Drat, I can't answer that one with nods. 'Cunard.'

Scott looks taken aback, it's probably not what he expected. But now I've started, words flow a little easier. 'Yes, the shipping line. Apparently one of their senior team was at the Awards Ceremony when I got my commendation.' I swallow, staring into the fire.

'She rang me and offered me a job. Apparently someone dropped out at short notice and they're offering me a twelve-month contract on a cruise, teaching basic chocolate making skills. Around the Caribbean. If I accept, I leave in ten days.'

'Wow, go girl!' Cherry's eyes blaze and she bounces up and down on the sofa.

'And you're upset because…?' Trust Scott to cut to the chase.

'It would mean a year away from all I'm building here. Before I've even settled in properly. Before I've made sure the murderer is brought to justice. My ex always said that I never settled to anything. That I always ran away.'

'And are you? Running away, that is?' Scott's staring at me with such intensity I feel I'm about to melt.

'No. Yes. Maybe. I don't know.'

'Yes, you seem to have covered most of the options!' He grins as Cherry digs him in the ribs but I have to smile. 'Seriously though, Cat, if this was a business issue in your former life, how would you have dealt with it?'

'Well, obviously, I'd have thoroughly weighed all the pros and cons, given it due consideration. And gone with my gut!'

'So, what's your gut saying?'

'That's just it. It's not saying anything.'

'Hmm, maybe it's just slow in waking up to all the possibilities.'

Cherry has a point. 'It would certainly give my business a boost. Get my name known.'

'Absolutely.' Cherry's bouncing again. 'And just think, a thousand cruisers each time – is that what you call people who go on cruises? Anyway, they'll all have a whole bunch of friends they'll tell when they get back home. It could send your sales stratospheric, you could make up orders when you're in port, and let's face it, these days you can deliver from anywhere to anywhere.'

Great point. It would certainly work. My heart starts to race. 'But do I really want to *see the world* and put myself under so much pressure?' My heart sinks again. *Why would I want to leave here and all I've built up?*

On the other hand, perhaps I'm getting lazy? Maybe it's not just my gut instinct that's gone to sleep.

And haven't I always prided myself on going outside my comfort zone, stretching myself? When did I last do that? I think of another thing.

'Oh, but there's Dagenham. What would I do with him?' I could never do that to the poor boy.

Cherry snorts. 'We'll look after him. Dagenham and Barking would have a whale of a time together.'

The fire crackles and a spark flies out. I could spend hours staring into a real fire, it's so mesmerising, the movement of flames, the constantly changing shapes as the logs burn, the rainbow colours, the distinctive smell, the... well, anything really that distracts me from what I'm wrestling with.

Scott tosses a couple more logs on and we all watch as the sparks fly then settle again as the flames lick them.

'Then, there's this dreadful murder business,' I say. We're no nearer solving it – which I'm not trying to... But I don't think I could run away for a year's cruise leaving a murderer free as a bird. It's just too soon.'

Scott and Cherry exchange glances but say nothing. My brain is thumping so loudly I'm sure they must be able to hear it, but it's all noise and no clarity It's so frustrating. When I was at the Agency, I was famous (or possibly infamous, depending on who you asked) for speed and clarity. Budgets would be set in seconds, staff hired or fired in minutes and an annual report assembled in an hour. Now, my mind feels as sticky as one of my chocolate caramel recipes. But business is one thing, this feels more about my whole purpose and all the reasons why I left London behind.

'Is this about Linton?' Cherry swivels on the sofa, her voice soft as velvet but strong as steel.

'Good question. But no, it isn't. I'd already made up my mind I wasn't going to pursue it, especially when I saw him hugging a dark-haired beauty. Then he cornered me at the Business Awards, and it turns out she's a rep and he's godfather to her son. Then he asked me to the Harvest Ball and I was so embarrassed by my behaviour that I accepted. Now I wish I hadn't. We don't exactly have a good track record. Maybe this gives me the perfect excuse:'

Cherry's eyebrows shoot up and Scott has the cheek to snort. 'What?'

'Maybe you just need to sleep on it, the cruise I mean.' The smile has disappeared from Cherry's face.

My gut rumbles and my eyes well up, and since I'm learning to trust my gut that must mean something important. But what? I review the last segments of conversation and when I get to Cherry's comment about sleeping on it my gut erupts again. It's worth a try, I suppose, although I'm not optimistic. We lapse into silence, broken only by the crackling flames, as we bask in the warmth of the fire and the sherry.

*

'Yuk, gerroff!' My face is suddenly warm and damp and there's a heavy weight on my lap. 'Dag? What the…?'

Cherry smiles across at me. 'When I suggested sleeping on it, I didn't necessarily mean straight away!'

I shift in the chair and look around. I realise it's got really dark and yet it's only… oh!

Cherry flicks on a switch, and a gentle pool of light gives a little more substance to the room.

'I'm *so* sorry. Sherry on top of lack of sleep…' I glance at Dagenham, who's now busily trying to clean scraps of mud from between his paws. 'And you ended up having to walk my dog. What must you think of me?'

'That you're tired and wrestling with a decision that could change your life. And, seriously, the dogs have had the best time. Look at them.'

It's true, Dag has given up on his pedicure and is fast asleep in front of the fire, his head on Barking's flank, the pair of them snoring contentedly like an old married couple. *Oh God, please tell me I wasn't snoring!* Hang on. 'How did you manage to fetch Dagenham?'

Cherry gives me an odd look. 'Oh, really, Cat, everyone in the village knows you lock yourself out so often you have to leave a key with Wickham!'

My gut murmurs and I realise the decision's been made, just as Scott slides around the door sporting a gravy-stained pinny and announces, 'Come through.' The lovely Cherry links arms with me. 'Will you accompany me to luncheon, m'lady?'

I beam at them both. 'Lead me to the Captain's Table. I'd better start getting used to it. Oh no, my passport...'

*

If you've ever planned a major upheaval, a tight deadline concentrates the mind wonderfully. Although, by the middle of the week, blind panic has set in and I'm only too glad to draw breath in the Coffee Emporium and review progress. I'm keen to keep my imminent departure quiet, not least because I still have a murderer to track down. So only Wickham, Skye, Rose, Cherry and Scott are in the know and they've been sworn to the strictest secrecy.

The conversation with Skye was particularly difficult; she was far from happy that, just as she was planning her big promotion of my confectionery, I was 'upping sticks and jetting off to the other side of the world' as she put it. But eventually, when I explained that as well as the boost it would give to my business, I also needed time away to come to terms with the whole sorry Linton saga, she reluctantly agreed that it was only a temporary postponement giving her time to consolidate her changes before we 'hit an unsuspecting world' the moment I returned.

Despite wanting to keep things quiet, what the villagers must be thinking as a cavalcade of delivery vans arrive at my front door, supplying me with a few lightweight machines, is anyone's guess. I'm still awaiting several months' worth of reading matter, and a surprising number of odds and ends, like maps and insect repellent. The closest shave comes when I pop into our post office photo booth and then ask how quickly a passport can be renewed if it's done in person, while ordering several hundred pounds worth of US dollars. I bet that raised a few eyebrows and occupied more than a few gossipy tea parties.

Ah well, be that as it may, I'm going to enjoy a few quiet moments to myself as I order my second coffee and another slice of Bakewell tart. I barely look up when the shop bell jangles, and then I see it's the Scottish policewoman. She looks as forlorn as ever, so I nod to her to join me. She looks around apprehensively, mouths her order to Skye and collapses opposite me with a sigh almost strong enough to rattle the crockery.

I may be impetuous and some would say even gobby. But I also know when to keep quiet and wait. It proves the right strategy because after a couple of minutes she wipes her eyes and smiles weakly.

'I've done it, Catherine. Asked for a transfer back home once this case is closed. It didn't go well. Mind you, at this rate, I'll be getting my pension first.'

I put my hand over hers and she flinches, then gives it a brief squeeze. Dag picks up on the atmosphere and lays his head gently on her lap. She strokes his ears.

'Ye've no idea how unfriendly and foreign it is down here. It's even worse now that I've said I'm leaving. I mean, maybe because of that, they're not telling me anything, but the only progress seems to be that we think the victim was stabbed where he was found. And as for why there were three knives. Oh, I really shouldn't have…'

'Don't worry, I won't let on.' But it's interesting and I notice my gut rumbles. 'There's something I need to tell you.' I look around and lower my voice to whisper level. 'I'm also about to leave, although only temporarily.'

The policewoman looks suitably startled and, I might say, even a little disappointed.

'I've been offered a year's contract running chocolate making workshops on a Caribbean cruise. They want me almost immediately.' The policewoman smiles.

'I'm really pleased for you, that sounds great.' She stares into the distance, wistfully and I guess she must be longing for some opportunities for herself. 'Look, I'm sorry, I have to go, I'm on duty in ten minutes.' She pauses. 'You won't let on, will you, about what I've said? Maybe you've got a better chance of solving this than they, we, have. And the sooner the better.'

She stands up, a haunted look in her eyes, and my heart feels for her. I realise how lucky I've been to be accepted so easily. And yet, I'm willing to give it up…? *Don't go there, Cat.*

I take a deep breath. 'Of course I won't let on. And, listen, if you just want somewhere to relax, or someone to talk to, you know where I am.'

She smiles weakly and looks sad. 'Thanks, Catherine, but I think I've said too much already. You're so kind.' Then she turns and hurries out of the door without a backwards glance, leaving me feeling sad too but also angry that Inspector Parva could let such a thing happen.

Dagenham marks her departure with a loud, disgruntled snort. He's far from impressed and regards the now frequent comings and goings with the greatest of suspicion. He's started barking like mad at any van or caller who pulls up within fifty metres of our front door and now follows me everywhere. He's often literally under my feet. He's taken to throwing out the most piteous little whines and, worse still, has gone back to a leaky bladder, something I've not had to deal with since the early days after the rescue centre. Dag now seems incapable of or unwilling to go more than two or three hours without relief, which is especially wearing at night. Even having him spend more time with Barking hasn't helped, although he does at least show impeccable manners when he's there. It breaks my heart and more than once I think it's all too much.

But giving in now would mean an animal, even Dag, runs my life which I've always said would never be the case. Although I never thought it would be this hard, or I'd be this tempted to give in.

After a particularly bad night, I decide it's time for some retail therapy and a thorough wardrobe renewal. This is the most dangerous part of the subterfuge, requiring a combination of online purchases and a manic day's expedition to Bicester Designer Village, under the supervision of a very excited Cherry. Her efforts to equip me with dresses and swimming costumes so skimpy I'd be sacked on the spot have to be knocked firmly on the head, although I admit her point about finding a suitably hot and wealthy companion (or two) is quite persuasive…

All of which soaks up so much time and effort – to say nothing of expense – that seven days have passed and it's the eve of the Harvest Ball before I even think about what I'm going to say to the good doctor.

Chapter 18

This time I've made sure I've got the venue right. Not only have I read the ticket so many times it's as dog-eared as if Dag had chewed it, but I've also asked several people, several times, until it's become something of a standing joke. The church hall looks magical, and I take my hat off (metaphorically) to those who must have spent hours if not days transforming it from, let's be honest, a very average church hall with a wooden floor and rafters marinated in the smell of old polish, teeth-staining tea and dance-class perspiration to an intimate, fairy light festooned grotto.

Hay bales line two of the walls and a few wooden chairs are scattered around a handful of tables, each with an assortment of corn dollies and tea lights in the middle. There must be about twenty people milling around, several of them darting in and out of the kitchen, as trestle tables sprout food, like mushrooms on a damp morning.

At the far end, on a makeshift stage, a quartet of musicians are tuning fiddles, a double bass, a saxophone and a keyboard. They're dressed in tight trousers, collarless shirts and waistcoats, with the men in the group sporting black bowlers and huge beards – which is the first hint that this may be more Harvest than Ball. A little unfortunate, given my long cobalt ball gown, chosen specially to glitter in the lights and hug my figure to best advantage. Given its plunging neckline and narrow straps, I'm not sure how I'll fare with the Dashing White Sergeant or Strip the Willow.

I smile at Red Street and Martin Dales, seated at a table to my left but neither responds. Maybe my dress isn't as eye-catching as I'd hoped, or they're deep in conversation, which immediately makes me curious. They hadn't struck me as the most obvious of companions but as I edge closer, Red spots me and they both turn round quickly with suspiciously guilty smiles. Hmm. Might be worth keeping an eye on those two. In fact, this evening might be a good opportunity to watch a few people and see if anything about the murder falls into place. I certainly need some inspiration.

Linton had inevitably texted to say he had a late house call and is a few minutes away, but to be fair, it is only ten to eight, so I walk over to the bar and join Boothby Graffoe, who's perched on a tall kitchen stool, holding a glass of whisky and obviously set for the evening. I'd not expected to see whisky on offer this evening and he follows my eye as I scan the bar drinks, then winks. 'Private supply, Cat.' He nods underneath of the bar. 'But I'll gladly share some with you.'

'Not my tipple, Wing Commander, thanks. I'll settle for a glass of red.' Hearing a drinks order, Perry Barr pops up from under the counter and nods warmly in greeting. 'Rick given you the evening off, then, Perry?' I smile. The two of them run our village pub.

'It's a matter of some dispute which of us gets the busier night, Catney. Naturally, I know it's me.' Perry grins, revealing a set of teeth so white and perfectly aligned he must be a dentist's dream patient.

I glance around. 'Really? Hard to imagine, with these numbers.'

'It's not the number of people – and, trust me, in another fifteen minutes, it'll be up to three figures in here – no, it's their capacity to put it away.'

Boothby rubs the edges of his wingspan moustache through nicotine-stained fingers and shakes his head. 'I reckon they've all gone to the old barn. Creatures of habit, every one of them.'

Perry notices my confusion and smiles. 'It's where we usually hold the Ball, in the barn. Authentic like. But they had an early harvest this year so it's already full.'

I'm fumbling around in the bottom of my velvet clutch bag for my purse when a long arm reaches over my shoulder and Carlton Curlieu, the local solicitor, announces in his rich baritone, 'This one's on me. And I'll have the same.' Then he plants a kiss on my cheek and nods. 'Looking lovely, Cat. Now, tell, me, are you ready to harvest all this evening's opportunities.'

'I certainly plan to plough every furrow, Mr Curlieu.' If he wants a battle of the puns, he's come to the right person.

'Hmm, I hope it doesn't go against the grain, m'lady.'

'Well, sir, if it did, I'm sure you'd keep me on tractor.'

'Don't call me Tor! Just call me when there's a hoedown…'

'Oh, give over you two,' Boothby mutters, although he's grinning like the Cheshire Cat. 'Make mine a double, Perry. I'll need it, now these two have got going.'

As it happens, he's saved from the humour, if not the alcohol, by screeching feedback from the amplifiers as the musicians explode into a frantic jig, setting our feet tapping. Carlton seizes my hand and leads me onto the dance floor.

Now, I have to say, every dance I've ever been to in London, and way back to my early teens, has begun excruciatingly with one brave couple in the middle while fifty others try to avoid their gaze and pretend they're in the most riveting conversation since Moses returned from Sinai with the Ten Commandments. A conversation that will continue for at least the next hour, if not for the whole evening.

Much Slaughter folk are built of sterner stuff. Within seconds, the floor is a mass of swirling bodies and I'm relieved to see that lack of skill is no substitute for enthusiasm as we twirl and cross and promenade around the room.

I clearly need to pace myself because, as the music finishes the opening number, I'm puffing like a decrepit steam engine, and I can feel a light sheen of perspiration on my forehead. I love music, but I'm usually a better listener than dancer – my sense of rhythm has a disconcerting tendency to waltz off and leave me mid-step. Tonight, however, I'm most certainly up for it, especially since it seems to be more country than classic.

Which is just as well as, before I can get near a seat, I'm grabbed by May Hill who's dressed in bright blue jeans, huge, brown leather cowboy boots, a frilly suede waistcoat and a truly enormous ten-gallon hat. In her wake, Scott and Cherry join the quartet, the latter both in evening wear. It's all very confusing but not the time to ask questions above the loud music, especially when every few seconds you're swirled back and forth or up and down. Which is not helped when, in a brief shimmy past Sandy, she squeezes my hand so hard I'm surprised the bones don't crack.

At last, dizzy and gasping for breath, and having covered every square inch of the floor, I'm back where I started. The music stills and applause ripples across to the band and to fellow dancers. I love it. I curtsy demurely at Scott, bow to Cherry and May and dart across to the bar, now several people deep. My heart lurches as I spot my date.

I hadn't noticed Linton arrive but, my goodness, he looks good in a deep, purple-black velvet jacket, white t-shirt, tight black trousers and black shoes with a broad cream stripe along the front. I reckon he's had his hair trimmed, it's in such a straight line, showing just an inch of lovely brown skin above his collar. When he spots me, his face lights up and as he leans in to kiss my cheek. My knees go weak.… 'Cat, what'll you have?' I desperately want to shout, *you* – but settle for 'a glass of red, please.'

'Excellent choice. Just what the doctor ordered.' I groan then spoil it by giggling, so we amble across through the dancing hordes to a quieter corner and perch on a straw bale. He gently lifts my hand to his lips – *be still my beating heart* – and plants the most delicate of kisses on the very tips of my fingers. 'Cat, you look – amazing. I'm so sorry I kept you waiting. But, my goodness, it was worth the wait.'

'Well, you're not so bad yourself, kind sir.'

We gaze at each other for a few moments, then he grabs my hand, his skin soft and warm. 'Let's dance.'

Somehow, I seem to have lost all sense of rhythm. In fact, I seem to have lost all sense of everything other than this gorgeous hunk who spins me round, links arms and sways in and out as the caller takes us through some dance or other with instructions I can hardly hear. It's all so wonderful. Then the music stops.

'We'll be back in fifteen. Enjoy the food. But not too much. You'll need all your energy to twist into the second half.' The musicians dump their instruments and are applauded all the way to the bar where Perry has been preparing an impressive line of drinks. Linton puts his arm across my shoulder and his warmth sizzles my bare flesh. I realise that at some point he must have discarded his jacket. My feet are throbbing. Where has the last hour gone? Thank goodness the evening's only halfway through. And so far, no hint of a wardrobe malfunction.

Linton propels me to the nearest trestle table, and I load a paper plate with ham, potato salad, chicken, green salad and rice. Well, dancing is incredibly calorie-burning. My date glances at my piled plate as it bends quite alarmingly and grins. 'I thought you'd want to avoid the beetroot,' surveying my gown appreciatively. At least, I think it's my gown he's appreciating.

'Linton, this evening is just amazing. Thanks for inviting me.'

He puts his head on one side and smirks. 'Isn't it a bit, well, "yokel-ly" for a London sophisticate?'

It earns him a playful punch, but I do make sure there's also a slight edge in my voice: 'Well of course we had barn dances – but they're just not the same in a posh hotel!'

His smile fades. 'Don't you miss all that?'

'What, when I can be in a village of friends, enjoying amazing food and where everything's produced in a five-mile radius? Hardly.'

'Local includes tonight's band, you know. A couple of them work on local farms and if you look closely, you might just recognise my receptionist.'

My heart sinks. If her hostility at the surgery is anything to go by, I'm going to spend the evening with her glare brighter than a spotlight: hardly the romantic prospect I'd hoped for. We settle on a hay bale and watch the hordes munch.

'So, doctor, were you brought up in the countryside?'

His bellow of a laugh rumbles around the room, above the chatter, and several people turn, then smile rather too warmly at their doctor. 'Hardly.' He doesn't seem to notice, thankfully or else he's got used to it. 'My parents are of the Windrush generation, and they settled in London. My dad got a job in the docks and mum did a bit of ironing for the neighbours. But as parents they were what we'd call pushy, nowadays.' His black eyes turn distant, reliving some memory. 'Anyway, suffice it to say, I ended up training for medicine in London. I left a few years later, after they'd both died, at relatively ages. But poverty can do that.'

It's odd to think that he was there at the same time I started out and during my wild twenties we could've met at any number of bars or clubs. To think, I might have had...

'Fancy some fresh air, Cat?' He grabs my hand, and as we thread through the crowd, several people turn to stare after us. More grist for the village gossip mill.

As we step outside, I shudder as cold air hits my skin. He wraps me in his long arms, and my temperature rockets to furnace level as I feel his body close to mine. When our lips touch I'm sure I'm about to melt, it's so soft and heartfelt and amazing.

Except moments later, he breaks away. 'Cat, I'm so sorry. You're missing the dessert...'

'Can wait!' Frankly, I'm having all my desserts, ever, in one melt-in-the-mouth moment. I snuggle into his arms, as a burst of some 1980s disco hit filters out to us. It's lost on me as all I seem to be capable of doing is staring into Linton's lush black eyes. He places one arm around my shoulder, and every nerve in my body tingles as I snuggle into him. He feels so comfortable and safe.

Linton lifts his warm, lovely hands to my cheeks and whispers, 'Fancy a drive?'

Since his cherished car is a vintage pink Jaguar, and this is my first invitation to ride in it, I don't hesitate. Well, that and never wanting the evening to end. Linton grins.

'And, before you ask, Cat, I've been alcohol-free tonight night, so I'm perfectly safe. Well, alcohol-wise, at least!' He wiggles his eyebrows.

*

Forty minutes later, we're perched on the retracted hood of the car in each other's arms, staring out from Coaley Peak over the M5 motorway with the River Severn glistening out of the darkness in the valley below. It's blissfully quiet, even though my ears are still pounding from the ball. And from the effect of holding hands and a series of kisses that have raised the quality bar way beyond anything else I've experienced. An owl hoots in a nearby tree and for a few moments a handful of stars twinkle in a velvet sky, before being swallowed back into clouds.

Linton has chosen a Julie London cassette (well, it's a vintage car) and as her sultry tones mix with the velvety night. I slide my shoes off. 'Come on, doc, let's dance.' I know – it's almost midnight, freezing cold and damp, but to go barefoot through wet grass in a skimpy dress hand-in-hand with someone special, there's nothing like it. Even if, afterwards, you will spend the next couple of hours thawing out. And to my mind, this version of *Bye Bye Blackbird* is one of the sexiest songs around.

As the track ends, we stand for a few minutes, gazing across the darkened valley towards Wales before my toes deaden and it seems wise to get warm. As we approach the Jag, Linton swings me round, and with both hands on my bottom, pulls me into his arms for a final lingering kiss. Yep, definitely getting warmer.

When I surface for air, I'm sure my eyes must be blazing like a tiger's in the night. 'It's much too early to settle down. Where shall we go next?' I murmur.

Linton merely wiggles his eyebrows. 'Leave it to me. Somewhere you once said you wanted to explore.'

Chapter 19

'Not sure if you prefer tea or coffee, so I've brought both.' I prise open one very sleepy eyelid and then giggle. My erstwhile dance companion is standing at the foot of the bed sporting a silver tray with a huge willow patterned teapot and an equally huge cafetière of the most gorgeous smelling coffee – and not much else. He climbs into bed next to me, causing a draught which reminds me I'm wearing even less, and he snuggles under the bedclothes, his arm cold but lovely across my stomach as I wriggle up to him. 'I hope you're enjoying my Bedside Manor?'

'I'm sure I must be, but I can't really remember.' I grin before turning over and stroking his chest, which is rather hairy, in a nice way, especially when I run my fingers through it.

'Surgery in three quarters of an hour, though, Cat.'

'No thanks! I think I'm alright as I am, doctor.'

'I meant, plenty of time for me to cook you breakfast, before…'

The carefree lover of last night slowly ebbs away, replaced by the respectable doctor. Shame. Especially when there's a conversation looming. I raise myself on my elbow, my free hand still toying with his chest hair. 'Linton, we need to talk about last night.'

I feel his muscles tense. 'Cat, I'm so sorry. I thought you…'

'It's not that. Last night was wonderful, if anything, too wonderful.' He looks completely confused as I struggle to find the right words. There's something I've agreed to.' Now he looks very worried. 'I've had an offer, one I couldn't refuse.'

'You mean there's someone else?' Panic races across his face.

'No, nothing like that. A job offer.'

'But that's good, isn't it? I mean, you wanted to set up… Oh, I see. Where is it?'

'That's just it. It's on a cruise liner. The company was at the Business Awards and they thought my chocolate making would be great for their passengers. And it would give my business real profile. I didn't tell you because, until last night, I didn't think our relationship was going anywhere, so it wasn't so important. If only the Ball had been a week earlier…'

'How long will you be gone?'

'Twelve months. And I have to start in a couple of days.'

'What?!' I have never seen a man look so devastated. His face looks as if it's crumpled in on itself then he pulls away and flops back into the bed.

I lean over to kiss him, but there's no response. 'It's only a year. We can have regular video calls *and* we can meet up when I'm in port.' The doctor shakes his head.

'Cat, you know my life doesn't work like that.' He bolts from the bed and moments later the shower door slams. I bury my face in his pillow, his scent filling my nose.

Then I crawl out of bed and get dressed, slowly, already dreading the 'walk of shame' home through the village, even though it's only a couple of hundred yards. It's probably better not to be here when Linton comes out. I can't bear to see the pain I've caused, and my heart feels ready to break.

*

My cottage feels cold and empty. I check that Wickham has fed Dag as agreed. My pup gives me a filthy look, but as I kick my shoes across the floor and throw myself into the nearest chair, he senses that there's something wrong, so he sidles up and puts his head on my lap. Unfortunately – and I never thought I'd say this – he's no consolation. I can't believe what I've just done. Nor how much it all hurts.

Numbly, I snatch my phone but the screen is blank. *What did you expect, Cat, a pledge of undying love? You've just dropped a bombshell.* Well, some response would be nice. Any response? I sigh. Isn't there some proverb about running off to sea, away from unrequited love? *It's hardly unrequited, Cat, after your night of passion*! Maybe not, but what about the next morning? And I'm getting nowhere with the unsolved murder.

I tap out a quick text to Scott, then I notice I've left muddy footprints across the floor and memories of barefoot dancing come flooding back. Seconds later, I'm wallowing in a sea of self-pity. Why does this always happen to me? What on earth possessed me to accept the contract and ignore the consequences? *Hang on Cat, this isn't just down to you. Linton hasn't exactly behaved like a beacon of light*. He has every right to be upset, but to flounce off like a spoilt child? He's adamant his job comes first, but when I say the same…

Then I catch a whiff of stale sweat and realise I'm in no fit state to receive guests, even Scott, so, as I peel off my gown and run a steaming shower, I send a text, *let yourself in*.

By the time I return, in comfy tracksuit bottoms and a sloppy top, with my damp hair tied loosely in a bun, Scott has set a roaring fire and the smell of fresh coffee wafts in. This man is a saint.

He casts an inquisitive look over me and smiles. 'Not quite as elegant as last night, Cat. But wasn't it lovely?'

'It was.' *More than you'll ever know, Vicar*.

'Didn't see you in the second half though. Nor the good doctor. No coincidence, I assume?'

Clearly one of the skills of a saint is to cut to the chase so I just blush.

'And I assume Linton is now aware of your imminent departure?'

I nod as another wave of desolation rolls over me.

'Which is why I'm here? Second thoughts? Regrets? Telephone number for the nearest convent?'

I smile, weakly, but even that helps a little. 'He knows. It didn't go well.'

Scott nods as he inspects the fire intently, then tosses another log on. 'Probably not surprising.' He looks at me for a few moments and, when I don't reply, adds, 'It's possible he might feel a little – used.'

'Nothing could be further from the truth,' I say, in my own defence. But it makes sense from Linton's point of view, I suppose. *What a mess.* 'What am I going to do? And don't say what do I want to do – because I don't bloody know, or I wouldn't be asking.'

Scott refills my coffee mug and pops into the kitchen to make a fresh brew. I'm not sure whether he wants some thinking time or whether he wants me to have some cooling down time but either way, it works. As he settles down again in the armchair, Scott reaches across and takes my hand. 'What actually is the problem, Cat?'

'What *isn't* the problem?' Okay, maybe I haven't cooled down yet. I glance at my mobile phone. Still nothing from my erstwhile lover. 'Number one, Linton and I no longer seem to be on speaking terms. Number two, last evening was probably one of the best times of my life – ever. Number three, I'm about to set off for twelve months at sea, which will nicely scupper any chance of getting back with Linton. Number four, twelve months of chocolate cooking now feels a life sentence. Five – I'm really going to miss Dag.'

Hearing his name, Dag lifts his head and licks my hand.

'Okay, so let's…'

'There's more.' Scott opens his mouth but keeps schtum. 'Number six, I've got a horrible feeling this is all about what's important to me.'

He nods. 'Exactly.'

I take a few moments to scratch Dagenham's soft ears, letting them run through my fingers and savouring their warmth. At this point in my previous life, I'd have walked a few London streets; now, my pup's fur is a great alternative for helping me assemble my thoughts. And I'm about to walk away from him – and the rest.

'There's no doubt it's a wonderful opportunity. I get paid to travel the world and it's a great chance to develop contacts for my business and, to be honest, I have been getting a bit stale. That's what I'd be turning down. But if I try to back out of the contract, it would be because of Linton so I'd be sacrificing my fledgling career for a man. Which, given my history with men, is sure to result in a double disaster. And he didn't suggest asking if they might need a ship's doctor.'

I shiver and reach for a woollen throw, wrapping it tightly around my body like a giant comfort blanket. Scott tosses another log onto the fire and gives it a good poke. Dag grunts and shifts to lie across my feet. I go on.

'On the other hand, is work more important than a wonderful relationship? Always assuming it can be called a wonderful relationship if…' I pause and glance at my phone's blank screen 'he's not even speaking to me.'

'Honey, I think you need to cut Linton a bit of slack. Remember, you hit him with this right out of the blue. I suspect he's as confused as you by this.'

'And how typical of a man, to deal with it by ignoring me...'

'Cat, in all fairness, you avoided talking to him until the very last minute.'

True, I suppose. Although how was I to know last night would be so fabulous and his body feel so right? 'And I know we're not talking about this, Scott, but we do still have a murderer on the loose. That's another bit of baggage else that'll travel with me. It's not just knowing there's a guilty person out there, it's leaving my friends in danger as well.'

'It's not your problem, Cat. You agreed to leave it to Inspector Parva. Which is another good reason for stepping away.'

My heart sinks. Which if I'm to honour my commitment to following my instincts, must be significant in some way. Although I've no idea what. I stare into the fire as minutes pass, but no inspiration emerges from the flames. Phoenix appears to be dead.

Finally, Scott clears his throat and my eyes swivel to him. 'Cat, I'm really sorry but I have a service in a few minutes. So, may I offer you a parting thought?'

I nod.

'It seems to me that you need to have two conversations and only when you've had those will your heart really know which direction is right. First, you need to ring the cruise people and see if that'll buy you a few days. Then you need a conversation with our good doctor... and don't tell me he's not texted you back. Face to face, even if it means you stage a sit-in at his surgery until he's finished.'

In my heart of hearts, I know he's right, but how on earth have I got myself into this mess? I used to pride myself on my decisiveness. There's a lot to be said for letting your head rule your heart. Which, in this case, would lead me to set sail. But even as I think it, my gut rebels and reminds me of Scott's recent Harvest Festival sermon, *Man shall not live by bread alone...*

'And, Cat, I'll be praying for you.' He pauses in the doorway, grins and adds, 'And for Linton! I've got a feeling he'll need it more.' Then he's gone.

All very well, Vicar, I think, but what happens if Linton still refuses to speak to me, if there's really no hope of a relationship? I can't bear the thought of losing him, especially after last night. But if I'm being logical, it was just one evening – a few dances, a nice chat and some very good... well, enough of that. And if I can't convince him there's a way to make it work, would that change how I feel about the job?

It's like standing in front of a huge mountain with no clear path. An old conundrum my first boss loved to quote floats into my mind: how do you eat an elephant? Answer: one bite at a time. And it doesn't much matter where you take the first bite…

I grab the cruise letter and dial, half hoping no-one will answer. But, of course, they do – on the second ring.

A couple of minutes later, my plea of *something's come up* has at least earned me a reprieve until the beginning of December, even if it's at the expense of any goodwill. It seems they're inordinately keen to get me. A small part of my burden has been lifted. Or, I suppose, a more apt metaphor would be: I've put down one of the heavy suitcases I'm carrying, even though I'll soon have to haul it up again.

Now for much the harder conversation.

Chapter 20

Well, it might not be chestnuts roasting on an open fire, but it's *my* fire in *my* cottage in *my* village, and I can't imagine anywhere I'd rather be cocooned, as the flames lick around the logs and the perfume of burning wood fills my sitting room. Add in Dag snoring peacefully across my feet, and Scott and Wickham settled comfortably on either side of my comfy armchair plus, courtesy of my neighbour, a large pitcher of homemade mulled wine, and courtesy of the vicar, a huge tin of (bought) very welcome mince pies, even if it is only the second week of November. It's a precious moment.

'Very apt company tonight,' Wickham says, smiling, his hand on my arm, 'the guardian of your property and the guardian of your soul. Got all bases covered.'

I want to shout, 'but where's the guardian of my heart' because over the last ten days, communications with Linton have struggled to reach even the formal and polite. I had a one word text and gave a one word acceptance reply, followed by another text the next day from him: 'OK?' to which I replied: 'Yes'. Since then, zilch.

Enough of the dark side. Tonight is about relaxing with two of my closest friends and remembering how lucky I am, with a warm home, good friends and an adoring pup. *A good job someone adores you, Cat.* Stop it!

'Now, Cat, lovely and cosy as all this is, you said there was something you wanted to talk to us about,' Scott remarks, staring into the fire, his voice quiet but cheery. 'I'm guessing it's either about the murder or the cruise?'

I nod as my heart sinks. Why do perfect moments always have to get spoilt by reality?

'I thought getting the extra time from Cunard would make everything easier but I've only got three weeks and nothing's getting any clearer, not with Linton, nor with the murder.'

I don't know if it's the warmth of the wine, the fire or the company but suddenly it seems obvious – my mind's made up. 'I'm going! If Linton's too blind to see what he's missing, well, that's his loss. And we've still got three weeks to solve the murder.'

'You mean, the one you're not investigating?' Scott grins and I throw a cushion at him, catching him very satisfactorily on the nose.

Wickham glances across at me, rather grimly. 'Inspector Parva's been back a couple of times, interviewed a few people and made some very general enquiries. But if you ask me, he's no further forward. In fact…' he looks at Scott who shrugs, 'it wouldn't surprise me if you got a visit in the next day or two.' Which leaves me wondering.

After the best night's sleep for ages, I'm bright-eyed and bushy-tailed, and waiting for the library to open the following morning. If there's any chance of the inspector calling, I need to get my mind back in gear. It shocks me how mushy my brain has become recently. It's as if all the recent conflict and confusion with Linton has wiped my memory like a malfunction on a computer hard drive.

So, what better way to get back up to speed than some research into juicy newspaper gossip about my suspects? My money's still on Martin Dales, our vet, and it seems the best place to start. Now, what exactly was that contretemps with Dean all about? I march across to Reception, enjoying the oak counter's smell of polish. It gleams in the weak early morning sunshine. Another thing I will miss… As I request back copies of the *Cotswold Courier*, I can almost already feel the big leather binders in my hands.

The librarian stares at me as if I'm some elderly woman who's forgotten where she lives, which is a bit of a cheek since I'm clearly at least a decade younger than him. 'Madam, these days…' He speaks slowly and loudly, emphasising every word. 'These days we have them online. Would you like me to show you how to use the library computer? It's really very…' I may have temporarily lost my concentration, but I certainly haven't lost my withering look when I'm being patronised by someone who can't even remember I've already spent time using his blasted computer. The suitably chastened man scurries away into the office, closing the door firmly behind him.

The computer takes an age to boot up, eventually informing me, rather rudely, it's *updating*, as if it's suggesting I might want to do the same. But at last, it deigns to assemble all the icons and permits me to enter my search terms. Underneath the desk, it trundles and whirs, before at long last granting me access to the *Cotswold Courier* archive.

*

An hour later, I have a couple of pages of notes ready to be printed and I set off in search of the librarian, hand over my coins in exchange for a code and attack the printer. Moments later, I grab the printed sheets, scanning them rapidly as I leave.

As Wickham predicted, Inspector Parva is waiting in an unmarked, featureless car outside my cottage. 'Ah, Ms de Barnes. I'm, erm, glad to see you're back safely. I wonder if I might have a word? A fresh perspective, perhaps?'

'Indeed you may, Inspector.' I treat him to a warm but aloof smile, while inside I'm smirking like a teenager. 'Come in. Coffee?' He nods and I decide this will be a kitchen-based conversation: formal and short.

'I hope this won't take long?' I say. 'I have an important engagement in less than an hour.'

I'm pleased to see he virtually squirms on the kitchen chair, looking very unsure. I carry on. 'I presume you're here to update me on your inquiries?' Cheeky, but, hey, what have I got to lose?

'Well, to be honest, we're not making much progress.' He twists his fingers together, gazes around the kitchen without seemingly finding any inspiration, and finally looks me in the eye. 'I rather hoped your time away from sleuthing might have given you some ideas?'

'Then you may just be in luck.' I can't prevent a smile forming, much as I might try. Well, okay, I didn't try very hard. 'I'm still convinced this is all to do with one of Dean Court's old cases.'

Parva nods. 'We thought the same. Trouble is, when you're a local bobby, you might only deal with petty crime, but there's a lot of it. Hundreds of cases in fact. And Court was the most meticulous of record keepers. I'm not surprised, there isn't much else to do but write detailed notes when you're policing a backwater. Sorry, no offence intended.'

Offence definitely is taken, especially since this is the second murder in a few months and I don't know many backwaters where that would happen, apart from in TV land. But there seems little point in pursuing it. Particularly when I know I'm about to score some very precious points in the credibility stakes. 'I've been looking back through old newspaper reports and I think I've found a few possibilities.'

With a theatrical flourish, I remove my notes from my handbag and toss them onto the kitchen table in front of him. Miss Marple would be proud of me. He glances at them with barely concealed scorn but the more he reads, the more intent he looks. 'Interesting.'

'I thought they might be worth looking into?'

He nods, tucks the papers into his pocket without asking and rises. 'Thank you, Ms de Barnes. You can leave it with us now.' He stares at me, more in hope than in expectation, I'm sure, since we both know the chances of me leaving things alone are zero.

'You'll let me know what you find out, won't you Inspector?'

He sighs, reluctantly nods and marches from the room just as a text arrives and my heart leaps. The policeman can see himself out. This is much more important. Although it does create a dilemma. *Are you free for lunch at my place, 12:30 today*? And it's signed *from your mortified medic*. The answer is yes, the question is, do I want to be? I feel sick. And angry and confused.

Well, it's got to be faced sooner or later so I suppose it might as well be sooner. I text *okay* as I set off for the *Crimson Courgette*, my mind buzzing. Thank goodness for friends to talk to.

The familiar smell of the coffee shop makes me well up. And the sight of Cherry and Rose lounging in our favourite alcove finishes me off so, by the time Skye gives me a huge embrace and an equally generous huge mug of hot chocolate, before plonking herself down beside us, I'm a soggy mess. The first few minutes of catching up are spent with me alternating between huge grins and loud gulps, much to the amusement of the other villagers scattered around the tables. This being a village, they know exactly what's been going on.

*

I can't believe it's 12.25 already. 'Time to face the music.' I grin and wince, scrambling reluctantly to my feet, before reaching into my bag for my purse.

'On us,' insists Cherry. 'The condemned woman deserves a hearty coffee break.' The three women each treat me to a big hug so I can leave feeling very aware of their support.

As I'm crossing High Street, my phone rings: *number unknown*. I don't normally respond to anything unsolicited, but sometimes I just know, so I peel off and amble around the Square.

'Good afternoon, Catherine. This is Christian Malford of Prestige Events, we met at the Awards lunch and I said I might have some business for you. Well, bless you, it's good news. It's come about much quicker than I thought. I've sent you an email with all the details and I need to talk you through them, urgently. It's a fantastic opportunity, if you can make the deadline. And, if it goes well, it'll be the first of many. Lots of our events have three or four hundred people, all of whom have family, friends, work colleagues… You'd be perfect.'

My feet have already changed direction and I'm back opening my front door before I realise. Thankfully, my laptop is already running and within moments I'm reading the email with growing excitement.

'Catherine, hello, are you still there?'

'Yes. Sorry. Just reading the brief.'

'And are you interested?'

'I absolutely *am*.'

'Then I'll need your proposal back to me by the end of tomorrow, including how you'll meet the deadline, especially after the last lot let me down. And the event is in two weeks on Friday 25th. Can you do that? If not, now's the time to tell me.'

'Absolutely. No problem. I'll get onto it right away.' This is *so* exciting.

Oh, my goodness, Linton. I tap out, quickly: *Sorry, something's cropped up – business. I know you'll understand* then open up a new word processing document and for the next two hours think and type like someone possessed.

Next thing I know, it's getting dark, and Dag is whining around my feet desperate for his walk-and-wee. And now I come to think of it, so am I, so I save the documents, type in a reminder for tomorrow and close down.

Perched in the bathroom, I take the opportunity to look at my phone. It's not good news. Linton's reply is typed totally in capital letters: *BUSINESS COMES FIRST. AS ALWAYS.*

'Oh, come on, that's not fair,' I mutter to myself in the mirror. 'One time.' Or, rather, twice. Why are men always so self-centred, why can't he just be pleased for me? This could be my big chance. Well, blow him, at least my friends will be excited.

By the time Dag and I have completed our favourite circular walk, I've updated Skye – who tries to sound glad for me even after I've told her this will b e the last order for a while, despite her burgeoning order book. I've also left a voicemail for the reverend. I unlatch my garden gate just as my neighbour emerges and I'm pretty much jumping up and down on the spot.

'Wickham, you'll never believe it. I've just been contacted by one of the most important events companies in the region. They want me to supply chocolate gift boxes for two hundred people at Cheltenham Racecourse. The fee would fund my entire cruise wardrobe and probably my drinks bill as well.'

He gives me a warm hug then put both hands on my shoulders, looks into my eyes and proclaims, 'It was only a matter of time, Cat. You're so good at it, so creative. Pop round later and I'll open a bottle of bubbly.'

'Wickham, it's a lovely idea but to be honest I've got so much to do. I really wouldn't be decent company.'

Once inside, I draw the curtains, stoke the fire with a pile of logs, grab a notebook and pencil, wrap my legs in my cosiest throw, settle Dagenham across my feet, and line up a box set of *Midsomer Murders* to play in the background. The Cotswolds at their very best.

Chapter 21

So, this is where Sergeant Dean Court held, well, held court. Today is the first time the museum's been open to the public since the murder, and my prompt attendance has been rewarded as I'm the only person here, for the moment. The duty curator is still pottering around opening up the spaces and I can hear her preparing the old courtroom on the floor above.

I peer into the preserved cell, trying to imagine how it might have felt to the prisoners. It's dim, dusty and disorientating, and so cold my breath comes out in clouds as thick as if I'd been toiling up the local hills.

As I sit myself down on the tiny bench bed, I'm struck by how numbingly uncomfortable the wooden planks are, even for sitting, never mind sleeping. How many people have sat on this exact spot?

There's a single barred window just above my head, the ten tiny panes letting in barely enough light to see the shadowy floor. Then I jump as a single bulb in the middle of the ceiling starts to glow dimly. 'Thought that might help a little, Ms de Barnes.' The curator's voice wafts in. But the bulb is pretty ineffectual and doesn't improve the ambience. *Perhaps that's the idea, Cat, after all, it is a cell.*

There are two sturdy metal hooks on the longer wall, just above head height. I can't decide whether they're for pull-ups to keep the occupant fit or a convenient space to hang coats or clothes – neither seems likely. They might be a good place to hang a body though. Which drags me back to the job in hand. Maybe Court met his visitor here, maybe he even had them sitting on this very bench? It would allow him to tower over them, in the position of power.

Come on, Cat, you're letting your imagination run away with you. Stick to the facts. What have you got?

I shudder, and not just from the cold, and kick the cell door closed, sending a very satisfying clang echoing through the building. The back of a cell door must be one of the most dispiriting sights imaginable. You're locked in. No-one wants to hear you. Your future's...

Oh, now that's interesting. In the wall close to the door hinge and almost at ceiling height, some marks have been carved into the plaster around one of the bricks. Not on the brick face, which would be what you'd expect prisoners to do, literally making their mark. Why on the plaster? You're hardly likely to stage a *great escape* through a single brick. For access to some pipe or other, perhaps? It's been done carefully, the yellowy-white paint remains intact on its front and there's just the thinnest cut into the surrounding plaster all the way round. Now that must have taken time and patience. And it's completely invisible when the door's open.

But again, it's only one brick, a very small space. I reach up and gently pull the brick forward, my hands shaking and my heart beating a little faster. Is this the clichéd hiding place, where the condemned man left a final note for his family or a note for the next prisoner who's about where to find the treasure from a lifetime of robberies? *Really, Cat, don't you think you watch too many Midsomer Murders?*

With the brick fully removed and standing on tiptoe I can just about see into the hollowed out gap, and realise it contains not a piece of paper but a data stick. It must be Dean's. After all, as far as we know, the police didn't find anything at his house and this would have been a suitably quirky hiding place. No wonder he was so keen to see people in here, it's a perfect excuse to keep an eye on it. And no visitor would want to be left alone in the cell, especially with the door shut.

Now, what to do with the data stick? It's evidence, so naturally I should hand it over to Inspector Parva. Or is it? There's nothing to prove it belonged to Dean. There are no labels, nothing that says *I'm a vital piece of evidence in an unsolved murder enquiry.* It might just as easily be where the curator keeps his stock orders. Well, okay, maybe not. But there could be innocent explanations. And then it would be yet more proof that I'm a complete idiot. Surely the police must have searched the cell, so maybe they put it back, waiting to see who comes to get it? Who knows, maybe even now the curator is on the phone and the inspector is racing to the scene, all blue lights and swerving traffic. Oh, good grief, what if the curator's in this as well? She'd need to turn a blind eye to the cell damage, at the very least.

Yes, obviously the best plan is to get out of here as soon as possible so I can check the contents, ideally with Scott to vouch for me. Everyone trusts a vicar, right? If it's nothing, I'll simply slip it back in place and no-one will be any the wiser and at least I'll have saved face. And if it's incriminating, then I'll be able to ring Glen and bask in glory rather than wallow in foolishness.

My gut rumbles and I can't help feeling there's about to be a breakthrough. What could go wrong? It's a great plan.

*

Unfortunately, that's not the vicar's assessment. 'Cat, I can't believe you'd be so stupid. Removing evidence from a crime scene is a crime in its own right, you know. Parva's never been your greatest supporter so he's hardly likely to cut you any slack.'

He's right, of course and I sink onto his sofa. How could I have been so stupid? My rush to solve the case before I leave for the ocean waves blinded me to the implications of removing the data stick and might well cost me – what? A fine? Surely, I haven't saved face only to lose my freedom? I can only plead a frozen brain and the malign influence of the cell.

'But, since you're here…' He shakes his head, as much at himself as at me, and leads me into his study. '*Then* it's straight on the phone to the inspector.'

I nod and blow my nose, feeling a shade better and hoping against hope my gut will be proved right.

Scott reaches under his desk and fishes out an old laptop, and plugs the data stick in. There's a perfectly good newer one on top of the desk. 'In case it's got a bug,' he says, answering my puzzled look. The screen lights up immediately with a police logo and Sergeant Dean Court in large red letters.

'Hah! Not even password protected, how arrogant is that?' Clearly Dean didn't believe anyone would find it.

My heart thumping like mad. I peer over Scott's shoulder for a better view and let out a small sigh of relief. It's obviously what I thought. The display consists of three folders. The first is labelled *SECRET SERGEANT – the mss* and when Scott clicks on it, it takes only moments to see it's exactly that, all four hundred pages of it. Tempting as it is to start reading, we both know we need to discover what else Dean thought was so important it needed a secret hiding place.

The second folder is simply labelled *Solved* and appears to consist of dozens of numbered case files which presumably were, as it says, solved. I feel a wave of disappointment wash over me, although I don't suppose it was ever going to be labelled *101 Things to Incriminate Me*.

The third folder, however, does look more interesting as it's labelled, *Crime DOES Pay!* As Scott opens it, however, we turn to each other in surprise. It contains only eight files, each labelled with three letters and numbers I assume would have been the case number.

As we stare at them, hesitating to dabble in what shows all the signs of being police material, I let out a low whistle. 'And you accused me of removing police evidence. Surely Dean wasn't allowed to keep crime records on his own data stick?'

We stare at the files. They're labelled SLA RST EJO OFA BVU MSM AWA FST, followed by four seemingly unconnected numbers, even when I try them as dates.

'Coffee, guys?' Cherry's voice behind me makes me jump. 'What on earth are you two…'

'Trying to spot links between files.' I scrunch my eyes after staring so intently at the small screen. 'The only thing I can spot is maybe SLA and RST are Sandy Lane and Red Street. But no idea on the others. Possibly other people Dean had some hold over? But I can't match them to anyone I know here.'

Cherry glances at the display. 'Why not open one of the files and see what's inside rather than just staring at the list waiting for something to jump out?' She shakes her head as if she's dealing with small children, then ambles away nonchalantly, pausing at the door to wink.

'Good idea, my love…' Scott looks sheepish and goes back to the *Solved* folder. He starts clicking on the files like a demented woodpecker.

Within seconds, the screen is filled with open documents and we start dipping into them at random.

After a while, we close the files in the Solved folder, since they're exactly what they're labelled and focus on the other eight. I turn to my companion.

'Scott, am I understanding this properly? It seems to me that the *Solved* files are just that, cases which Court was involved in that led to a prosecution or at least to a caution, so they were signed off.'

He nods and I'm starting to feel excited that we're onto something. 'And obviously the *Crime DOES Pay!* ones are unsolved. So, that title might refer to the criminal getting away with it, for then crime does indeed pay?'

He nods again. 'Makes sense, Cat.'

Except that, and this is what excites me, my moment of inspiration: 'But what if it doesn't refer to the criminals, what if it refers to Dean?'

'You mean, Dean profited from them not being solved?'

'Exactly. We know he had a reputation for scrounging food and drink whenever he could. What if he sometimes agreed to turn a blind eye? For some favour in return, maybe money or something else?'

Having studied the contents, we turn to each other, my heart pounding and my gut bubbling like a witch's cauldron.

'Time to face the music, Vicar, and hope that what we've found outweighs Glen's anger at how we got there.'

Scott dials a number. 'Inspector, we've discovered something you really need to see. Urgently.'

*

The next hour passes more slowly than watching a kettle boil. And by the time the doorbell rings, I'm feeling sick and more apprehensive than I can ever remember feeling in my whole life. The third and fourth coffees haven't helped. I'm remembering I promised not to interfere in the case, and I don't suppose Glen will view finding the data stick, removing it from the scene and then studying every single thing on it as just a harmless curiosity. And he probably he has a point.

My tension isn't helped when my phone pings with a reminder about the proposal for Prestige Events. Oh well, I'll have to come back to that this evening, hopefully with all of this dealt with.

The fury on Glen's face as Scott brings him into his office does nothing to reassure me and his voice is colder than the air outside. 'The reverend informs me you've been interfering in my crime scene, Ms de Barnes.'

'Inspector, I didn't exactly say…'

'Despite my explicit instructions – and your own agreement, I seem to remember.'

My face burns bright red and another wave of feeling nauseas rolls over me. This is not a man you take lightly, as I suppose any number of villains have found out.

'And as if that wasn't enough, you've also removed vital evidence from my crime scene.'

Any hope he might view this benignly is disappearing as rapidly as my confidence.

'And you've been reading confidential police records.'

'In fairness, Inspector,' Scott points to the screen, 'as you can see, they're not actually marked Confidential. We had no idea what was in them until we'd opened one.'

'At which point, naturally, you closed them all down? No – I thought not.'

'If we'd done that, Inspector…' I admire Scott's bravery in trying to get the irate investigator back onside. 'we wouldn't have made the discovery that might just unlock your investigation.'

'I'm perfectly capable of unlocking my own investigation, thank you.'

But then a ray of hope: Glen hesitates. 'However, since you've got this far, you might as well show me what you've found. And tell me what you think. While I think what charge I'm going to bring against you. *Both of you.*'

233

'Actually, Inspector, it was Cherry's idea, back at the vicarage.' Oops.

'Oh great. So, it's not just you two, you've now broadcast it across the whole village.'

I open my mouth to reply but rapidly think better of it. 'As you can see…' I nod to Scott, who's hovering the cursor over a folder, 'apart from the manuscript, there are two other folders, *Solved*, and the other one.'

'Go on, Catherine.' I think there's a chance I may have impressed the policeman…

'The folders are very different sizes.' Again, Glen nods.

I'm starting to enjoy this. I feel like a conjurer about to produce a rabbit out of a hat. 'What's interesting is, if one of the folders is labelled *Solved*, you'd expect the other to be *Unsolved*. And that's exactly what it seems like. And, you'd expect the unsolved folder to be the bigger one: with more statements, needing more resources, using more police time, that sort of thing.'

Glen is now nodding his head up and down like one of those toys you see bobbing in the back of cars. 'That makes sense.'

'Except that it's the opposite. The eight 'unsolved' files have barely a page each. The solved ones often run to a dozen or more.'

The police officer leans forward and stares at the hovering cursor. 'But that's ridiculous. Why on earth…'

I try really hard to keep the note of triumph out of my voice, honestly I do. 'I think, Inspector, Dean Court had a very definite plan for using them. Or rather, for using the people who committed the misdemeanours. And I think you'll find at least one of the names inside the *Crime DOES Pay!* folder particularly interesting.'

Both men stare at me, then at the screen as the vicar opens the file I'm pointing to. Glen reads for a moment, then announces in a determined voice, 'I think I need to have another word with our Ms Lane.'

Chapter 22

While we wait at the vicarage, Cherry serves a massive tray of coffee, scones and all the accessories. It smells divine. She looks from Scott to Glen to me. 'My, we do look serious.' When no-one responds, she lightly pecks Scott's cheek. 'I'm off now. Need to meet the man who's inspecting my drains. Back tomorrow.' Scott nods, squeezing her hand. She stares at him for a moment, then smiles at me, nods to Glen and leaves the room, just as the doorbell rings.

'They're in the study, Sandy. Go straight in.'

As Sandy enters and looks around Glen gives a curt nod and I smile, noting she doesn't seem her usual confident self. Whether it's the vicarage or the company, who knows. Scott stands and with a warm smile, pulls a dining chair out and stands in front, waving our visitor to the armchair he's just vacated.

'Ms Lane, please be seated.' Glen's formal police voice, which I'm sure comes directly from the police manual, and has been honed over hundreds of interviews, clearly doesn't improve Sandy's confidence. Glen sits forward in his chair, his hands on his knees. 'Ms Lane, we've discovered some new evidence in this murder business.'

I bristle slightly at the 'we' but remind myself that I promised not to get involved, either then or now, so I simply watch Sandy as intently as I dare.

Now seated, Sandy runs her hands through her untidy grey hair. 'Sorry – you caught me on the hop, Inspector. I wasn't quite ready to… leave the house.'

She looks paler than usual, her wrinkles are more pronounced and she has dark rings under her eyes. I realise she's not wearing makeup. She's also wearing an old baggy jumper covered in bobbles and a pair of battered blue jeans. I feel quite disconcerted, as if I'm intruding on something intimate. She's not her fashionable, elegant self.

Glen produces an evidence bag containing the data stick, and waves it in front of Sandy's face. She baulks slightly, but whether it's out of guilt or just the suddenness of Glen's action, I can't decide.

'Anything you'd like to tell us, Ms Lane?' The Inspector's voice is soft and encouraging.

Sandy pauses, takes a deep breath then straightens her back. She looks him directly in the eye. 'Nothing I haven't already told you and your officers, Inspector. Several times. The truth.'

'Ah yes, "the truth, the whole truth and nothing but the truth". But *is* it the *whole* truth, Ms Lane?'

She hesitates for a split second. 'Of course, Inspector. Why, what are you implying?'

Glen holds up his hands, as if in surrender. 'Nothing at all. Just wanted to give you the chance to – well, never mind.' He leans back in his armchair, interlacing his fingers and gazing at her in silence.

'The thing is, Sandy…' I blurt out, 'I, we, found some old case files.'

Sandy deflates like a punctured balloon.

Glen lifts his finger to his lips and whispers, 'Including your case file. There are some details you chose not to put in your statement.'

'Inspector, it was years ago. I can assure you there was no attempt to deceive. Why would I?'

'Indeed, Ms Lane, why would you?' He stares at her. 'But – we'll come back to it. You see, there were two sets of case folders. And yours comes in the more interesting set, the ones with little information, because for some reason Court didn't seem to investigate them properly. Would you care to enlighten us why that might have been?'

I watch her wince. 'Sandy, Dean noted on the folder that held your file, "Crime DOES pay". Was he blackmailing you?'

'No, of course not. How would I know why he wrote it? Was I worried his memoir might rake it all up again? Yes, of course I was. The facts of this case are exactly as I've told you.'

Glen leans forward. 'A caution does seem a little, shall we say, generous for an assault.'

'Inspector, there are two things you need to understand about this case.'

I can't help smiling as she slips into her magistrate voice, even after all these years. I can imagine she'd be quite something on the Bench in that upper room just a few hundred metres away. Sandy continues.

'While I did slap the man across the face, in full view of dozens of witnesses, you need to consider the context. I'd been the victim of what nowadays we'd call a sexual assault and the slap was a direct result of the assault. In those days, it was the only way to make a point.' She swallows hard, and Scott hurries from the room, returning with a glass of water.'

'Thank you, Vicar. And if Court's files say anything different, well, then, I'm afraid it's a lie. Now, if there's nothing else?'

I'm full of admiration for her dignity as she stands and makes her departure.

Glen simply shakes his head. 'One down, one to go.' As if on cue, there's a knock on the office door and in walks Red Street. A greater contrast with our departing suspect would be hard to imagine. He stamps across to the vacant chair, plants himself on the edge, ramrod straight, and fixes Glen with an angry glare. 'Really, Inspector, this is too bad. I do have things to do, you know, I can't keep dropping everything for your every whim.'

Glen raises an eyebrow and stares back, the silence lengthening, so I take the opportunity to inspect the man before us. Unlike Sandy, he's impeccably dressed in a black roll-neck sweater under a Harris Tweed waistcoat and a jacket. His well-cut trousers are, I suspect, moleskin, not to everyone's taste but they suit him. His tan trainers have blue laces, and as he studiously folds one leg over the other, he reveals a pair of trendy red and white bamboo socks. The man really is quite something. Although as yet the jury's out on what that something might be.

'Mr Street, some new information has come to light.' Good grief, now I'm starting to sound like the inspector. 'I'm sorry to rake over old ground, but would you mind telling us about the events leading up to your daughter Evie's death?'

He switches his glare to me, his eyes boring into mine, then he shrugs and rounds on Glen. 'Is this really necessary, Inspector?'

'I'm afraid it is – in the light of the new material.'

Street sighs and stares out the window. 'She was 17 when she was killed in a road accident. Hit-and-run. Dean was the investigating officer, but he never found out who was responsible. Which was almost worse than her death, not knowing what happened or having anyone to blame. At the time, the sergeant and I spent hours, days together going over it, he was adamant he'd left no stone unturned – but in the end – nothing. We just had to let it drop. My wife couldn't take it, it destroyed her. And then she was diagnosed with cancer the following year and was dead within six months. That maniac murdered two people, three if you count my ruined life. And, even worse, they got away with it.'

Glen pauses a few moments, before asking, 'Was Dean reinvestigating the accident again recently?'

'No – when we came across it in the research for his book, he just said it was… too painful for him, his biggest regret. And he knew it must be for me too.' His voice cracks and a single sob rolls out from his throat.

He looks a shadow of the confident man from just minutes ago.

I lay my hand gently on his arm. He recoils but his eyes are empty and lack focus. 'I'm so sorry, Red. Thank you, we won't take up anymore of your time.'

He nods, hauls himself to his feet as if his body weighs a ton and shuffles towards the door, accompanied by Scott, who takes his arm and helps him out.

For the first time, Glen looks upset. He stares into the garden for several moments, then sighs. 'Well, we didn't get very far. With either of them. I'll take the data stick back to the office to look at the stuff in more detail.'

He looks up as Scott returns. 'I assume you made a copy?' Scott blushes. 'I thought so. I suggest you both look at the memoir and leave the police files to me.'

'Of course, Inspector. But now I'm afraid I need to shoo you both out. I've someone coming to see me in a few minutes, and I need to prepare myself.'

*

241

Over lunch, the clouds vanish, replaced by the deepest blue sky. I need some fresh country air in my lungs and some exercise so I can clear my mind.

'Right, Dag, let's …' he's already pawing at the front door, his tongue lolling, 'get your lead!'

I wrap my favourite scarlet cashmere scarf tightly around my neck, add a black gilet and button my blue duffle coat snuggly to the top, even though the toggle will stick into my throat. I might get throttled but at least I won't get cold.

As I pull the door closed, I sink my hands into thermal gloves, and we head down Cowley Road past the Rec and out of the village. Halfway up the hill, I turn to savour the sight of the Cotswolds stone houses glowing golden in the sun, a handful of thatched roofs and the quiet meandering streets. Not for the first time, I realise why so many poets and musicians have been inspired by the Cotswold's beauty and peacefulness.

But this walk isn't just a workout for legs and lungs, it's a wake-up call to my brain, so I swing back and set off at such pace my pooch glances up in surprise, panting and his tongue fully outstretched. Within a couple of minutes, I'm much the same. Not a pretty sight.

To be honest, Red's words have hit me harder than I want to admit. How unimaginably horrible it must be to lose your wife and your daughter in such a short period of time. I mean, I've never been particularly drawn to having children but to have had and lost…

Life is so very fragile. I remember him staring at the woman when we were in the Coffee Emporium and my blood runs cold. Was he remembering his wife and daughter? And there was me thinking he was eying her up. He even said she reminded him of someone, how could I not have realised?

I stop and when Dagenham trots back to see what's going on, I grab him and bury my face in his damp fur. How could I have been so insensitive?

Dag pulls on his lead and as we set off towards the top of the hill, defiance sets in. I have so much to be thankful for. I have a fledgling business. I have a bunch of great friends. I deserve to be in a loving relationship, and if it's not going to be with Linton, well then it will happen with someone else.

At the summit, alone and gazing over the woods and fields, and the cluster of houses, I mutter, 'Life's too short!'. Then, having checked I'm alone, I bellow at the top of my voice, 'LIFE'S TOO SHORT!'

Dag looks up, utters a single woof of support, and continues his sniffing mission.

The air up here is clear and fresh, and I fill my lungs with deep breaths while I tap out a brief text.

*

A few hours later, Linton and I sit at my kitchen table sharing bread, cheese, and a very decent bottle of Sangiovese. And a conversation we should have had weeks ago. He's looking particularly dashing in a crisp white shirt, red velvet jacket, black trousers and a black velvet bow tie. He's clearly taken my text about a simple supper to heart. Unfortunately, I'm wearing not very fetching black legwarmers and a very unspectacular loose-fitting cotton dress, also red, but in a shade which clashes badly with his jacket. Not that we're sitting close enough to offend the eye.

I top up Linton's glass, which empties the bottle, and cross to the cupboard for another so I can refill mine. 'I've been talking to Red Street.'

Linton's eyebrows shoot up higher than his glasses, but he doesn't say anything. I take a large sip of wine. 'He told me about what happened to his wife and daughter. And the impact it had, still has, on his life.'

Linton nods. 'I know. I wasn't here at the time, but people talk.'

'Something struck me then, it's pretty obvious when you think about it. I just hadn't. Thought about it, that is.'

This is proving much harder than I'd anticipated, scampering down the hill, so I bite into a piece of Double Gloucester cheese, savouring its tang. 'They probably had a wonderful relationship. And, to be honest, Linton…' I stare into his eyes, those wonderful, deep lakes… *Get on with it, Cat.* I shake my head so I can choose my next words carefully. 'that's exactly the sort of relationship I want.' My companion jolts, his eyes narrowing, his forehead creasing into a frown. 'For a while, I thought we might have it as well.'

He opens his mouth, but I raise my hand to stop him. If I don't get this out now, I never will. 'I still think we could. But…' I take another deep breath, staring beyond his left ear because it'll be fatal to look back into those eyes. 'I can't deal with being constantly stood up. No doctor can possibly have so many medical emergencies. You're not respecting me.'

Linton does a good impression of a fish, his mouth gaping and gawping. There's a long silence. His face has gone very red and he's breathing heavily, his fingers curled around the table edge. Then he speaks. 'That really is the most unbelievable thing I've heard in ages.' His deep baritone voice starts as a whisper but grows louder with every word. 'Might I remind you, Catherine, you were the one who stood me up not two days ago. How is it possible that my medical responsibilities aren't a valid reason for missing a date, but your chocolate making is? Unbelievable!'

'On *one* occasion. I've lost track of how many times you've cancelled.'

'Catherine, they are people who need to see me. It's my job.'

That really is the final straw. 'And my chocolate making is what, a nice little hobby?'

'Well, isn't it? You don't seem to be putting much effort into it. Not like you do with this murder investigation. Frankly, I have no intention of being, at best, only number three in your priorities.' He jumps to his feet, knocking the chair over, glances back, hesitates for a moment and then stamps out, slamming the door. Dag growls and I'm left spitting feathers. How could I have thought it would work with such an arrogant, insensitive, pig-headed…

I grab a poker and ram the dying embers of the fire into oblivion, then stamp upstairs and throw myself on my bed, certain I'm as likely to sleep as to fly to the moon, especially since I've got a nagging feeling I've forgotten something.

Chapter 23

The next thing I know, my alarm is blaring and it's seven am. My head is throbbing and my mouth is as dry as the Sahara. Yesterday's clothes smell decidedly unpleasant and I strip off as quickly as I can and throw myself into the shower.

Half an hour later, having put on a sloppy fleece onesie, I boot up my computer and stare at the screen through barely open eyelids.

Oh dear. Emails flagged *Urgent*, especially those with the whole header in capital letters, are never a good sign. And when I see this one is from Prestige Events, I want to be sick as, too late, I remember what was nagging me last night. They have a point, I had promised the proposal by the end of yesterday. But there was Inspector Parva to impress and conversations to be had with Red and Sandy. And then the disastrous encounter with the doctor so I think my lapse is very understandable. Unfortunately, as I'm reminded in the opening paragraph of what looks like a very long missive, I knew the deadline and why it was so important... Ah well, it's not yet 7 am, I can still get something to them before their day starts. Especially if I use the proposal from those people who let them down – perhaps start with a cut-and-paste job? Panic settles in.

Shortly before eight, when Dag's wines and nudges have grown from persistent to desperation, I tap the final few keys, hit *send* and breathe an enormous sigh of relief. No self-respecting business should open before 8 am. Especially in the Cotswolds, where pretty much the only people who set foot outside of the door before nine are those on the school run. Job done. The first of three deadlines today.

The second is much more straightforward. Forty-five minutes and one medium-length doggie walk later, I'm ready to hand over my chocolate packages the moment Skye opens *The Crimson Courgette* and treats me to her first coffee order of the day – admittedly my fourth.'

Which leaves deadline number three, the one I'm dreading. Glen has summoned me to what he laughably calls a 'case conference' at the Vicarage. Which irritates me because it's my safe space for cosy chats with my cleric companion. Hang on, is this a sneaky way to stop me investigating? I'm *not* investigating, of course, just having a few informal chats. Well, if it is, he's doomed to failure. There are plenty of other little hidey-holes I can inhabit, even in a cosy village like Much Slaughter. Where there's a will... or in this case, dead body. *Hardly appropriate, Cat.* True, but it makes me smile and I really need something to lighten my mood.

When I arrive, deliberately half an hour early, Scott answers the door and there's no sign of Glen, or Cherry either. 'She's still at her house in Much Snoring. It seems her plumbing's even less robust than we thought,' he offers. *Great pals always know what you're thinking.*

I grin and follow him into the main part of the house. As usual when Cherry's away, I have to shift a pile of folders and books before I can sit down, and Scott has to remove a pile of dirty dishes before he can serve my coffee. But with friends, you don't need to apologise or explain.

'Are you okay, Cat? You look rather pale.' Scott squats beside my armchair.

'Sure. Just a lot going on at the moment.' *Never a truer word, Cat.* 'I'm fine.'

He pauses, looking right into my eyes, then shrugs and stands. 'If you say so. Now, before our beloved inspector puts in an appearance, did anything strike you from reading Dean's memoir?'

'To be honest, Scott, I haven't looked at it. Been rather preoccupied with some business stuff. Anything strike you?'

He shakes his head. 'Nothing we didn't already know. As far as I could tell. It's four hundred pages long, so I couldn't do more than scan it, and I had some vicar-related things to do. Maybe the inspector and his team will have found something.'

'I thought the book was our area and he was looking at the police files?' Even as I say it, I know there's as much chance of Glen not reading the manuscript as me not reading the police files.

Glen arrives as the last chimes of the church clock are dying away. He looks tired, with sallow skin and dark rings under his eyes. He flops into the chair and tosses a bulging manila file on the coffee table. 'Nothing new.' Even his voice sounds tired.

Scott carefully moves the file to serve Glen's coffee and, rather than starting to read the contents, which is what I would have done in his place, simply deposits it carefully at the side of the policeman's chair. 'Maybe we should start with reminding ourselves what we know, Inspector?'

'Quite right Vicar. The old motive, means and opportunity, eh?' Oh dear, when he reverts to clichés, you can tell his heart's really not in it. I wonder if he's getting pressure from above. None of us seem to be getting any closer to finding the culprit. He sighs. 'Both Sandy and Red's stories check out.'

'Maybe we should start with them, then, so we can finally eliminate them?' I murmur, cheerily. Glen just shrugs and Scott nods. 'Good idea, Cat. Kick us off.'

'Okay, well, first Red Street. There's no doubt he had opportunity: he admits he was due to meet Court at the museum on the night of the murder to take some photos. He insists Court didn't turn up. But we only have his word for that. If he was lying and Court did turn up, then he's likely to be the last person to see him alive. He's certainly strong enough to kill him. And he owns several sets of knives in one of the best equipped kitchens for miles.'

Glen raises an eyebrow.

'Before you ask, Inspector, I saw them through his kitchen window. But as for a motive, he was helping Court and as far as we know, they hadn't argued. What on earth would he gain?'

Glen says nothing, just stares out the window. But perhaps he's one of those who listen the hardest when they seem to be listening the least. Or maybe he's just picturing this case joining his own file of *Unsolved*.

Scott nods. 'I agree. And we haven't discovered anything pointing suspicion back to Mavis.' I nod and he continues, 'The only possible motive for Mavis was the photo of her clock. She might have lied about the inscription, but we know she had romantic feelings for him and she admits they had meetings in the museum, just the two of them.' I can't imagine anything less romantic than that gloomy, claustrophobic hellhole. I shudder as I picture them and it occurs to me, 'Hell hath no fury like a lover scorned…'

Scott interrupts my chilling train of thought. 'What if during one of those trysts she noticed the loose brick? Maybe she found the manuscript and panicked about what he'd written about her?'

In my mind's eye, I scan the cell, then shake my head. 'The open door completely masks it and I don't get the impression Court would have been keen to be in there with her and have the cell door shut. Besides, even if she had discovered it *and* she'd managed to get in there alone to get the data stick out, she'd have had to smuggle it out, without him noticing.'

Scott sighs and nods agreement. 'Did you find anything, Inspector?'

He shakes his head, sadly. 'Even when he 'lost interest', she'd neither the height nor the physical strength to kill him. So, unless she found something we all missed, I think it's pretty safe to rule her out.' Scott and I nod. I carry on.

'So, next, our vet, Martin Dales. Let's concentrate on what he's told us. He noticed the sergeant always seemed to be on police duty for the hunts. He also said Dean seemed highly sympathetic to the hunters if any of the anti-hunting brigade were there – apparently quite a few of them ended up in custody, without anyone seeing them do anything wrong. Plus, Martin has a whole wall of animal rights posters in his waiting rooms. Is it so far-fetched to think they had a violent falling out over their contrary and clearly passionate views? I mean, neither of them is exactly a shrinking violet. Martin is certainly big enough and he's no stranger to knives.'

'What about opportunity, though?' Scott's face creases into a frown. 'Given their history, I can hardly see Dean opening the museum for a cosy little chat, can you? Nor dropping his guard.'

'Unless Dean was blackmailing Martin over something? Maybe some dubious animal rights stuff?

Maybe they'd arranged to meet that evening? It's a perfect opportunity for Martin to…'

The inspector swings round and glares at me. 'Do you really think we didn't think of that? Dales has an alibi.'

We lapse into silence, each of us trying to knit the confusing strands into some sort of meaningful picture. My gut rumbles as an idea forms. 'Inspector, what if the bang on the head and the stabbing weren't at the same time?

Scott nods. 'You mean, two different people? One knocked him unconscious, then someone else dragged him across the floor and stabbed him?

Glen snorts angrily. 'Unless he was having a parade of all his victims, it's too much of a coincidence. Nevertheless, he extracts his police notebook from an inside pocket, licks his pencil and scribbles a few notes, then flips it shut and puts it back, as he purses his lips and resumes staring out of the window.

Scott sighs. 'We mustn't overlook Sandy Lane. I'm sorry to say it but she does have a history of violence…'

'Oh, come on, Scott, we only know of the one incident and from what she says, she was much more the victim than the perpetrator.'

'That may be true, Cat, but she admits Court knew about it. What if Court was still holding it over her head and the prospect of his memoir tipped her over the edge? After all, we know she's into yoga and swimming so she'd have the determination and the strength to finish him off.'

We all stare silently, letting the thought meander around our minds.

'The trouble is, as far as we know, she didn't meet him at the museum, unless she was lying in wait on the off chance, which hardly seems likely on an autumn night...'

Scott breaks off as Cherry hurtles through the door, flings herself into his arms and liberally covers him in kisses. 'So sorry I'm late darling. It took the plumber far too long to unblock me!' She wiggles her eyebrows at Scott and then me, then freezes as she spots Inspector Parva. 'Oh my God, I'm so...' She blushes, pulling her frizzy chestnut hair across her face. 'I didn't.... Coffee? Cake?' She grabs the tray and scuttles away to the kitchen, leaving Scott shaking his head, his face as red as the village postbox.

'So, are we agreed, then?' I mutter, desperately trying to keep a straight face, while noticing Glen hasn't twitched a muscle. Either such bizarre interruptions are a common feature of police investigations, or he really isn't on top form today.

'Are we agreed, then,' I repeat, 'that we can discount Sandy, as well as Mavis and Red? And that Martin has an alibi.' I lace my hands together and place them on my lap in best Miss Marple fashion. Unfortunately, it doesn't help.

Neither Scott nor the inspector look convinced, so we resume our 'let's stare out of the window' impasse. The uncomfortable silence continues until there's a knock on the door and Cherry floats in to deliver a tray crowded with coffee and three different types of biscuit, now the consummate vicar's partner.

It's a welcome diversion and we munch and sip.

'You know what's really bugging me?' Scott puts his empty *World's Best Vicar* mug on the tray. Why drag Court across the museum? And why three knives? It must be staged, so what point are we missing?'

My mind slides back to the inside of the museum as I stared through the window at Dean's body – he wasn't wearing a coat. Which suggests he'd been there a while. So, what if he'd been there all along and hadn't been home? Maybe the murder had seen a light on? Someone in the village who had a good reason to be around unusually late? Dean was expecting Red, so he might have left the door unlocked. Although how the murderer would manage to open the door, cross the tiled hallway and get close to Dean without him hearing anything, well, that's a different matter.

Any further puzzles will have to wait as an *Urgent* email notification pings on my phone. 'Sorry, guys, I need to look at this.'

Moments later, I'm staring at my phone in disbelief. The email is short, sharp and to the point: *Very disappointed…. missed promised deadline… took no notice of anything I said… looking elsewhere.*

And in one short email it feels as if the bottom's dropped out of my world. Here am I in the wilds of the Gloucestershire countryside with no romance, no murderer and no future…

Chapter 24

Village Sunday mornings can sometimes feel as if the world has ended and you've been left behind. There's even less life than usual. *The Crimson Courgette Coffee Emporium* doesn't open its door until 10.30 am and our local pub, *The Boar and Nightie*, remains locked and barred (pun intended) until midday.

Pretty much the only movement comes from the fifty or so people who, at 9.59 am, are bustling their way to the church of St Cyril the Obtuse for the 10 am service. I creep in ten minutes early so I can be safe in a corner before the last minute rush and thereby avoid any contact. It's not that I don't like my fellow villagers, but being social has a time and a place, and for me this morning is neither the time nor the place. I just want to be left to sit in silence. And, if I'm honest, to wallow in self-pity. Although if the Divine were to choose this time to reveal some guidance about my hopeless future, it certainly wouldn't go amiss.

My chosen spot gives me the perfect vantage point to see who's there, providing I can recognise them from behind. And has the added advantage that the only person who can see me well is Scott as he leads the service, and he does keep staring in my direction, probably wondering what on earth I'm doing in this unfamiliar pew.

Divine finger pointing towards murder suspects is noticeably lacking. Nor is it doing much on the romantic front: not a single eligible male is there, not least because only a handful are under seventy. There is Red Street, however, and I realise I've been staring at the back of his shaved head for rather longer than I should have. There's another rumble in my gut but he's dropped off the bottom of the eligibility list and I have absolutely no intention of allowing him back, so this time the rumble must be more hunger rather than hint.

Seeing Red focuses me on matters murderous and I glance around the pews to see who else is gracing the Divine with their presence this morning. Sandy is diagonally opposite, in the front pew, her head shrouded in a trademark cream hat whose circular brim is as broad as her shoulders. She's wearing a heavy coat in the same shade of cream and large, dangling silver earrings. But however intently I stare at her back, I get no sense of her involvement.

On the far side of the church, several rows back, Mavis is wrapped in a huge, black woollen coat, with lines so sharp you'd risk cutting your finger on them. Her statement outfit shows her to be every bit the prim and proper lady, but it seems to me her shoulders are drooped, and she doesn't quite inhabit her clothes the way she normally would. I also notice that she doesn't join in the hymns, another first because, as she often reminds us, she does have a classically trained voice.

The only one missing is our vet and I wonder if, rather like Linton, he often gets called out at the most inconvenient times. Can't be much fun, maybe that's why he's single? Which reminds me why I'd nipped out of yesterday's meeting – before that wretched email wiped everything else from my mind. And as I remember, something else clicks into place.

Luckily (if Lady Luck ever ventures onto church premises), we're almost at The Peace and in the general hubbub of people sliding out of pews to greet each other, I can slide out of the building unseen, or at least unchallenged. Time to seize the bull by the horns or at least seize the vet by – whatever you seize a vet by.

One of the paths through the churchyard comes out by Martin's house. Thankfully his car's on the drive facing the painted tunnel on the garage door and when I put my hand on the bonnet the engine is still hot. Normally I'd take the path around the back to the surgery but today, the front door feels more appropriate. It also means he spots my approach and is standing guard in the doorway. 'Ms de Barnes.'

'Martin, might I come in?'

He looks me up and down, shrugs, stands to one side and waves me in. 'First door on the left – I assume this is a social call?'

Now that is a good question. How would you describe a visit in pursuit of a murder inquiry? I smile and follow his directions.

'Sherry?'

I nod and perch on the edge of a formal Chippendale armchair, resting my hands on the green upholstered arms. Martin drags a small mahogany table beside it, produces a silver coaster and brings me my drink in a beautiful cut glass goblet. It's so different from the sanitised clinic it's as if he inhabits two different worlds. Or is two different people.

Horn-seizing time. 'Dr Dales, I'll get right to the point.'

He remains standing, his back to the fireplace and, although he's not particularly tall, he seems to tower over me, and I wonder if that's deliberate. In a Victorian novel, his presence would be described as brooding, perhaps even menacing.

'I wonder if you'd tell me where you were on the evening Dean was killed? If you'd been out on a late call, you might just have…'

'Ms de Barnes, I have said this before to the police. I did not kill Sergeant Court. Now, if that's all…' He moves closer towards me and my heart jumps.

'No, no, I'm sorry, that's not what I meant at all. I just… wondered if you might have seen someone else? After all, High Street isn't exactly teeming after dark, is it?'

He stops, mid-stride. 'I can assure you, not only did I not kill him, I wasn't even in the county that night. So, no, I think you can safely say, I didn't see anyone. What I will tell you – since, in a perverse way I rather admire your persistence – is that I sent a very strongly-worded letter to the odious man warning him to be careful about getting too closely associated with the hunt, especially as a police officer. And, yes, as I told Inspector Parva, I do have a copy. I also have his arrogant reply.'

He crosses to a beautiful mahogany bureau, takes a single sheet of paper from one of the compartments and hands it to me. Scrawled in a spidery black biro, Dean had written, '*It's you who needs to be careful. I still have lots of friends in the Force and you'd be amazed what they could book you for, if I talked to them. Watch out.*' Nothing else.

'And before you ask, of course, the police have seen it. Now, while I appreciate your zeal in trying to find someone to blame, unfortunately, today, your famous sleuthing skills have failed you.' I bristle at his patronising tone. 'I have, what I believe they call, a "cast-iron alibi" – he marks out the phrase with quote marks – 'I was at a vets' conference in Nottingham and the hotel CCTV will confirm that I didn't leave the building until 10 am the following morning. Now…' He raises an eyebrow, his left arm pointing towards the door.

Okay, Cat, maybe just stick to chocolates. Much less humiliating. And let's be honest, you're better at it.

Which is why on his return from church half an hour later, Much Slaughter's vicar finds a crestfallen Catney crumpled on his doorstep.

As I sit in front of his roaring fire, legs stretched out and slowly warming up, my mind slides back to the

261

museum and I picture the perpetrator, he, or she, dragging Dean across the floor and taking such trouble to drape him on the motorbike. Each step would increase the risk of being seen, so it must have been both deliberate and important. Along with using three knives. A clear message we're completely missing. What was the point?

My gut rumbles. Oh, my goodness, what if…?

Inspector Parva is far from delighted at being disturbed during Sunday lunch – Cotswold lamb with all the trimmings, as he's keen to mutter down the phone. He's even less delighted when I tell him I'm on my way to confront the killer.

*

The ceramic piece on the windowsill looks decidedly odd, misshapen, and while I'm waiting for the offered afternoon tea, I pick it up. On closer inspection, it looks incomplete, as if a large chunk of it had been broken off. The underneath provides no clue and I'm still staring at it when I hear the door behind me open, accompanied by the welcome tinkle of china cups on saucers as a tray is put down.

My host carefully tugs at the seams of his expensive denim jeans as he folds into an armchair, his shaven head glinting slightly in the light from a large brass standard lamp; it's still early afternoon but like so many old cottages, small windows mean lamps are lit for most of the day. He tugs each arm of the orange roll-neck jumper into place and carefully pours the tea from a Wedgewood pot. 'I think we agreed Earl Grey, Ms de Barnes, so I assume you won't be taking milk?'

I smile, even though my heart's beating louder than a ticking grandfather clock and nod. 'Quite right.'

There's an uncomfortable silence as we sip our tea. It's blisteringly hot but I suspect neither of us knows what else to do.

After an eternity, I finally pluck up the courage and fix my gaze on him. 'I know you killed Sergeant Court, Mr Street.'

He tenses.

'It was when I focused on why the victim was draped on the motorbike, I realised it had to be something from that part of his police career. Which led me to wonder about the significance of the number of knives. Why three? So specific. What was there in his career that made the number three so significant? Which was when I remembered something you'd said – and it all fell into place. You told me that when your wife and daughter died, three lives had ended.'

In a sudden movement, Red leans across the table, his elbow catching the tea pot and sending it crashing to the floor, spilling tea across the cream carpet. He hardly seems to notice as he reaches for the magazine rack underneath, and reverentially places a large blue photo album on top of the table. It falls open at a page filled with snaps of the three of them at the seaside, blue sky, ice-creams, kiss-me-quick hats and such happy smiles it brings a lump to my throat, despite what's unfolding. He runs his fingers over their faces as tears drop onto a page already grimy from years of touching. 'May I show you?'

I nod.

We're still exploring the photos when Glen bursts into the room and I lift my hand to stop him.

Without prompting, Red looks up, his eyes filled with tears and vacant. 'It wasn't exactly difficult you know, Inspector, persuading Court to come to the museum. He was such an arrogant monster. The moment I told him I wanted a photo of him on the bike for the book, he couldn't wait to pose. He walked across preening himself as if he hadn't a care in the world. He was always bragging about how the bike helped his policing – he thought it symbolised his power. In the end, it was ridiculously easy – I simply got him to stare out of the cell as if he were remembering all his derring-dos and then hammered him with one of the truncheons he'd so helpfully taken down from the display. Dead simple to wipe it and put it back. Literally.'

Red finishes the last of his tea and turns over a few more pages while Glen and I look on, as if time has stood still.

'And for me, it was the perfect form of justice.' He stands and throws his shoulders back, his chin raised, sadness replaced with defiance. 'His life ended on the very machine that ended the life of my Evie. Stabbed in the back, one for each of us. A nice touch, don't you think, kind of poetic. Stabbed in the back, just like he'd done to me all those years ago.' His voice trails away as he flicks one of the photos out of the album and lifts it to his lips.

I put my hand gently on his arm. 'He blocked the investigation, didn't he, Red?'

Red nods. 'All those years, he pretended he'd investigated a crime which he had no intention of solving.'

'How did you find out?'

Red turns to me, his eyes red and rheumy. 'The fool gave me several old notebooks to archive because he said he didn't need them for his book. That struck me as rather strange and being nosy, I thought I'd have a little root around in them.'

I bristle. Surely they're police property not for members of the public to browse through as if they're in the library. *Oh come on, Cat, that's, exactly what you'd have done in his place.* True.

'Anyway, one of them had a loose page sticking out. Seemed to be notes in Court's handwriting about attending a burglar alarm going off at Tarlton. It was signed off at 10.05 pm. I was just going to slide it back to stop it getting damaged when I saw it was dated the night my Evie died. Now I know Evie's accident took place around 10.10 pm because she'd phoned to say she was leaving her friend's house and her phone was smashed in her pocket at 1012. But Court reckoned he received the radio call at 1020 while he was at home. That's when I realised there was no way Court could have been in the village at that time. But he might well have been roughly at the accident spot. So if there were only one set of tyre tracks, from a motorbike, they'd have to be his. And finally it all made sense. Oh, he rushed back to town and managed to get here before the accident was reported. But he was the one who killed my wonderful Evie.'

He pauses as two police cars with flashing blue lights screech to a halt outside and five officers march into the room, while Glen pronounces the official words. I don't think either Red or myself really take them in.

'That ornament, by the way...' He stands and nods at the piece I'd been examining earlier. 'It's a model of the Wedgewood memorial on Bignall Hill at a place called Red Street, which is why it caught my attention. The memorial was chopped back after a storm in the 1970s. Used to be three times the size. Amazing how much damage a single act can do, isn't it? Seemed rather appropriate.' He holds out his wrists as he's led handcuffed out to the waiting police car and a gaggle of curious villagers. I burst into tears and Glen hesitates, before awkwardly putting an arm around me.

Chapter 25

Scott's text had been brief and blunt: *Meeting tonight 6.30. Coffee Shop. Bring Dagenham.*

If that had been my old boss, even as MD I'd be expecting the sack – at the very least. It's a tone I've never experienced before from Scott.

To say I'm apprehensive when I arrive would be an understatement. *The Crimson Courgette* is in near darkness, only a couple of lamps glowing dimly from the till and some other electrical device, so I check my watch. I'm on time, so I push on the door. It swings open and as I walk in, the light in the far alcove clicks on, illuminating Scott, Cherry and Wickham grinning like maniacs in the shadowy corner. As I move in their direction, another light comes on, highlighting Rose and Skye Green and Carlton Curlieu, also grinning mischievously. In an orchestrated move that feels like the curtain rising on a West End show, they all stand, raise flutes of champagne that glisten in the half light, and chorus, 'Surprise!' Another figure appears at my elbow, and this really is a surprise, Chief Inspector Parva hands me a bubbling glass. I get another surprise as he's actually removed his trademark sunglasses.

'Ms De Barnes, Catney, I never thought I'd say this, but thank you for your help.' He raises his glass and the others follow suit and thump their tables. Everyone stares at me but the lump in my throat prevents me from making any reply. The inspector puts the back of his hands to his forehead, feigning shock. 'Well, that's the second thing I never thought I'd say: Catherine de Barnes is lost for words.' Which produces resounding cheers and another round of table-thumping.

Dagenham startles me with a loud bark of approval, then settles his head back on Barking's flank underneath a large radiator where they've already made themselves at home. I'm delighted my pooch can enjoy friendship as much as I do.

Scott wanders across and puts his arm around my shoulder, just as the door behind me opens and there's the biggest surprise in an evening of surprises, Linton Heath hurries in, flustered and sweating. I'd have thought he'd be avoiding me like the plague – as it were. 'I'm so sorry. Full surgery.' As he quickly scans the room, Skye beckons to him to sit on the spare chair between her and her aunt. The vicar lifts his hand and the room quietens. 'This isn't a night for speeches…'

'Don't make one, then,' calls Wickham, 'we get enough of them on Sundays.' Tables are struck again, accompanied by catcalls and words of agreement.

'But...' *loud theatrical groans and laughter,* 'I couldn't let the chance pass to say how grateful I am to have Cat as a friend. Even if she does drive me mad sometimes. And to say how much I admire the way she's stuck with solving this mystery like a dog with a bone.' Both hounds look up at the phrase and lick their lips, causing even more merriment. Scott turns towards them and puts on his saddest face. 'Sorry, boys, none of – those things I can't mention. But your treats are coming.' The pooches thump their tails on the floor in anticipation. 'Anyway, Cat, you stuck to your guns and as a result, a murderer is on his way to prison and our village is once again a safe haven.'

Truth be told, I *am* rather proud of my part in apprehending the villain, as they say, and very glad not to be currently halfway across some ocean or other crammed into a tin can. *Ever thought you might be missing something about the joys of cruising, girl*? I sashay across to join Cherry, who's patting the seat next to her and welcomes me with a massive rugby-scrum hug. 'Brilliant job, Cat. I have to say, my money was on Sandy. She seemed the perfect person to blackmail, a wealthy woman, with a shady a past. Not hard to imagine that retired policeman getting too greedy… All very *Midsomer Murders*.' There's a huge guffaw from Carlton and a gale of laughter from Rose and Skye rolls across the room, leaving Linton grinning. He glances at me and I turn quickly back to Cherry.

'If I might have the attention of that unruly mob in the corner!' Scott laughs, to whoops of delight from the other table. 'Our beloved Chief Inspector did ask if he might say a few words.' Mock groans accompany the police officer as he manoeuvres himself towards the centre of the café.

'Don't worry, I'll keep it brief,' he says, to resounding cheers from the assembled crowd. The inspector smiles, which certainly makes him look a lot more pleasant and actually quite handsome.

'I know there are those amongst you who thought I'd been dragging my heels…' More laughter as he turns to me and I blush. 'but there was a lot going on in the background.'

'That's what they all say,' chortles Wickham, stroking his beard knowingly.

Glen smiles. 'Indeed. On to other matters.' He turns to me, his face stern. 'Ms de Barnes…' Oh dear, it's back to my formal title. This can't be good news. 'Before I tear a strip off you for the stupidity of confronting our main suspect on your own, *and* for interfering in my investigation against my specific orders, I have to ask, what changed your mind? You seemed dead set on the vet.'

'Oh, I knew it couldn't have been Martin when he told me… Oops.'

Glen splutters. 'Don't tell me you confronted…?' Which produces another gale of laughter and several raised glasses. He has the good grace to simply shake his head in mock disbelief.

I smile serenely. 'Good job I did, though. His alibi made me concentrate properly on what message the killer wanted us to get. Did he deliberately drape the body on the bike, or was it simply where Court happened to fall? And why three knives? Which was when I remembered Red saying the accident destroyed three lives. Of course, it destroyed his daughter's life because she died in the accident. But it also destroyed his wife's life because she couldn't cope with the emptiness and the not knowing. And then she got cancer. And finally it destroyed Red as well. Three lives, three knives. It all made sense.'

Glen turns to shake my hand. 'Cat, you did a really good job working it all out. Thank you.'

Linton rises and starts to lead my friends in yet more applause, along with whooping and stamping of feet. 'On behalf of the Much Slaughter community, we're grateful, Cat. And on my behalf, I'm proud as well. And I'm sorry if I haven't always said that.' He moves to stand at my right hand side and suddenly I realise we're holding hands. Wonders truly will never cease.

Scott comes to stand on my other side. 'Of course there's another reason we're partying tonight. And it's one tinged with sadness. Cat, we also want to wish you *Bon Voyage*. We'll miss you more than we can say. And we have a small gift for you.'

Skye emerges from the shadows with a huge wrapped box almost as big as herself and I squeal with a mix of surprise and intrigue.

I carefully remove the tape from the outer layer, to find an interestingly squidgy parcel taped to another folded layer underneath.

After more careful unwrapping, I discover a smart new apron and then I giggle as I open it out. Each of my friends has a caricature face printed on it, under the heading, *Bon Voyage*. 'I love it! Thank you, guys.'

'Keep going,' Wickham calls, 'and preferably with a little less care and a little more speed. I do have a shop to open tomorrow, you know.'

His encouragement earns a round of cheers, so I rip off the next layer in double-quick time.

This layer produces a huge envelope with a card totally filled with scrawled messages, so many it looks as if the entire village has contributed. By now, I'm so close to tears I don't trust myself to speak, so I simply smile and mouth 'thank you.'

The next layer proves to be the last and when I tear the wrapping off to reveal a state-of-the-art silver laptop, I really am speechless. And the tears refuse to be held back. As do the sobs.

Wickham comes forward and places a fatherly arm around my shoulders. 'For video calls. And we've each pre-entered our details so there's absolutely no excuse.'

As the laughter spreads, Rose flicks on the remaining lights, revealing a long trestle table laden with the most delicious looking sandwiches, quiches and salads, and at the centre a huge chocolate gateau that looks very familiar. 'I thought you wanted that to sell, you rascal?' Skye shrugs as I hold out my arms and we hug.

I jump as I feel a hand on my arm. 'Cat, I'm so pleased you've settled into the village. And I'm so proud that now you've solved this murder, you can put all your energy into getting your business off the ground. Even if it is on a cruise boat.' Linton's eyes are warm and gentle and when his hand slowly slides down my arm to squeeze my fingers, a huge shiver ripples down my spine. My gut, however, is confusingly silent.

Linton is all I could ever want in a man. He's warm, sensuous, I can hold a decent conversation with him (and an indecent one as well, it seems). Dagenham likes him – and I rate his judgement very highly. He's also pretty good in at least one other area...

But he's hardly what you'd call reliable on the diary front. That's also true: I could never be sure he'd turn up, however good the reason. On the other hand, the Harvest Ball was one of the best nights of my life and he felt so right in my arms. And it was so romantic dancing on the grass under the stars. And I'm about to sail off into the sunset for twelve months.

He squeezes my hand again, the tingle drawing me back into the moment and I realise we're now alone at the table.

I slide my other hand on top of his, luxuriating in the warm tingle it brings, and stare into those beautiful dark eyes... 'We need to talk.'

He nods, a flicker of concern passing across his lovely face. 'I know.'

'If we're ever going to make this long-distance relationship work, even have a reasonable chance of it working, we need some ground rules.'

'The question is, Cat, do you want it to work?'

I gulp. Now I'm on the spot, the answer suddenly feels crystal clear. I nod. 'Yes. Do you?'

He pauses and my heart sinks. This is typical of my luck. Just as I finally make up my mind one way, he's going the other. 'Well, doctor, that's fine.' I start to leave.

'No, no, you misunderstand Cat. This is really big for me. I've not felt this way for years. Not since – well, that's a story for another day. But, yes, I really do want this to work.'

Slumped back in my chair, I turn and lift his hands. 'Then we both have to be honest.'

He nods. 'And understanding.'

I smile. 'True.'

'And…'

'Hang on, this is starting to sound like the intro to some tacky TV game show.'

He lifts my fingers to his lips, kissing them so lightly my whole body shivers. 'I was going to say, fun!'

'Ah, well, that I agree is exactly what the doctor ordered. But, Linton, it's big for me too, and I've no idea how I'll feel when all I can see of you is on a small screen. So let's just take it carefully, shall we, and see how it goes?'

We move in for the romantic kiss, just as a loud voice echoes across the party.

'Sorry as I am to break up this cosy gathering,' Chief Inspector Parva struggles to his feet, brushing pastry crumbs from his chest and wiping chocolate smears from his mouth, 'duty calls. And, for a change, it's not a call to Much Slaughter.' Which produces loud cheers and yet another round of table rattling. My friends really are a raucous bunch. As he reaches the door, pausing to smile in my direction, I shout across the hubbub, 'And I promise, no more investigating!' He turns, stares at me for a moment, restores his sunglasses and walks out.

Will Catney be able to keep her resolve? Will her relationship with the dishy doctor survive a life on the ocean waves?

Find out in Mass Murder *– the next in The Cotswold Capers series, when locum vicar Norman Cross is found battered to death in the nave of St Cyril the Obtuse.*

Coming shortly…

Acknowledgements

Shannon Cave, via ALLi (the Alliance of Independent Authors), has once again done ana amazing job as my Development Editor. How she can retain so much detail and spot inconsistencies in plot and text I'll never understand!

Ellie Stevenson, my copy editor, continues to not only round up missing full stops and commas and so much more, but also gives such experienced advice.

Emma O'Brien has again drawn such wonderful artwork that really encapsulates the essence of Much Slaughter and its amazing characters.

A number of people read early drafts and gave helpful and encouraging comments, particularly Marcus and Deborah Nolan, John Weston and Alison Hesketh, I'm also grateful to Sian Davies and Gary Knight for their comments. A fresh pair of eyes adds so much and even if I've not always taken the comments on board, they've always prodded me to think more deeply.

I continue to learn so much through excellent articles provided by
REEDSY(www.reedsy.com) and
ALLi (www.allianceindependentauthors.org).

Indeed, to all who've read, advised, encouraged and challenged – simply THANK YOU.

About the Author

Peter Hyson was born in the area of Nottingham that shares his name. Over the ensuing decades he's worked in a host of different areas, geographic and professional, as a teacher, professional swimming coach, radio reporter, video editor, business consultant and facilitator of leadership retreats – to name just a few. This means he's met a wide variety of people and backgrounds who've enriched his experiences and none of whom appear in any of his novels.

He's married to Hilary and between them they have four amazing children with two fantastic partners and two grandchildren all of whom bring such fun and joy.

Peter also helps run a Retreats business in the UK and around the world.

The Cotswold Capers series

If you've enjoyed this book, please leave a brief review.

For extra material and to be among the first to hear about Catney and Dagenham's future adventures, sign up for our quarterly newsletter, *Continuing Capers*, at www.peterhyson.com

And look out for their next adventure, *A Mass Murder*.

And if you missed the opening novella in the series, here's a taster for The Taste of Murder…

The Taste of Murder
a novella

the forerunner to

The *Cotswold Capers* series

PETER HYSON

Chapter 1

'Oh, no, not again.' The loud click confirms my worst fear. I pound on the locked door even though there's only my pup inside and again regret the penalty for being the only person in the village of Much Slaughter to lock her door. I'm locked out. And I only popped out to collect my Monday morning milk order – yes, we do still have doorstep delivers, part of supporting local producers.

With a sigh, I pull my thick velvet dressing gown tighter around me, slip through the rickety wicker gate, my fluffy slippers squelching in the mud, and knock on my neighbour's door.

'Sorry, Wickham.' He's already dangling my spare keys and grinning from ear to ear behind his whiskers. This is not the reputation I'd hoped to create in the village. 'Glad I caught you before you left for work.'

'It's Monday, Catney. I don't open the bookshop till ten. I'd offer you coffee, but...' He averts his gaze, his blue eyes twinkling under bushy white eyebrows that must have taken all of his 68 years to nurture.

Face burning, I beat a hasty retreat. 'I'll call in later and grab a coffee with you. Thanks.'

Safely back inside, I glance in the hall mirror, grateful my dressing gown not only covers me neck to knees but also hides the absence of nightwear. Not bad for a 42 year-old, I reckon, as I toss my golden curls and sashay upstairs.

Showered and dressed, with minimal make-up applied, I'm almost ready to face the day.

But first, the call of homemade muesli, Greek yoghurt and local strawberries. Plus, my special treat, a steaming mug of freshly-ground black coffee. To my mind, a healthy start to the day gives you permission for a few little extravagances later. Especially if they're chocolate.

After breakfast and two mugs of coffee, it's time to pull on an apron and a pair of thin plastic catering gloves while humming the opening bars of '*Hey ho, hey ho, it's off to work we go*'. Well, we all have our own ways of preparing for our daily routines, don't we?

I snatch a tea towel off a tray of coconut pyramids and break a slab of dark chocolate into a freezer-bag before grabbing my wooden rolling pin and hammering the chocolate into smaller fragments. I heat some water in a saucepan, empty the chocolate fragments into a bowl and place it over the heat. This is one of my favourite parts, watching the dark blobs slowly melt into a wonderfully rich smelling sauce. My mouth's watering.

Once it's all fully melted, I swirl chocolate over each macaroon and carefully place it on a sheet of greaseproof paper. Next, the best part: running my finger around the bowl and blissfully sucking the remaining thick gooey chocolate.

A cold wet canine nose against my bare ankle makes me jump. 'Won't be long, Dag.' I toss a treat into my golden retriever's eager mouth and enjoy a few moments tickling his floppy ears, before I change my catering gloves and take another tray out of the fridge.

A few minutes later, thirty-six neatly wrapped cellophane packages are ready alongside my wicker basket. Just in time, I remember to add my latest touch: thin cardboard pennants in the shape of medieval knights' flags proclaiming CATNEY CHOCS.

'Right, Dagenham – time for your...' My gorgeous pup is already pawing the door, so I clip the leash onto his collar. Dag lollops down the paved path, tail spinning like a propellor, eager to greet all and sundry.

At my gate, we both pause to sniff the summer, the scent of new-mown grass and flower-strewn banks.

Near the main part of the village, the bank flattens into a wildlife strip planted with daisies, buttercups and cowslips, already alive with butterflies.

The *Bound to Please* bookshop has its own colourful display of window boxes and hanging baskets crammed with magenta petunias, white geraniums, bright red fuchsias and what look like daisies, but can't be. The smell is amazing and Dag sneezes loudly. I dodge half a dozen fat bees, their hairy legs already pollen-laden, and open the bright red wooden door, setting the brass bell tinkling.

The bookshop owner, my devoted neighbour Wickham Skeith, has already settled his waistcoated frame into an upholstered green armchair and waves me to its twin, across from a low wooden table set with two large mugs and a cafetiere of steaming coffee. Dag lollops off to nestle into a huge dog cushion underneath the window. By the time I'm settled, my damson and gold dress draped over my legs, my lovely pet is snoring loudly and twitching in time with his dreams.

Wickham pours the coffee, glances across at the dog and smiles, his rheumy blue eyes twinkling. 'Seems like he's been here forever. You too.'

'Yep – six months now. And I don't regret a day of it. Can't think how I lasted so long in London.' I lift the mug and take a moment to savour the rich tang of his coffee which he orders specially from the importer, while my body relaxes into the upholstery. 'Mind you, there are those round here who'll still see me as an outsider even after ten *years*, Wickham.'

'Catney de Barnes, don't you dare take any notice of them. The general opinion is, you've thrown yourself into village life good and proper. Much to everyone's surprise…' He glances over his half-moon spectacles. 'And pleasure, of course.'

'Oh dear, do they think I'm being too pushy? I've just been trying to meet people.'

'Well, perhaps at first. You can't blame them.' He wiggles his bushy eyebrows, then looks serious. 'Every village lives in fear of outsiders, hell-bent on the rural idyll and then complaining about noisy cockerels and church bells.'

'I know, Wickham. I've tried to be sensitive and low-key, but I need to keep myself occupied.'

'You have, Catney. After all, you've only joined, what, five committees?' He grins. 'Oh and become well-known for your chocolate goodies.'

I smile. 'Which reminds me.' I delve into my bag and remove five cellophane packages like a conjurer pulling rabbits out of a hat. 'A little thank you for rescuing me earlier. Don't eat 'em all at once.'

'You should lock yourself out more often, kid.'

'I'd never keep up with the baking. Now, I really need to go. Fête Committee in five minutes.'

'You lot still planning on having that ridiculous TV chef open it?'

'The committee's very excited. Well, most of us, anyway. Dag, come on, boy.' Dagenham raises a sleepy eye and promptly sinks back into the cushion, already snoring.

'Leave him be for now. And leave me in peace with…' Wickham flicks an invisible speck from his tweed waistcoat and reaches for one of the macaroons.

Moments later, I'm shouldering open the heavy oak door of the village hall, just as the church clock ends its eleven chimes.

'Morning, all. Perfect timing, eh?' I mop my forehead with the back of my hand and pause as the hall's smell of stale polish, musty air and stewed tea wafts over me.

The sole person in the room looks up from the wooden trestle table and runs his finger round the inside of his clerical collar. He's wearing a dark suit, well-fitted without looking overly expensive. He tugs down his jacket cuffs.

I speak. 'Scott, thanks for sending the agenda round last night. Didn't have time to read it, I'm afraid, but…'

'Clearly not, Catherine. Otherwise, you'd have seen the meeting started at ten o'clock. I'm afraid we've already finished.'

Oh dear, I think, *if it's Catherine I must be in trouble.* For the second time this morning, I blush. 'I am SO sorry. I didn't think anything in Much Slaughter got going before mid-morning.' This isn't helping, I can tell.

'Yes, we do realise that's the common perception of the outsider.' Scott glowers, pushes his spectacles back up to the bridge of his nose, then bursts out laughing, running his hand through thick black hair. 'Sorry, Catney, couldn't resist.'

'You absolute terror, you really had me going, there.' I slip into one of the empty chairs. 'So, where is everyone? We need to get going. Only a few days to go…'

The vicar clears his throat. 'Erm, the meeting did start at 10 and we actually have finished, I'm afraid. But don't worry. Trot back to the vicarage with me and I'll fill you in.'

With a couple of mighty strides, he's out the door. And I'm literally trotting behind.

The High Street is already busy with meandering tourists causing us to weave in and out as if we're following some complex pattern.

I smile as I watch him make a path for us through the throng like he's the rugby player of his youth. Friendship is a precious thing, especially when you're new to a place – although I never thought I'd number a vicar among my closest companions. But then Scott Willoughby is hardly your typical vicar: he's in his still in his forties so half the age of most other vicars I've known, he's still got his own hair (quite a lot of it actually) plus he's one of the kindest souls you'll ever meet, and his dog Barking is Dag's best mate. He's also got a live-in girlfriend, and a whiff of scandal from his previous post to boot. Definitely my kind of clergyman.

'Right, Scott, fill me in on the fête decisions.'

'Firstly, it's a *fair*, not a fête, or you'll offend an awful lot of people. Sorry.' He bumps into a young woman who has suddenly stopped dead in the middle of the pavement and is clicking off photos as if her life depends on it.

'The fet… the fair? What did I miss?'

'The main thing is this celebrity chef bloke has confirmed he'll open it. People seem to reckon he'll bring in the crowds. Apparently, he's well known in – certain circles.' He wrinkles his nose and I smother a giggle into a cough. 'Reckons he'll be around for a few hours as he's got some business or other in the area. The committee thought you might be the one to meet-and-greet, given you're in the same line of business.'

'Making a few novelty chocolates for special occasions hardly makes me a chef.'

'Yes, well, you weren't there so the committee decided.' He pushes his glasses up again and flexes his broad shoulders. 'Anyway, I reckon the word's already out. Saw a whole load of strange women nosing around Rose's Tea Shoppe yesterday. I reckon it's his fan club.'

As we draw near the bookshop, a crowd of brightly clad women ogle the window where Wickham's added a rolling video to his display of books, artfully scattered around a large cardboard cut-out of beaming CELEBRITY CHEF LEE CLUMP. The woman taking photos is now busily recording the shop front from every conceivable angle.

Scott turns as we pass. 'Well, at least Wickham will be happy. Unlike some others.'

'You mean, because of the rumour about Clump's business plans?' Several people swivel to stare.

Scott's reply however is lost in the general hubbub, by which time we've reached the vicarage driveway.

'Is there anything else I'm down for, apart from being the bit of fluff on the arm of our celebrity chef?'

I'm unable to stifle a laugh at his look of horror. 'Don't worry, just joking. I can't imagine me being just a bit of fluff on anyone's arm, can you? Not my style.'

Of course, if it was the *right* arm…

Chapter 2

'Better late than never,' I announce, staggering into Ye Olde Tea Shoppe, looking forward to my regular Tuesday morning tete-a-tete with my friends.

'And better never late.' Scott looks solemn but there's a twinkle in his dark eyes.

'Oh, come on. What's twenty minutes among friends?'

'Not an idea I'd like to follow with the services at St Cyril the Obtuse.' He lowers his head to look down his nose at me, grins and shuffles along the padded banquette to move various dirty cups and plates onto an adjoining table. Minus his dog-collar, he looks almost normal, especially when he smooths his black hair back and runs his hands down his khaki chinos. He glances towards the bottle-glass window, under which his dog, Barking, lies snoring loudly in the usual Old English Sheepdog way. Dagenham flops beside him on the padded cushion.

Rose bustles over and serves my regular black Americano and a generous slice of her famous Bakewell tart on her signature willow-patterned crockery, then sinks into one of her cushioned spindle chairs. I still find it odd to see her in her 'work' gear of sensible shoes, black dress and white lace apron rather than comfy-fit trousers and sloppy jumper, her long pepper hair cascading freely over her shoulders. But I have to admit, at work she looks a decade younger than her 57 years.

These coffee rituals had been set up to 'help me settle in' as they described it, make sure I would 'fit in' was how I'd taken it. Now, I wouldn't be without them, they're such a useful source of lively debate and gossip. Even the vicar's been known to impart the occasional juicy titbit. Mind you, he and his girlfriend have also been the source of some juicy gossip themselves.

Halfway through devouring my delicious tart I'm startled to find them staring at me.

'What?' I don't mean to sound irritated, but must they be so nosey?

'You're clearly not yourself, Catney.' It's Rose who speaks but Scott nods.

'Bad night.'

All that does is raise their eyebrows.

'Okay, okay.' I sigh. 'I kept waking up feeling really, well, uneasy. And I can't work out why. Usually it means something horrible's about to happen. It's as if I sense it in advance. I got it shortly before my husband walked off with that floosy.'

'Well, that's one thing we can guarantee won't be happening.' Scott smiles and gives me a small hug. 'But, seriously, any idea at all? I mean, you're happy here, aren't you?'

'Now I'm a totally free agent? Absolutely. I loved doing my chocolatier course and the opportunities it's bringing, something to get my teeth into. Sorry, no pun intended.'

'No pun taken' Scott grins. 'Well, we'll just have to have more coffee and cake while we think. My treat.'

Rose nods and goes back to her kitchen.

My mood improves slightly, especially when Rose carefully places the new items in front of us, the delicious aroma of freshly baked scones making my stomach rumble. Even after my generous slice of Bakewell…

'Catney, update us on what's happening with this so-called celebrity chef.' Rose sounds rather grumpy. I know he'll bring us more trade, I'm just not sure how good the crowds'll be for the village , all the extra things we'll have to put in place. We might even need to book a medic.'

'Actually, that's already in hand, courtesy of our local, home-grown medic, the redoubtable Linton Heath.' I feel myself blush.

Rose winces, her sallow wrinkles creasing her face. 'I've heard the chef's already been paying secret visits, planning some business venture. That's why he agreed to open the fair. No disrespect, but we're rather small fry for him really.' I giggle and Rose glares at me. 'Sorry, Rose, just the idea of a celebrity chef and small fry...' Scott shakes his head but also smiles.

'All very well for you, Catney. But if he decides to take up residence, the competition could finish me off. They're hardly queuing at the door, are they?' She sweeps her arm across the shop, and I realise we're the only customers. One of the reasons I really like the place is that it's quiet and relaxing. It never occurred to me that it's not exactly good for business.

'Mind you…' Rose lowers her voice and looks around guiltily even though we're the only ones here, 'he is very good looking.'

Oh, my goodness, she's blushing. 'We'll have to see what we can do, Rose.' I nudge her in the ribs and wink.

Rose looks pensive. 'He reckons he's already got local council support. "In his pocket", he said.'

'How on earth did you hear that?' Scott leans in and the arm of his jacket drops into a blob of cream on the gingham tablecloth. 'I wonder who he meant?'

'Two newspaper reporters were in here talking, last week. Amazing how many people think I'm invisible just because I run the place. They reckoned he's after some local premises for a posh restaurant he wants to call *Meat &Greet*. Really got them smirking, that did. They reckoned it all sounded very fishy.' I splutter coffee back into my cup but no one else seems to have noticed either the pun or my blunder.

'Anyway, thankfully I can't see it coming off. Far too much local opposition.'

Rose starts as the door opens and a tall woman, in her mid-forties, and in overalls, marches in. Her sleeves are rolled up above her elbows and she's sporting a large plastic safety helmet, pushed back and showing her dark hair.

'Morning, May.' Scott half stands and waves to her to join us. 'What's it today, tree-surgery or wood carving? I'm assuming it's not mayoral duties, given the clothing. We were just discussing Lee Clump's visit and his posh dining plans.'

The woman tosses her leather gloves onto the floor and throws herself into a wooden chair. 'Great idea. Need some fresh blood in the place. Just think of all the rich and famous it could attract. And heaven knows, there're enough of them and their money around these parts.'

Rose's glare as she slams May's drink on the table risks curdling the milk. 'Yet another outsider wanting to take over a village property for over-priced fripperies from a dilettante ne'er-do-well.'

I burst out laughing. 'Oh, come on, Rose, don't beat about the bush – tell us what you really think.' She glares. 'My family's been here for three generations and my dad fought tooth and nail to keep this village going. People like this chef geezer just want to ride roughshod over us locals and our traditions. Which, since you're our mayor, is exactly what you should be standing up for, May Hill.'

'Good for you, Rose.' Scott slaps the table with his very large palm. 'If only more people were prepared to stand up and be counted. Not that I'm taking sides, of course.'

Rose stares out the window as if accusing anyone passing by.

Within minutes May has downed her coffee, and her buttered scone barely saw the light of day. She pauses then speaks. 'If you're talking about someone on the inside, I reckon it's that Councillor Barnard Castle bloke. Never did trust him. And I don't buy that eye-trouble story of his for one minute. Convenient excuse to get out of doing any work, I reckon. Only out for 'imself, that one.'

'That seems rather harsh, May,' Scott murmurs.

'Well, that's my opinion. Take it or leave it. Now, if I'm away any longer, my treetops will've grown another ten…' She freezes and stares.

Framing the doorway, hands on hips, is a young woman not much more than a teenager, a mop of tangled bright red, green and blue hair streaked across a hot and sweaty face. Her long, flowing dress, decorated with stars and moons, seems far too thick for the warm weather and she's laden with a massive backpack. She looks around slowly.

'Hello, Auntie Rose. Skye Green's reporting for duty.' The youngster's face lights up as she races across the room – well, as fast as her flowing robes and heavy load will permit - and enfolds Rose in a huge embrace accompanied by the clatter and tinkle of her numerous bracelets and bangles. Rose remains as still as a statue, then slowly and tentatively folds one arm around the girl.

'How are you, Auntie Rose, you look so great, for your age.'

May smirks, Scott coughs and I'm just lost for words (which is not something you'll often hear said).

Skye slides out of her backpack harness, dumps it on an empty table, smiles brightly and holds out her right hand. 'Skye Green. Rose's niece. From London. Come back to look after the tea shop for a little while. And then hopefully take over.'

Scott is the first to recover. 'Scott Willoughby. Vicar.' It's Skye's turn to look taken aback. 'Ah, yes, sorry, no dog-collar. My day off.' At a touch over six foot, he towers over her and she nods up at him before turning to beam at the rest of us.

I take her hand, struck by how thin she is. 'Catherine de Barnes. But most people call me Catney. Or Cat. Newcomer.' Now where did that come from, I wonder, having spent the last few months trying to pretend that's exactly what I'm not?

She turns to our final member. 'And you are…?'
'May Hill.' May doesn't move, caught up with watching as the silhouette of Leonard Stanley, our village librarian, scurries across the window.

To find out what life-changing adventures are awaiting Cat and her coffee crew, order the full e-book here: **https://www.amazon.co.uk/dp/B0C2CR8MNL**

*

Keep up to date with my quarterly newsletter for more stories, characters and special offers at either:

peter@peterhyson.com or

https://www.peterhyson.com or

follow me on LinkedIn:
https://www.linkedin.com/in/peter-hyson-962b61271/

Milton Keynes UK
Ingram Content Group UK Ltd.
UKHW020053300924
448990UK00005BA/113